THE SELVES OF QUINTE

THE SELVES
OF QUINTE

by Marcel Moreau

TRANSLATED FROM THE FRENCH
BY BERNARD FRECHTMAN

GEORGE BRAZILLER · NEW YORK

Contents

THE SELVES OF QUINTE

At Home

Jeanne was waiting for Quinte. He was ravenously hungry. He dipped his finger, like a cook, into the night. When he reached the last monument on the street, which had been erected after the destruction of the cemetery, he saw the light, which was like a photograph of a hollow laugh in the sky. It was the apartment, the dreariest apartment in the world. He stumbled, but instead of falling he had rather the impression of getting up continually. When they had rented it, it had smelled of linen to be washed, and now it smelled of linen that had been washed, thanks to Jeanne. The light that filters into the apartment looks crumpled, slightly soiled, as if it had barely managed to squeeze into narrow pipes and as if daylight here needed to be washed. "We ought to . . . ," thought Quinte. His idea did not take shape. Much annoyed, he threaded his way among scaffolding where, pushing aside a lantern, he unintentionally scattered the contents of a box, of nestfuls of flakes and plasterwork. There were no pretty curtains in his home. And the windows are set so high that in order to survey the street when a noise issues from it, they have to stand on a stepladder and hold on to the window frame. In order to remain in that position, they have to overcome all kinds of cramps and, in his particular case, ominous cracking sounds around the spinal column, that's what hurts. They are therefore no longer interested in the street . . . They content themselves, if they are athirst for exteriors, with looking at the rear landscape with its great variety of hanging underclothes, ripped perhaps by dreams of rape (and among them the eternal red handkerchief of some unknown person), with sweaty brats in the dirty yards. Impossible to leap out. They must domesticate asphyxia, disenchantment. Space takes shape around itself like allusions to space. And the gardens are inaccessible. In a clod of earth, each animalcule is a globe-trotter. And they do not seem to notice that the balcony, the few square yards of white concrete which enjoy daylight, is missing, that the others have one. They live in a dark slogan . . . "And all the rest is just poetry," cried Quinte to himself when the lighted window had disappeared and he reached his door. He glanced behind him, there was nothing, yet he distinctly felt that he was being held back, the soft plume of the darkness molested his neck, belly . . . and . . . hips . . . with a . . . memory. And between his legs the slow peal of the stately glands in the damp, hairy tower eager for services . . . That was yesterday, in the bedroom. He shrugged his shoulders, entered with all his might. He had a feeling that an iota of night remained on his body, a black hair. He shuddered. Then his skin was light again, his body was at home, as if snapped up by the stairway switch. He lumbered up the old, discolored stairs where a half-breed had killed his mistress one Sunday with a kick in the behind. The stairs and he together were a lot of fatigue, and half-wooden, half-fleshy groans which were reduced in his hearing to a hubbub of consonants, especially *r*'s and *c*'s, and even cedillas, played a certain role therein. They so disturbed the silence of the house that there seemed to be silence only where they were together, the stairs, his vision of the angry half-breed, and he. Only what is perfectly calm can be disturbed. For one would have thought that the noise was extracted better-fed, better-modeled from the silence massed there like a dump of faded echos of toneless voices, and that the silence itself *launched* the noise. The noise rose up, acquiring forms, slender forms in the soundless, silent space that revolved about him, like a dressmaker's dream at the feet of his model or the quiet drunkenness of a verminous lover on his knees before a naked countess. Halfway up he stopped to dissect with his gaze his hand which was on the banister, it was long and damp, gnarled, it looked like an unfinished or botched *mascaron,* and, when it moved, like a pulverulent toad, because of the greenish-gray gleams of the grimy light. He recognized the flow of his veins, he squeezed the hard, round, bonelike support. A smell of broiled meat. He thought of a fire in an abattoir, his nostrils were full of impressions of iron, of sacrifice, of funeral pyres. Then he went up two steps at a time, as if to touch an infernal spectacle at the top. "Hello." (Hello, hello a thousand times, shit a thousand times.) They kissed. It was a lack of air, nothing but aspirated *h*'s, a last breath, tenacity zero. No moistening either, nor tongue between. Two old scars had bumped into and then repelled each other for fear of awakening the wound. He cast a sidelong glance at the table. The dullness of it was mad. It was set: bread which he imagined dry, twisted meat, and a black, anthracitic wine, a thing impossible to drink, that remained stuck in his throat. He tossed his napkin into a corner. It collapsed. He inquired, with his mind elsewhere:

"Was she good?"

"Yes, a slight toothache."

The chair turned. He felt himself sit down on it. The whole seat slid into his flesh, which was traversed by snakes, knives, thorns. She sat down opposite him and they began to eat.

"You're losing weight," he said to her when she stood up. Yet, when her back was turned, she seemed to be swelling, to be growing huge fruits in her dress.

"I know."

She sat down again, after making a vague dance step. Her eyes bobbed up in front of him, half closed above an orange clinging to her mouth which streamed with juice and tears. His face clouded over. She began to contemplate him, looking for the word, the subject of conversation that would put some blondness into all that. He got the bulk of his impressions from something new in his bread, in his meat, but he was thinking nevertheless of a woman's face searching his, hands in a trunk before the big journey. To unearth what? He coughed, a leaping cough. She was perhaps right in wanting to talk, in wanting to hear him, after a dozen hours of separation. But he could not communicate because his mouth was full, and his heart, and his soul too, no doubt, whereas the separation had an opposite effect on Jeanne, it left her with lots of breath, little appetite, a great readiness to receive and give ideas, words. News. In the evening, he alone was filled, mind and limbs, with all the things from outside, so much so that he felt he had enough of them, that it was a pleasure to be silent, to stop moving at last like a weary, sated animal that feels within itself its latest acquisition of life. The wind jarred on the windowpane in its frame. He raised his head, but did not go so high. He met his wife, and she was all intense. Then he stopped seeing her, and he managed not to think about her. Yet she continued to be intense. He vaguely recognized her beauty, her direct beauty, arrows of charm shot by tireless archers. On Jeanne's face, elucidation and mystery reign each in turn. Nothing is connected with anything there, everything is departure, arrival. The nose, the mouth, the eyes thrive on the disharmony. They are an ensemble of mobile riches there which can be admired only one by one, in the gap between two moments of abyss. At times, brief torments go by which alight there black as crows and which immediately fly away, white or motley. This expressiveness is an aviary, an excessive seaport, this sadness is expressiveness on strike, a paralysis, an effacement more beautiful than all the rest. It is a beauty saloon, men enter, drink, get drunk, all men are sailors in the eyes of women. "What women?" he asked himself.

Quinte muses: "Three years . . . that makes three

years . . ." Today they are dullness itself, a kind of incredulity makes them waver slowly when they are face to face, an incredulity broken by the desire of one, who detects it himself, to grope in the part of the other which, he thinks, belongs to him, although he does not clearly discern it, through a kind of meatus. At times, when he looks at her, he has the impression that he is scratching her, superreally, and that a corner of his own presence in her is suddenly going to appear. From time to time, she seems to be awaiting a phenomenon, a garish light like the one in which they had seen each other before the wedding night, in a hotel room where there were mirrors. She remembers: that time her body had felt like a spinning top and a greasy pole, paroxysms! They had uttered cries, cries uttered by eternity. Who uttered the cries? Their revival of the event was a chimera, one mustn't wait for it but periodically imagine it had recurred by means of love scenes which were nothing out of the ordinary. Married life definitely meant salvaging, putting together odds and ends every day with a less and less awkward effort. And there was Jeanne's soul. Her secret exercises probably had no little effect on the mixtures of her physiognomy. If one could have revealed and spread it, perhaps one would have seen in it a thick tangle of doubts and dreams, of sarcasms and hysteria, all of them transformed, in passing, by beauty. What astounded her, beyond the rhythms, was that having agreed, out of love, to live in imitation of a man, she followed him docilely, despite herself, even in the abatements of that love. She was weary at the moment, her presence was vague, uncertain. What remained was the intensity, which cannot be explained. But is it not true that to be intense is also to thwart her fatigue with a greater fatigue of a contrary nature?

She imagined his love to be discreetly weary, prostrate within her like a breathless athlete whose beauty and dead weight she bore. He was not observing Jeanne with his sidelong glance but the flowers on her dress. He adored her, in a way. But actually he did not understand that maltreated, twisted sentiment which always feigns rectitude. He sometimes thought about "love's lofty task." He would imagine himself waging a husbandly combat. But he hardly knew which, nor did he know the name of the adversary or of the weapon with which he fought him (it was not important enough to be the answer to these questions; there must have been something else in which it was only a straw). An exhausting combat, not insipid, which, by good fortune, did not leave a taste of chalk on his lips. And that struggle had its hours of brightness, when, for example, she was sick. The problems would then fall away, the masked adversaries would then pull away from each other, all that remained was an immense beach, which was his love for her. She heard him eating. The sound from his mouth traveled all the way to her ear. "Perhaps he's thinking about his lonely youth, a festive atmosphere, an atmosphere of intoxication. I'm sure that's what he was thinking of the last time he said to me, 'Aren't we happy?' Perhaps someday I'll use the astonishment into which he throws me . . ." He was suddenly bitter. He put down his fork and its tinkle made him note that Jeanne was no longer there (where is she? in the toilet?). Then he tried mentally to begin a novel: his hero was very much in love with his wife, very sincerely in love with her, but at the same time he saw himself led, by the very same sincerity, to commit acts referred to by the usual morality as being exactly the betrayal of Love. In addition, the hero harmonized his divergences perfectly, the relationship between them was one of complicity or kinship. When he got to that point, Quinte gave up his projected novel, he had the impression of having unconsciously reached the surface of a crime story or of having tried to deal with ordinary destinies. Although relatively annoyed, he gave his character a name: Jean.

A scandal that does not break is not a scandal, and if evil is not scandalous, it is not evil, why may it not even be good, thought Jean to himself. Jean felt an indefinable joy and even pride in the very dismay at being a husband, father, and pervert. He pressed his wife and his daughter to his heart, and the warmth he gave them, the caresses he lavished on them were not those of his fatherly and husbandly love in all their purity, they were also those which had been shaped, even refined and made more charming or profound by the marginal practice of other loves with other means. And he thought, for example, of his debauches with a weather-beaten fortuneteller.

He realized that he had continued the novel in spite of himself. Although he had no intention of writing it, he thought that a novel could take shape in that way. He knew his sketch by heart. But Jean antagonized him. For at bottom he was a yielding character, without consistency, as soft as cheese, it was hard to make him stand up, to find him after losing him. Moreover, Quinte was afraid of literature. The child's name was Thérèse. She would be like her mother, the same measured charm and a face divided into quiet areas (the cheeks and forehead) and scathing areas (the mouth and eyes). But Jeanne had, in addition, certain oddities around her neck. Thérèse would never have that neck, hers was a foreign neck, it was not her father's or that of any living member of the family. Multitudes of such necks could be seen in day nurseries. Naturally they had started to love Thérèse deeply. Their heads had touched above the cradle, etc. One day, because she had laughed at both of them in a perhaps extraordinary way, they had hugged as when they had been engaged, by the waist. And their fingers had mingled, etc. At certain moments, the mere sight of her made them feel a kind of tacit respect for each other. The child was perhaps a link, that's what's said in pulp fiction, she looked as if she were present, as if she had loomed up there, between them, like exquisite hedges, like the inexplicit means of being together. But today it seemed that each of them tended rather to love her for himself, neither of them dreamed of enclosing himself in that sentiment with the other. Jeanne came back (from where? from the toilet?). Her breasts, which were half expelled from her bodice, breathed health, horticulture, white milk. She had in her hand a newspaper with blood on page one. She yawned, but it was again the opposite of a grimace, it was a gluttonous deformation of the lips. Everything she did was against ugliness. Seeing him bent over his plate, she felt like laughing out loud. One of those joyless laughs whose cause one detests when one knows it, one hates to be tickled and one laughs, she did not know the cause, she laughed at not knowing why she felt like laughing. She vaguely feared that behind it all might be contempt. One could have written that it was not love that those bodies lacked, nor was it that their hearts were closed to harsh tokens of affection. Something was going on behind those difficult masks, or else it was what was not going on that rather hurt them while striving not to separate them and even not to suggest to them the mere idea of a separation. But no doubt this something, these unconniving forces, this big gummy knot which could not be resolved operated underground, short of the explorable, not within reach. It was perhaps a want of inspiration or a loss of formula. There were a thousand million answers to it! In love all hypotheses lead to an incomplete and one-sided truth less strong than a supposition. No amatory truth which is not everything vile that can be said about it, said Quinte's *Jean*. He did not know. Neither did she. And they continued their stubborn effort toward an unknown point in the future where a friction of souls would perhaps produce a new spark, then two, then three, until there was a flaring up, a flaring resurrection of erotic origins . . .

Then Quinte closed his eyes, which ground a bit of light. That was how he passed time in those twilit hours: with questions that could be answered only with other questions. Jeanne gave answers to questions she did not ask herself, for she was there chiefly as an observer. She lived her female life as an unsummoned witness.

The time that flowed intrigued him. It was like the suspension of a hearing, one awaited the resumption of the trial. (Jeanne had disappeared again.) Quinte thought of something else, of his goal. A great Goal, the exact contours and particulars of which still eluded him, but toward which he felt himself wanting to tend, and in truth did tend, inexorably. For the time being, he was content with knowing that "the success of his project depended on the extraordinary union of an aspect of his body with an aspect of his mind." Nothing more. At times, he has the impression that the future is imprisoning this goal in its star-excited jaws, and at times the feeling that he is accumulating it by chance in his being. In short, he was moving toward something gigantic, indubitable, the summit of which he saw both inside and outside himself. The important thing to note was that this goal had not yet been reached, or at least that every time he approached it the goal *rose* higher, so that he had to start climbing again. In any case, as he devoted all his strength to it, it was not possible that it would not someday be granted him to be able to go no further. Perhaps he himself would then be the Goal, would have become identical with his goal. It is no doubt right and proper to give a name to each of the reasons for exaltation that man chooses for himself. Quinte, however, did not name his. It was perhaps an animal or mineral. He wanted perhaps to have a very large number of brothers, simply that, although the word "brotherhood" was practically unknown to him. He was looking for brothers, and perhaps those brothers were not men, they were kinds of brothers, kinds of men in the form of things. In any case, it seemed to him that he was constantly accepting orders and directives, and it had to stop. Surely he would rebel. "I want what I know to be foreign to me and what I create to be new," he thought. To create! To refuse to be the onlooker of others. To listen only to the amazing will to turn his back on the spectacle. The idea struck him. Jeanne had nothing to do with it. Perhaps she thought she was the center of his universe, but he knew that what moved him at that very moment was precisely a universe in which the center could not be distinguished from the rest. He was going to join the Club and his joy was profound. He was no longer the same. Though Jeanne might look at him as she did yesterday, he was sure that he had changed, that he was at the very least transformed by joy. This joining was not a brutality of mind, it was the consummation of a . . . of a . . . maturation, the origin of which . . . He tried to find the right thought. His past had become all dark . . . The origin of which . . . he wanted to insert the word GOAL, though end . . . beginning . . . were more . . . suitable.

He tried once again to recapture the idea, the vision, the scene which by devious paths had led him to that most grave decision. He did not remember a precise shock, the only thing that resembled a memory was the picturesqueness of a procession . . . fog that day, heads no hats . . . In order to have a basis, like everyone else, in order to be able to say "the first time I saw that I realized that" he had helped his memory reinvent the memory of his remarkable vacation in . . . For it was not possible that he had not taken a vacation that year. He told himself a story that had been lived at the crossroads of the real and the imaginary, like a puzzle stretched between memory and experience, and it took place in a city called No Coal; my uncles had invited me, I was sixteen, I was already screwing. By consolidating, by continuing to store the images he retained of his stay there, he had succeeded in making it the starting point of his project. It presented itself somewhat like a tale. Once upon a time there was a big village surrounded by extraordinary mountains, the land there was not particularly good, workable, the liquid that drooled down men's faces expressed the lowest order of sweat (of all sweats, those which have not been produced by the union of sun or love with the energy of the senses are the most . . . unlovely). At that time he had not seen, but now he *saw again* the façades of the houses which were eaten away by a hard dust, a kind of oxide, the gray faces of the children whisking like owls along the winding catafalques of the streets, a lame breeze came down from the mountains, and the old women were grave and waistless in their dark, heavy dresses, the men-coughers were sitting on the concave thresholds, their eyes were curious about everything and nothing, as if that were the only way of being tragically dreamy there in that village, they became forgetful of the slow invasion of death, and as soon as one came near them, that death was almost palpable, one thought of a monkey-musician squatting in its thoracic cage, in the process of plucking the cord of the superannuated bronchia, and they were absorbed by that game in which the biggest gob of spit that came out would be etc., etc., the most meaningful; in the only whorehouse, where the knickknacks were pale and cracked like old bones that have been abandoned by dogs, the heart of darkness convulses and wheezes, the lamp has been put out and skinny Negresses are being quietly sawed by men's sex organs. He was more than sixteen, he could, it was allowed by Big Marthe. A tear there pelts like rain. Even the fairs there are dark, to say nothing of the fact that they swarm with people, but that is less certain, and the fair booths have a tone of vespers. I also remember the miserly sun. It was its parsimony that made the people so sad, it was a grace when its alms pierced the clouds, there was a kind of solar cruelty, on Sundays the people got dressed up to wait for it and it did not come. With their night eyes looking up to the sky, they prayed to the light in manly fashion, they had rolled up their sleeves, what were they hoping for, the reddening of their forearms no doubt, etc., an extraordinary breed of petitioners ignored by, by whom after all? They would scourge themselves to have sun, but the quadriga sets elsewhere, in lands to which we never have access because this is No Coal and we never leave it; the hoarse barking of the dogs makes a din in the kennels, nothing in the region is more desolate than rainy Sundays, with the sound of the perforated eaves, the forming of mud on the sidewalks, the sticky pavestones, the returning of the last strollers to their cells, one sees water lashing panes as if to fell their feeble lighting, one sees trees weeping convulsively on the trenched ground, at times a melody crosses the street, or a smell of fried potatoes, it is a precious perfume, and that is all, the water has washed away hope, and when darkness joins forces with its squalls, one sees the two of them swooping down faster than ever on all things, huge pots of thick dye, water and darkness fall, in a frenzy of blackening everything as they pass, and of blackening even more what was already black by the force of circumstances, and during this time, in the houses, the men smoke, shuffle cards, listen to the broadcasting of a song. I roll in the white sheets, one would think that the gardens are the theater of all the murders in the world, there is madness at the windows, sexual desire, the fever that crackles, and there was the following day, when dawn threw its dragnet on the road, pulling back those shoals of men toward all-powerful fishermen, invisible or still asleep at that hour. And to orient those cohorts, those cyclists, there were cathedrals of hatred, with huge wheels for rose-windows. A little tauromachy without glory, without a crowd and without light began again. He has poured his imagination, his force into the tale, he believes in it, it is, he stops believing in it, and it still is. And the story continues, its elaboration is unforeseeable: it requires only, not so much that he read the Club newspaper, but that he talk to himself about reality, that he rouse in himself the true legend. One day (wait, it's memory that, memory that . . . Ah yes, that's it), one day, when he was in the room where he lived, he heard cries . . . he went to the window . . . and he watched the rambling procession of people moving along . . . That time, the sun gleamed oddly, and he was able to see . . . eyes . . . welling up . . . on charred faces. They did not seem to be going to the festival of which there had been so much talk in the village for the past few weeks. Supernatural drums gave rhythm to the march, legless cripples and one-legged men brought up the rear. The whole town had an air of wrath, the flags were raving on the staffs. "What's eating you?" he cried. But from such a distance his voice had no chance of being audible. The tale unfolds within him, breaks up, dissolves, takes shape again unexpectedly, at times the words are lacking, or else there is an excess of words which becomes the Obstacle, the sentences tear at each other, kiss each other, the hymn grows, the legend swells. The goal . . . takes shape. But what goal . . . Art? . . . barrenness? . . . aristocracy? . . . revolution?

No! Tragedy!

Jeanne was there again. She is thirsty and squeezes an orange. He, half dreaming, intercepts the sound, the sensual colors, the play of opulence, the hot game. Thérèse is asleep, said Jeanne, he knew that.

"Hasn't my father written?" he asked Jeanne.

She shook her head, rather negatively.

"My father's indifferent."

His father had no goal. He made his wife happy and other women too. He believes in God, fornicates, and poaches. When he poaches, he looks as if he were fornicating (he caresses his gun, breathes hard, embraces trees, he shows the whites of his eyes), and when he fornicates he looks as if he were poaching (the woman is a prey). The father is kindness itself. The great problems leave the father cold, actually the father believes only in moments that are lived potently. The mother is unaware of his misconduct and shuts her eyes to his little faults, happiness is a blur.

Quinte delicately takes the newspaper from Jeanne's hands.

"Have you seen? Another revolution . . ."

She did not answer. She was tired of hearing about the revolution. He could have talked about something else. But his half-beaming face betokened no words or ideas other than those she already knew. She sighed.

"Where?"

The steaks were bleeding in the plates, one peppered, the other not. He liked pepper.

"You think he's going to come?"

"Who?"

"My father . . ."

"How do I know? Does your father worry you?"

It was not his father that worried him but what his father was doing at that moment. He often felt like sneering at him or taking his women away from him. He thought: "I descend from my father, but in order to return to him I must descend even more. When I was born, I can see him from here, he bent over my cradle and opened his eyes wide. I grew up and he said nothing to me about the Goal. He smelled of piss. I might have lived like that for a long time, in ignorance, I might have continued being the newborn babe for him, since he looked at me with the same round eyes when I was twelve, good and uncomprehending eyes. When I told him the story of No Coal, he laughed at me. Fortunately I found what I needed, all by myself. And tomorrow I'm joining the Club."

"Anything new?" he finally asked.

"Yes, a little while ago, at the crossing, I witnessed an extraordinary sight. The light had just turned green. And not a car moved. The drivers didn't notice. The weather was nice, it was very sunny, and they were laughing, with their heads out. They gave the impression of being able to live that way for a long time, in the same place, lollingly . . . Have you ever seen anything like it?"

"No . . . And finally . . . did they get going?"

"Yes, of course, when the light turned red . . ."

(She's wrong, thought Quinte. She took red for green.)

"Tell me, where are we going for vacation this year?" she asked.

"Vacation?"

The question took him by surprise. He scratched his head. Jeanne was still so young and light, so white-skinned, she seemed made for driving at wild speed over dusty roads, for wearing a transparent skirt in faraway countries where the men have eyes only for women. It suddenly seemed to Quinte that he was being confronted with a choice: to concern himself with her, or the rest, the terrible rest of men and things. Then everything got mixed up again.

"We won't take a vacation this year," he said quietly. Jeanne's face collapsed. Because of the light that was dancing on it, because too of all her tics, he imagined her very delicately alighted on a swarm of bees. He already saw them coming out all golden. He was afraid.

There was only *his* vacation. Walls leaning on his shoulders, *that* was his foreign land, his exoticism. All his life he had gone from room to room through the long tunnel of streets. In case of need, they were covered with landscapes and their roads, their immutability, and with subtle reversals of situation. At times, a promise of sun nestling in the darkness. He loved those rooms as a creator loves the retreats that weigh effectively, with all their hermetism, on the productions of art and science. He did not ask himself in what way he resembled the creator. It would have been enough for him to feel himself creating. At the office, at home, he was the prey of forces that made him believe in the existence of a work that depended on him. The same would happen at the Club. He had been carrying it for too long.

An action without a definite cause puts him into the state of one who is, not because he thinks, but because he believes and loves. Within him, as a result of the convergence of these two forces and of his own presence at the walls, a stage is achieved on which a goal lavishes unintelligible encouragement. And he was afriad of letting go, the thought of an escape made him draw back, the thought of fields and woods. Outside, it was the opposite that prevailed. The very opposite of his aspirations was gathered outside, waiting for him to come out. Quinte looked at his "opposition" with loathing. At times, with his nose against the window, he would see it from afar, he would spy it in the distance, slightly false and casual, spotted with light. "If I were out there, in the distance, I would lose the impression of vegetating, of being sheltered from degradation. People would oppose the loftiness . . . of the truth . . . which is inscribed in my being."

Jeanne dipped her finger into the orange juice. He sabotaged that sweetness by licking his finger, which was covered with pepper. He collected pepper. In little metal boxes with blue flowers, labeled and lined up against the wall on a small shelf. Irritating names could be read there: pili-pili, cayenne, paprika, curry, and others which he had invented: Ahic, Okourou, Hysteria.

It so happened that he was looking in their direction. His eyes were seeking them. But he saw nothing. His gaze had scanned the room in vain. He was disappointed. He realized obscurely, in that minute, how eager his eyes were for volumes, for masses hooked alive to a nail, or attentive on a stand, or severe on their feet. But his eyes actually furnished nothing they touched upon, or, rather, the objects, as if endowed with a vile shrewdness, began to stop existing, just as easily as that, no more noisily than a wasted breath. His repeated glances vaguely created not emptiness but barrenness around him; sterility suddenly covered the long, angleless wall and the infinite floor. The lamp alone seemed to him to shine, on unquivering planes. Jeanne resembled freedom. He had only to touch her to feel likewise free, delivered from faked living. He devoured her with his eyes. He liked to hang from that discreetly overflowing and generously clear flesh and to come. She had never been an obstacle, he could never forget that. She had permitted without a word or gesture what he was in the process of becoming. But Jeanne was disturbing that image of peace —he was remembering it fervently at that very moment— with her trivial desire for a vacation. He said to her anyway: "Jeanne, let's not talk about vacation today . . . I have something else to tell you. I'm joining the Club tomorrow . . ."

How often she had heard him harping on the same old string! One day, a blond, pink-cheeked fanatic, of the chaste kind, had come to the house to talk to him about the necessity of joining it, or something like it. Quinte had listened to him, with his head bent. And when he lowered his head, it was a sign that his resistance had been broken down by arguments he already knew. And the other had used flamboyant language: "We're all united . . . Things have got to change . . . You're in favor of justice, I suppose?" Etc. And they had clinked glasses, spilled a glass on the new tablecloth, complimented everybody.

He saw Jeanne turn to him. She looked as if intelligence were emerging from her head. Or else it was hatred.

"Do you think you'll like it?" she asked sternly.

"Yes, I think so. Our age needs men who proclaim what they are. I've got to learn what I am. And besides, one can no longer rely on oneself alone to love or hate.

One has to be supported by others, by the people in the Club!"

Jeanne saw stars. She threw herself on an old couch.

And he, feverishly:

"I've been feeling for years that that's where the answer is, in that Club, that it's there in front of me, that it's inviting me to fulfill myself in it. I hear the song of its circumference. I don't know . . . I can't stand it any more. It's destiny. I'll have friends." He was raving. He was imagining himself very strong, even formidable. He shook his head and laughed.

Jeanne was not laughing. It was the first time he spoke in a sincere tone, he must not be interrupted.

"Of course," continued Quinte, as if to himself, "I have a path . . . to clear before me, I probably still have lots of things to forget: prejudices, quirks . . ."

She also said:

"You're not meant for adventure . . ."

He felt himself turn pale. He would make every effort to forget those words, which he knew were fundamental.

"You'll have to reject everything, all the little, simple things that you like," said Jeanne soberly. "You'll have to see things in a big way."

"Yes, see things in a big way," said Quinte. "You understand me, that's good."

"And will you attend meetings?" she asked.

"Yes, meetings, perhaps symphonic meetings. There'll be music."

"What else goes on there?"

"We'll all be in agreement," yelled Quinte, flapping his hands.

"How can everybody be in agreement?" murmured Jeanne.

She's educated, he thought. She's not dumb. He discovered that truth, suddenly.

She was thinking of that big blond fool who had brought "that" here. She remembered his name: "Jean." Jeanne felt as far removed as possible from the idea of a club. Suddenly a wave of deep, extremely personal life seemed to unsettle her from head to foot. It was an extraordinary movement of thirst, of consciousness, of knowledge, which were not yet linked and went through her flesh. She was trembling: I'm a woman. She wanted to have nothing more to do with that Jean.

A crust of bread was drinking up the meat juice in the middle of the plate. Her slender hand flattened a tuft of hair above her right ear. She thought: "He has lost his bewildered look. It's as if he finally understood something whose meaning had been escaping him for a long time. And yet, it's not enthusiasm, it's still, as always, stupefaction . . ."

His lowered eyes kept staring at the empty plate. He had just heard doubt expressed about agreement. And that hurt him slightly. He wanted to think, however, that he had exaggerated his wife's voice and that he had overestimated the gravity of the words that had reached him and that kind of threatening, secret meaning. What he had heard could only be a burst of innocence, indeed hardly that. She had stood up and then sat down facing him. Quinte's free hands moved toward Jeanne's, which she had placed on the table. Covering them with his, he tried to remember in a ferment what those four hands had built, caressed, torn up together. He pretended to be seeing the slender happiness that wound its way between the fingers. He also thought of their eyes, of a quartet of eyes, extraordinary eyes concerned with harmonies.

Harmonies?

And so, from harmony to harmony, from little pact to little pact, they came to love each other for good, with their arms dangling. The pale, vibratile course of married life stretched out between them. Concord meant standing together on an impossible ledge. She had obviously meant another harmony. But he was thinking of accord in general. At the present moment, he did not believe, as she did, that every accord is a bringing together of errors and, if it lasts, their harmony. Then he raised his eyes to the starlike skylight. How depoetized it now was! With its unbleached wooden frame and its glass drowned in the lamp, it was no longer impressive. "The stars which don't deceive are higher." He shrugged. The room might have resembled a nest. Luckily, it put him in mind of a cage, tirelessly. The pepper was burning his tongue, the garlic too: a drop of beef blood which gleamed on the plate dazzled him. Life crowded to his lips. The moment he was living through was such that a joy had to be invented urgently.

"You're beautiful, Jeanne."

She smiled and stood up. She liked the unforeseen return of the vaguest words, even of lies, with their shreds of genuine acts. It was, once again, the universal compliment. From time to time he emerged that way, without fanfare, valiant and vacillating, at the surface of a stagnant indifference. It was then that she wished the word would not fly away, that it would remain there, enigmatic and, as it were, *skimmable*. He heard a sound and the quiet voice that murmured, "I'm tired." She never called him by his first name. Thus, the words she addressed to him gave off a strange sound which betrayed distance, incompleteness, failure . . . In fact, it was as if their very intimacy suffered from this emptiness, that it retraced its footsteps whenever the emptiness seemed to it insurmountable.

She was already moving off, supple and upright, how shall we put it? . . . a flame. Yes, standing there in her red dress, she did indeed seem to be a high flame that was spared by the wind. He felt like crying out, against all likelihood: "Come here so that we can talk it over!" But he said nothing, as usual. He felt violently weary on his comfortless chair. Beneath the skylight was the useless stepladder, and inside was the worthless, flaccid night in which the vomit of lamplight seemed to be drying. Moreover, Quinte had nothing to say except things that were very confused, things to be stammered. He knew nothing about the Club. But he wanted the Club to be.

They had met in a silly sort of way. Until then, what had excited him in women was their *length*. Their cajoling litheness. "Wherever you put your hand, there they are, like ivy that twines about itself and about the earth, but at ground-level, at man-level." At times, however, he compared them to sleek, swift insects, fit only for rushing, all black, up men's trousers and climbing to love along their legs.

One day, at the movies, Jeanne had appeared to him, strangely motionless, or rather set on her mobility, sitting on it like a conqueror. It seemed to him that by accident the woman had just interrupted her winding, her gliding into men, as no woman had ever been able to. Her two uncovered knees, seen from the higher level where he was sitting, resembled two generously exposed breasts, the very same white ones that she proffered under her chin. She looked as if she had four of them. Never had he seen a woman so rich in breasts. And they did not move, they were an excellent presage for him, very proper, very quiet. She had gone to the movies to kill a disappointment. A lot of people in the theater. A dirty film was playing, full of orgies, but it was there, and only there, that it had seemed to her possible to dig in, to give herself up to a patient training of her nerves and heart, she had laughed, she had almost taken a liking to all men. And Quinte had said to her, more than an hour after he had settled near her, "I think I've seen you somewhere . . ." "In the same darkness?" she wondered. And he immediately added the daring words that produced in her the effect of a desire that was food for her need to be desired: "But it's true that such beauty is never seen except for the first time . . ." "In the darkness," she repeated to herself, "in the darkness . . ." He entered the bedroom. The most dramatic of all the rooms was the bedroom. The woman's head was already resting on the pillow, like the result of a beheading of a pale, pure, ancient Pentelican statue. It was there that he had shown himself most virile and most gentle, most filthily smitten too, it was there that he had thought seriously that he was betraying the whole world, that he had conjured up the most feline images of another love, and also dreams of total laziness, and also the model of dark nooks where one did good illegitimately. "And illegitimate good is evil," he thought. And now the regular swellings of the bed covers were Jeanne's body. He did not put on the light. He wanted to see as little as possible that too precise face, that dovelike mouth in which a single sigh would have seemed to him unbearably ferocious. He took a few silent, supple, but graceless steps. His leather slippers responded noiselessly to the effort of his foot, he felt a kind of gratitude toward them. He undressed in the lighted corner of the room, outside of which were no perceptible lines or tonalities. However, when his eyes had grown accustomed to the darkness, he soon saw the moon bluing the shadows delicately; with her kind of emotivity, she seemed, by skimming it, to be pushing aside what kept things from appearing. Then, as if the result of meticulously gentle pulling, a set of furniture emerged, influenced, richer. Thus "unpaved," polished, the humble articles of furniture suddenly had style. She looked at Quinte with all the force of her eyes that were exposed mainly to the darkness. She saw his short, smooth hair, his beaked nose, his swarming temples, and, when he took off his shirt, his indigo torso, the subtle muscles which made her think of the play of knives chiseling some masterpiece under the skin. She did not move, she did not admire, she was seeing it for the thousand and first time, and of course she was a bit groggy. And yet a certain desire, which was trust in the Uncustomary, vaguely animated her. With her gaze, which he could not see, she tapped the casing of her husband's body with little lance strokes. Perhaps she was seeking the chink into which she had only to disappear so as to fall smack into the inaccessible. She almost mused: "It's not there, in his flesh, behind that fine leather which boasts deep health, that turpitudes accumulate . . . It's odd . . . one would even think he doesn't deceive me, that there are no 'foreign rooms' in it." The idea of a full embrace came back to her, that which circumscribes the individual who is gripped in so exact a mold that in his dream of rigor he does not imagine that someone else could get his little finger in. His amatory past still rumbled in his flesh, with its impurities, some of which had been learned willingly, others by force, with its lessons of intoxication and abundance. She rebelled noiselessly. She wanted a man. Her body was already rising up in waves toward this one's hands because he happened to be there, at that moment. She was going to fill those hands which were slowly taking off his trousers in a jar of moonlight, those eager hollows, she would literally cram them until her excess of pleasure could well up and flow irregularly between its fingers. Soon harmonious curves would come into being along the course of the incalculable fingers, of the soft, bronzed pommels where they would be enshrined. She shuddered, and yet her desire remained vague, undecided. The frenzy that she felt in her skin served to surmount the initial desire, the pure one, which remained vague and undecided in the depths of the burn.

A certain respite was born. The flesh, the evening, the silence, Jeanne saw a new respite arise out of the triple conjuncture of the Beautiful. Soon the problem would be over, the poor little asthmatic sound of the usual relations would no longer be heard. Only the hoarse joy of the shattered brakes could pierce the darkness. In the uncoarse intoxication into which they would be plunged by all the arcs of their bodies which slackened into each other, themselves drunk with so many simultaneous targets, they would not remember anything about day or tasks. Had she been asked to fix that night to the wall with eternal nails, she would have done so. Had she been requested to nail herself in a night without hope of dawn, nothing would have prevented her. She felt ripe for occult assaults. Anonymous or not. But the day would break, morning, noon, above all noon, most beautiful noon, the hour when there is surely sun and vacation elsewhere, when, with a flapping of wings, a kind of world-wide voluptuousness crossed the space not far from her, impossible to follow with the eyes, impossible to follow in any way. Quinte went to bed. He said nothing, did not even look at her. She was saying to herself, at that moment, that if her husband died it was not grief that would lacerate her, it would be the huge stele of the habits they had contracted together that would be lacerated within her, causing her face to make a grimace and a sound comparable to grief. When the bed stopped creaking and Quinte's pallid head had remade its hollow, which was still half made from the day before, in the pillow, he turned his blind attention to the hesitant shapes of his discomfort. His eyelids closed heavily, he saw red and black. Through the slit which they left him, he saw the ceiling, which seemed to him lower than usual, and the big, cobweb-like chandelier, closer than ever to his fall. The menacing, calamitous moonlight which looked like a column of lead half overturned by barbarians. It was all like a desert organized as a semblance of life . . . "Life, what is one to think about life?" But things must not be pushed too far. Shudders, right against him, were undermining the false peace of visions. Ardent calm had now set in, the moment had come to open his body to love and sleep. Those level-headed powers were lying in wait behind each other for his signal, he heard their anxious breathing in the shadow, they were an Indian god, not far from him, with their many arms, inclined to absolute brawls. Would he keep this appointment? Too late: if he had tried to flee, the room would have shrunk to her and him together. Besides, his desire got under way punctually, at the very Swiss hour of nocturnal collisions and tender lamplight services. Thus the major functions are organized in rites which by themselves fix their extreme instants so exactly that they could "clock in" in the maze of dubious time. He tried to think of something else, of tomorrow which was going to change him because he would join the Club, how odd it was to think of the Club, of the goal, when one has a naked woman at one's side. That word immediately created a fever, the very idea, necessary and vital, that the flesh is not everything, that one must be able to think of other things which prolong it toward a terrible salvation. And Jeanne was thinking of her Destiny.

He waited, she waited. Apparently they were both afraid of engaging in the big match, of touching early morning too quickly, of being stranded among their puffiness and the rings under their eyes. In that minute they were still fresh, but tomorrow everything they apprehended would reign, a smell of cod-liver oil would start loitering on the sheets, similar to the tired triumph of the senses. It was true that there was also Thérèse's first laugh, her first not-serious fall of the day. That alone was no doubt worth getting up for. Meanwhile they awaited the decision, the very spirit of decision. "What's new at the office?" she asked. Even that voice was naked. He answered with his rough, dressed voice: "Nothing, still the same enemies." Why was she bridg-

ing those two woes: being here, being there . . . all
those employees, bastards. He had always made an effort
to be outgoing with them, in order to understand
them, to absorb the manifestations of their "intelligence"
but without knowing either why or how, he had seen
them reject him while seeming to welcome him, it
was not he who kept away from them nor they who
kept away from him, but because they never responded
to the hopes he placed in their words and gestures,
it was as if they were driving him away . . . "I'm
cold," said Jeanne. They exchanged a few words about
the coldness, but it was manifest that their voices were
weakening, that they were decimating their words, not
without emptying them first of their substance. Soon they
stopped speaking except in a foul gurgle broken by sighs.
On the other hand, their movements had grown ampler,
their gestures had become bolder, they made veritable
inroads into the neighbor, there was a great traffic in
moods. It was almost a revel on the high seas. The sea
threw them up, naked and knotted, polypous, on a bluish
shore. They unlaced slowly, carefully, with inexplicable
pauses at the damp swellings, which they were incapable
of naming then and there; they were no longer held to
each other except by distant complicities, except by a
stringy touching of fingers or the impromptu meeting of
breaths. The sad voyeur perceived on their bodies the
mark of arid bubblings. It was because the sea had swallowed up the initial charm, and he could judge once again
the strange infirmity of bodies at that stage of the day.
Without moving a muscle, he surveyed, escaping from
the injured eyes of each of them, in front of a fleecy

square, the slight cohort of hazy consciousness on its way to sleep. Quinte dreamed of a goal, of a Club, of a terrible individual power. It was a huge swelling of the body and the mind, a dream. But she, what did she dream about?

At the Office

The office is in a building whose hideousness alone tends to putrefy the rest of the avenue, which is reputed for its fine jewelry shops. With its rheumy windows, which cannot be opened because of a defect that evoked, at the time, the sarcastic remarks of the ousted contractors and behind which hundreds of gazes discreetly swallow a frightfully glaucous and snotlike light; with its air of being abandoned, of having its corridors and stairways and even its offices encumbered with wax dummies that stand with their arms spread and their eyes unproductive and blue, the structure nauseates those who love immense, healthy things, the sea, the overwhelming works of sculpture of all ages, the pyramids scraped by Ra. And yet people work there rather powerfully. Boring publications are printed there which seem never to leave the place, for activity is greatly reduced when they are circulated, also humor magazines, also excited sheets whose headlines flounder in a red and blue mud and which are snapped up, when evening comes, by the mammas and papas eager for the latest unwholesome curiosities of the day, which was tiring, but not so much so that the misfortunes of strangers and the perniciously illustrated novel lose all their allurement, alas! And, as every morning, Quinte had pushed open the door and smiled at the obesity of the ushers sleeping in their chairs, he had walked a few yards, then had stopped in front of a painting that hung awry between two metal closets that swarmed with figures and names more numeral than the figures. He had fled, holding his head in his hands and crying "Ow!" The corridors, at the end of which there is always a waiting room, are so long that they end in a point like rails. Beyond the walls, which were scratched by excessive moving of furniture, could be heard the homophonous lisping of the employees in the process of acting, bent over the frightful white and gray autumn of the official papers littering the tables. Quinte passed people whose hands he refused to shake. His ill grace went unnoticed. "A sacred little gesture, without much meaning," he thought. He climbed two at a time the steps that led to what was called "the middle landing," where amorous appointments were generally made, where, also, people conspired, where there were odorless flowers that resembled basins. A lot of people everywhere, perhaps it was because of an event. In the offices that he

walked through, gatherings of quiet, smiling men, men
who were indifferent, faces choked by envy, ridiculous, or
as if poisoned by the emanations of a dream. Someone
called him, but in vain, he was running, out of breath,
intransigent, since he felt like saying to their faces:
"Someday you'll be changed! Even though a corpse is a
corpse, if someone violates it it's nevertheless violated!"
Today, as a consequence of his strange behavior, he
found no excuse for them. They were swine, they visibly
tended toward zero, they played at being small-timers at
the brink of nothingness, without realizing that a revolt
exactly like his was awaiting them, a welcoming and transforming, almost maternal revolt. While covering the distance that separated him from the shop, he thought of all
those who model, elaborate, and rectify the forms of the
world without its being clearly and indubitably apparent,
and he was furious at being unable to be where there
were such men with invisible hands, where were their
hands? Hands are all alike, those of the pianist who
strokes the keys and those of the stableman who caresses
rumps, they teem and if they are gigantic it is not on this
earth, what is the secret of hands? He kept feverishly re-
peating to himself the magic words: "The Club! The
Club!" It was there and only there that he had any
chance of seeing hands dismantled and clarified for good
. . . The Club was perhaps an excellent observatory from
which to distinguish the hands that act on the world. But
these employees obviously do not believe in all those
things; they believe in nothing, unless in the sex organ,
in its incredible dimensions, in its yellowish showers . . .
Tick tock tick tock. At his right, on the next floor, a
known figure rose up furiously: it was Wasmes-Bô, an

emaciated fanatic with a blue face. He looks as if his long, inflexible neck were perpetually impaling his head and as if the latter were being brandished and parading by for a carnival of vaguely hilarious onlookers. Squinting, grinning, and itching undo his face, and when he gesticulates he seems to be cutting up the image of yourself that you give him. People whisper that he is crazy, that he has a terrible secret. Why, moreover, does he give the definite impression of breaking loose even when he makes only the most trivial of gestures? Why, why? Quinte, rather fascinated, slowed his pace. He moved toward that man, who put so much of himself, particularly his ugliness, even into his weaknesses and fits of abstraction *that he seemed never to fail.* Wasmes-Bô did not speak, he never spoke, and yet Quinte listened to him. In his breath of an eater of things whose nature was never known but which must have come from far far away, there were no doubt words, words which had only that vehicle for falling into your ears, but he did not utter those words, he had no voice. And Quinte felt like sniffing that man, like copying his aphonia, his deep violence, but first his Success, which soared, which manifested a black, hawklike joy in the depths of his eye sockets, though he did not at all have a brilliant job in the firm. Quinte and he were the only ones who could stand facing each other that way without flinching, but with a frightening intensity of expression, a savage impulse wracked by the facial muscles, not like chess players, no, but like chess players pale with anger from whom a fleeing madman has just taken and run off with pawns. They went into the shop together. Machines, machines! Hubbub, hubbub! The workmen, the workmen! Quinte began a sentence: "Tell me, Wasmes-Bô

. . ." Whenever Quinte wanted to talk, he had a pain in his voice, which was ready to rise . . . To say something, though at the same moment there was no doubt something better to say, that was enough to grip the heart of any man in whom the best and not the good, the worst and not the bad are striving. He was sure that his speech had never been anything but a shadow of what it might have been, and this drove him to despair. But he was like so many others of his breed who long for the supreme and who die, contrary to their wish. "What is it like elsewhere? Are women more beautiful elsewhere than here?" he wondered. Wasmes-Bô continued both to be silent and to influence him, for his way of being entered him venomously and drove the sensitive people of his instincts to indefinable rebellions. Quinte would have quartered himself to possess a single one of Wasmes-Bô's hatreds, a single one of his loves. Streetwalkers cruise for trade in his eyes. They are beautiful, they have wool on their behinds, they are unscoured, and they have mouths and sphincters that could sever your organ in the twinkling of an eye. He burst out laughing. How literary everything is! Quinte heard a belch. "Wasmes-Bô!" he cried. He had disappeared. He closed his eyes. The adventure shook itself in the dust of dreaming. He began to stroll through the shop. A new sensation jerked his body and soul. He thought it was anger, that it had just been given to him for life and that, whatever he did henceforth, he would have to exist for it and by it and to exercise over it, for the public weal, only the domination that was necessary, no more. He will always be confronted with a disturbing nothing, whether hilly or smooth, and even with transparencies that will have to be hated and overcome by a struggle deep within him that will clamor with hound and horn for its frantic, torrential, irritated liberation through the fatty adversity of others! Yes, it is indeed hatred that haunts him. He must have someone, right away, to spurn. And it will be Ponche . . . Glory be to my hatred! My mildness was thus only an exaltation postponed by circumstances, by fear of the hue and cry! All those men were little broken willows bent over the back of a fleeing mirror, residual waters, sludge! . . . A last branch is still erect toward the sky, a kind of shameful desire impels it, nothing resembles sexual desire more than the desire not to die, they both betoken death. And that branch is called Ponche, just as all men who do not bow to my law will be called Ponche. Quinte now remembers. He had been taught in the past to hate, through a devious and antiquated kindness, in schools, in families, and hatred is now an adult, monstrous presence that awakens within him and recognizes places and asks at once for a glass of blood or for flayed breasts, for naturally it's hungry, poor thing. No one quite knew what department Ponche was in. He was not exactly a clerk or exactly a workman. Unlike Wasmes-Bô, he was an average man, of an averageness that reminded Quinte of the darkest hours of his mediocrity. But the staff was composed of men of that kind, and Wasmes-Bô overwhelmed them all because he was ugly in an ardent, mysterious way that was all his own. Let average men go away, let them disappear from our sight, average men have no goal, they are not disposed to the ineffable adventures of body and mind! . . . Quinte knew nothing about the rules of the Club (did the rules exist?). But he assumed that they would not ask, or even suggest, that he love Ponche. His tolerance had been limitless, but it was no doubt a thing of the past, since that morning, since he had taken the bus and the bus had broken its brakes going downhill and in the shuffle he had been able, for a few seconds, to squeeze against the door a screaming woman with a bluish face but a lily-white neck, a woman whose physical implications were aggravated through a black dress to the crackling of which Quinte's flesh responded with obscene torsions . . . Furthermore, the day had begun very dangerously, because of the weight that had fallen on his feet, because of a toothbrush that had broken in his mouth. And even earlier, the dawn had been impressive when he had gone to the window of the former spyings, and the ringed bellies of the droves had burst by the billion, as if from an apocalyptic enema whose squirts were demolishing the order and decorum of ideas. And in the moistening of the ephemeral surfaces, and in the non-watertightness of the sex organs, in the retroversion of the leaves on the big inoffensive trees, he had seen the Lack, the Emptiness of his soul running, jumping, dancing, and he had also seen the stern talisman of the gulfs plunging and surging in his blind artist's eyes. He would never again build his existence; he swore that he could never again live according to the plans and laws of other men. Exclamation points sputtered in the gaping, crushing jaws of the futures, and his life had imagined it was unique. And besides, what is tolerance if not to tolerate waiting for the hour to strike for oneself to be intolerant, with impunity. He moved from machine to machine, he touched the steel of a lever, of a handle, as others pushed aside branches of trees in a forest. He wanted to pass, to get through to Ponche, but on the way he came up against the object, the sovereign object of modern times which calmly devours the choice parts of our vitality. It is here and there, it reigns everywhere. Quinte suddenly thought it urgent to use all his resources, all his nerves, and all his outpourings in the execution of a tremendous project which would be to break the rigidity and inadmissible coldness of the object, its foul immobilism in which too many men are tempted to recognize the end of their confused aspirations and to conform to it. Thus the only thought in his head at that precise moment was to see his life hurl itself against objects, his fruitful, injurious life, which was as burning as the fire holes of big American kilns. He did not lose sight of Ponche, who was squatting over there, attending to long and short pieces gathered on the floor. His long sleeves, from which his hands hardly emerged, as if they had been sprigs of lily-of-the-valley, moved now to the right, now to the left, not to pick them up, but to judge their weight. Quinte's glances ran over that back which they furrowed with God knows what visions. Ponche, who was standing, was a tall fellow, not good-looking, pale and too clean, with sandy hair. Loose gibes were springing up around him, and he seemed to be listening to them with a certain attention. In a corner, men were telling ribald stories comparable to some obscure puzzle of vices and excrement, a puzzle that had come out of some sordid brain, then they talked about a change of speed. Quinte leaned against a post on which it was customary to write or pin dubious tributes to woman. Ponche, seen from here, was no less detestable. He was standing. He was a tall fellow, not handsome, etc. "That man must have a deep aversion to great deeds," thought Quinte. "He spends his life avoiding them, dragging from subterfuge to evasion. He lives only indirectly. I realize why I hate him: he's weak . . ." All that remained was to pick a quarrel with him, to imagine a destructive pretext (he surely loved Moussia). Ponche was part of his goal, he was a not-to-be-neglected aspect of his future adventure, a live but condemned element of his history. He announced to me my forthcoming power, the future unfurling of my gesture over the world. Quinte clenched his fists, but as if to squeeze a sparrow: with a certain restraint. Ponche's face, seen through the inextricable growth of the machines, filled him with a circumspect fury, very different from the flashing of mystics. Ponche was biting his nails. "They probably take me for a spy," thought Quinte, who also thought of Wasmes-Bô. He withdrew, without apologizing to someone for walking on his brief case. He crossed the shop in another direction. He was hungry, he would have gladly sucked a slice of bacon or snatched a revolver from the heavy panoplies of astounded collectors. There was a ringing. Almost at once the too-loud noises expired, while an odd joy cheeped. Hundreds, perhaps thousands of men, for the more men there are, the *smaller* they are, blocked the halls, obstructed the winding stairways which the directors never used. They began smoking terrifically, the slow, sustained suction of a cigarette mimes the highest delights of the body, they were not smiling, they were possessed by Nicot. The eyes shone, dirtily, and from the drawing to the exhaling there was a short path where the vulgar forms of desire were expressed. There were all kinds of damaged faces, some were vitriolized. Luckily for them that they indulged in the weed, that they looked as if they were dragging at a little white poem. There were some who seemed to chew the smoke before releasing it, and others who shifted a reddish, spongy butt from one corner of their lips to the other, the mouth was like a billiard scoreboard. Quinte went to urinate, men crowded around the toilets, on top of each other, and they were shaken as in the frightful suburban means of transportation. Someone dashed a bowl of water under the door of an occupied booth. There was a roar of anger, with a cough in the middle, and then laughter. Quinte, dazed, nodded, went out. Presently all those fellows would be going home and it would be sad, for there is a drama in every family. He saw a scarab of oil in the process of spreading, of having feet. He did not recognize any of the men. Yet they were all there, as they had been yesterday, and they had a name. "Why am I here? I have something to do, somewhere else." He no longer remembered. Then a wave of hatred tilted him sideways, like a boat on the sea. Ponche was quietly looking in his direction, without appearing to see him, his hair was smooth, a slender mustache was jigging above his puffed lip, and there was something that opened cautiously, like a trap door, over two gold teeth. There was nothing agile in my hatred, it was inside me, like a big slab, a big slab of pepper and garlic, a big slab of sulphur and suffering. Perhaps a fine incision was made over the whole surface of his being. He did not quite know what it was, then he ventured a gaze toward that of the other, though without managing to meet it, for it was a gaze that remained in his eyes, eyes without flashes, inexpressive. Was that what mildness was? The man seemed to be blushing; in any case, his paleness was not the same as usual, and he lowered his head. Hearts leaped, in certain breasts, like toads; in others like garters. Quinte said "yes" to someone who did not ask anything. Moussia crossed the shop, or she was getting ready to cross the shop, no she had already crossed it, it was that everything she did was so turbid, she seemed frightened at seeing herself surrounded by so many unoccupied men who unleashed their gazes on her, some the way one unleashes a pack of hounds, the others the way one simply "slackens." She realized, or did not, that they all dropped a certain conversation for one of which she was the subject, totally, and that perhaps a man who had begun a story with the intention of edifying or astounding found himself forced to break off because everyone had stopped listening to him, and because, after all, he too felt like getting an eyeful. Perhaps she felt that heavy, collective shift of attention toward her person as a noise and as a resonance of shunting. For a moment she even resembled a fledgling that is frightened by the giant onlookers encircling it, undecided. Then she collected herself and had a weak smile for everybody, a smile specially created for going to a group, a smile which parted the lips only unconsciously, which nevertheless vibrated beyond her like the poisers of Diptera, quite the opposite, in short, of the *private* smile which goes to the lover or the friend, and that black head of hair, so famous in the firm, well! it seemed red this time and the reason was that it looked as if it were licking her bare, quivering shoulders like flames (not flames that ruin, but that create . . .), and that head of hair was also, in the depressing atmosphere of the shop and before the fired eyes of the men, like a savage break-through of light in the darkness, and Quinte had the definite impression that she was putting new life into the collapsing of things and men, that she was exhuming the buried drives of dynamism and desire, in that barren universe she was exercising a pull that brought ancient shudders to light, and her passing snatched man from a pedestal and put him back in the saddle on a certain steed, fierce and temperamental, real insatiable life, spurred by the teeth of our ghastly laughter that digs into its hemorrhagic flanks. Moussia also symbolized luminous skin and clean, diametrically hygienic clothes, we would like to have washed with her, to saponify her gaze on us until we felt it sliding over our skin and mingling with our sweat; to make tremendous suds with her body against my body. And the uncertain odor that descended to her from her face and arms, like the train of a gown, light and all but invisible, the extremities of which went wavering beneath the men's nostrils, that odor was majestic, it was the total adorning of the air! Moussia glided sumptuously over the floor, the spectacle was like a stray fairytale, the more ardent males whistled, older ones shook their heads, said a few rapid words to their neighbors, the kind of words that helped them to stop desiring in silence deep in their hearts, with an adoring, idolatrous hatred, like oppressed brutes, greedy rapists. Had the mystery of the flesh suddenly become clear and glowing for one of them, God knows with what chanting of humiliated senses the innocence of savagery would have mingled! But the energy of the eyes is a sufficient beast. That was the best that could be done, since they could not pounce and gauge in their unhinged paws that lovely, unbreakable, and inaccessible body! A few of them growled, Moussia had touched the edge of their torment. With a twist of her hip Moussia had split their callous thickness, others called out to her in vain, particularly a dirty redhead. She was about to reach the door, and they would hear the fading of her footsteps, which was to the floor tiles what lapping is to water, Quinte was observing Ponche, and a kind of pyrotechnic eroticism was glowing in the redhead's wild stare. Quinte was no longer looking at the girl. Had he looked at her very well? The moment she was about to disappear (was it possible . . .), he kept his eyes fixed on some rare point of his grandiose projects which was buried in the enemy neck. Moussia left, Moussia had left, and at first the hubbub hesitated to decline, then declined very quickly, the slackening was most perceptible, the fire fell back to its ash, the blood subsided into its vascular darkness. To be sure, a bit of alcohol still flowed in the men, clinkers wandered here and there in gestures and the pupils of their eyes, but of the woman, strictly speaking, there actually remained only a swaying of all things, only a multitude of ideas which had been stopped and punctured in their impetus and the air of which, having become gloomy again, made the tatters oscillate up in the rafters. The first time he had seen her was in a streetcar, she was in front of him, a mass of black hair, and he wondered what kind of mask there might be behind those cascades, perhaps an all-white one, or a grayish-brown one, with a pink little snuffling nose, then she had turned around forcefully, like a woman pinched in the behind, and that face had leaped into Quinte's great joy, which had been hollowed by appetites, which was open like a grave that awaits a corpse, that face with the wavering luxury of its eyelids, with its art of melancholy, with, in the unknowable union of perfumes and the soul, the sober eldorado of foretokened charms, in the center of a burning intelligence and of the somber and infinite light of the race. Since then, he did not dare look at her too much, he did not like people to look at her too much, because he had had a feeling that she was a virgin and that he would someday be called to protect her against himself and the others. She was Moussia, and he pursued her with that vow, which was like a long, illusory, uneasy, desperate shadowing.

Something other than primeval hatred was now dominating him, a kind of visionary ardor stronger than all the evils and all the duties of the world and than all the accumulated things of *being* which were laid out in a circle around him; a kind of sensual will, frenzied but apparently without an object, one of those events that happen superhumanly to man and end in convulsive failure in the grip of the imaginary.

Everything that still resisted was flattened on the opposite wall, like a remnant of dirty snow which had been thrown there in a ball and the outline of which, now that it was almost melted, recalled, by chance, progressively, the face of an enemy, or of an ancestor. His hands were stroking tubes. It was not a threat of death, it was like existence (or experience) blocked on one of his slopes, like a switch of life that he would have had only to turn on or off in his head . . . In the latter, there was a sudden cry like that of a trio of drunken revelers; he did try to take his bearings, at a given moment, but each of his questions stood up and then collapsed theatrically in his mind, ideas flew like achene tufts, lightly, slightly defunct, and the images which he had thought the hardest, the most firmly rooted, slowly broke down at his approach into a cloud of dust. He bent down! He picked up a screw! A most precious little act. . . . "There was an enormous number of wax vestibules . . ." And there he was again communicating with the part of himself that was eager for his words . . . he felt he was drinking his words, incoherent, preposterous words, presumptuous words, of which he was no longer in control. "Why should I believe, why believe?" He was not seeking salvation, he was afraid of salvation, he would have gladly done evil so as not to be saved. "No plenitude for me!" he cried. In paradise, it must be impossible to struggle, to want to spread doubt, to have enemies and a controversial ideal. On the contrary, one finds oneself with all those others, those terrible others who have done us such harm and who resemble each other and whom I resemble, and who also resemble infinite tatters, it is those infinitely quiet souls, the fetus of which can be perceived here below in certain host-white gazes, that must be avoided at all costs. And besides, there was the uniformity, which he rejected in advance, the too perfect laws, the too straight paths. Make way for drunkards! And what do the souls say to each other, could they even talk to each other, since to talk is already to sin against silent purity. Really, he saw nothing up there but the same monotony everywhere, nothing but the equation of big and small, whereas on earth there were billions of bodies, myriads of gestures, and incalculable additions to every known thing, and that was what he had to believe in, in his solitude . . . He did not believe in the gentleman-who-was-crucified, he would say: "He was no doubt a Tarasque, a people amused itself around a Tarasque, on a mount . . . and those nails were as harmless as cloves . . .

Crucified with cloves ha ha ha!" And he was shaken by a frightful negation. Yet he liked the story, he liked to read about it in scholarly books, and however fabulous he was tempted to find it, at times he read it with a heavy heart at the thought that, after all, it might have happened, and even that it had happened to some extent if only because so many people have believed in it for thousands of years. There was no way of taking a step in the street or in dreams without encountering a religion; to be born was in short to be promised to some religion or other, the world was teeming with gray-eyed ecclesiastics. An abjuration was always a conversion, there was no getting around it, nothing to laugh about: religions were in the air, they jumped unexpectedly on the man who, thinking he was fleeing them, was actually swallowed up in one or the other. Denial was vain, he was there, propped up in an armchair, in a prayer, in a sickness. Quinte thought that in the Club there would obviously be no religion, which corrupted the atmosphere, and that contrary to what happens morbidly elsewhere, the members could love each other without rites and without necessity. Even the hard-working unbelievers who surrounded him resembled a kind of collective sprouting of the sacred. Even with airs of rationalized swaggerers, even with primitive or enlightened little ways of being secular, it is never very hard to embody a parish; at bottom, each man contained enough obscure religiosity for the forms of a church to be born of all of them. There were complete, organized religions, full of dogmas, unfriendly, and others that lived hidden or disguised in men's reason. A perpetual sound of Mass buzzed in his ears. At the Club, there would be no Mass, it would be too stupid. He was sure that he behaved like a man who had no religion. In addition, he wanted to be allowed to attempt to love without effort, without help. He would very much like to be *free* to love, to change his love and way of loving, and, in case of need, to dig a knife charitably into his neighbor's belly. Loving was almost that. The pleasures were there, against his limbs, against his wavering health, and they became accessible, they had white flanks, they opened beneath his steps like legs of a hysteric, he had only to bend over slightly to watch them operate, and it smelled good, the odors had the shape of barrels, and they rolled. Then he looked up, not to the sky, impossible here, but to a kind of flying outline, which was still the earth, between sky and earth. He loved that earth, he loved it with a frightened love, somewhat like the fascinated terrors of the Middle Ages. At times, sadness stole over him, he felt powerless to avoid useless words and acts, the ambient religions, the viperish habits; he would have liked to spring just like that, straight off, from an essential column and await the death of everything, and his face closed, but really a closing, which drew his skin down. Very strong desire, no doubt the strongest, the desire that has lost its itinerary, that knocks about everywhere, zigzagging, starved, steeped in pride and filth, gaudy, growling, desire was perhaps for him the one way of loving, the only one he had really cultivated when he was very young, when people hid from him the realities of life; he desired to and fro, depth-wise and height-wise, unknown things which were intertwined for better or worse, fleshy, wormy, cheery things whose supreme beauty was in fleeing from him, who pursued them breathlessly, *that* was his dear damnation, for there is always something to desire, at any time of day and in the night itself, when one dreams: *dreaming is only a reclining of desire;* he was quite ready to believe that love is not what lies beyond desire, in the sating that welcomes it with its powerful trumpets, but that love is the desire itself for love: an ingenious pain, a state in which one suffers perseveringly and in which a bitter experience of the fact of living is suddenly expressed in a forest of incomplete images, in a savage and enlightened knowledge . . . What he feared was that desire might be arranged, laid out in a circle around him, like any religion.

At that very moment when he was thinking of Moussia, he was rather grave, he wanted a certain thing from her, it must not have been Peru, for in her eyes there were only soft flashes, only "aged" flashes, flashes that looked as if they had already been used. In the lavatory, he was in the lavatory, buttoning up his fly, he saw his stern face, which capsized, which was perturbed by the movements of the gesture. He was not laughing. He was refusing joy. An idea occurred to him, interesting in the flowing of the water from the tap: "One does lasting things only in a state of gravity, lasting things can be done only in a state of gravity, not to laugh is not only moral, it's efficacious, instructive." He started to laugh. He was thinking of Moussia: "She has a reddish kidney." But Moussia was not alone, there were a million flies on her, on her virginal light. People are terrible when they visit your inmost thought, it is as if they were going to devour you, devastate you, rob you, from within, and the sound they make is zzzzzzzzz. Quick, an anthropicide! to kill man in his inmost thought, quick, Madness if necessary! Even those who had never had any influence on him, even those who had frightened him only slightly, they were all there. Quinte shook his head. It was not possible . . . Moussia had no navel, she was the first woman, and they dared . . . A statue with a winder, the only one of its kind, the only one of its kind as are all beautiful things before the insecto-maniacal verve imprints its crap on it!

He was now at the heart of something. In order to get going again, he would have needed a new language, foreign, unintelligible words. But he did not want them, he liked French too much, each French word is a gift to oneself as soon as one utters it, even when it is a howl in the night of wolves, but when they are, as now, devices of the devil that run madly around a slip of the tongue, no doubt a slip of the tongue, in a big bare and fatty space where one felt ridiculous because everything there jeered at oneself, he surveyed something-or-other where he had talked to himself, he wanted above all to situate that kind of choked little laugh he had just heard which was comparable to sabotage, paralyzing the play of a strange troupe of sad, fragile, panting marionettes. "Only questions are true, they don't lie . . ." The head, a tiny gymnasium swarming with all kinds of athletes in the process of exercising variously (with noise and irony) the head. He ran his hand over the skull of the former executive director. How smooth and round it was! One would have thought it was made of marble, but no doubt it was. He took pleasure in stroking it as if it had been his own, moreover it gave him that impression, an impression of homogeneity. He felt like stretching out and sleeping blissfully, as when one has picked up, as the saying goes, the thread of one's ideas. Nothing was now easier than to live, than, for example, to light a cigarette. He lit a cigarette, and it was a miracle of earthly simplicity, flame, smoke, tobacco that reddened, an ash, clearness. It was peace, deceptive peace, his favorite kind, the one you feel when the green light goes on and suddenly a thirty-second bridge is thrown between you and the person waiting for you across the street. Going ahead is then pleasant, irresistibly easy. It is like a few yards of intense life to cover between two lines of an impatient death.

So Ponche was there. Quinte felt only a little chilly. He uttered an unstressed, meaningless *ah* that seemed to emerge stealthily from his mouth, or rather from the sleeping or dying world of his throat. He understood, he did not understand that sudden unavailability of so much hatred which not so very long ago had been tribal, devouring. It very nearly seemed to him like a laboratory hatred that had been transferred from a boiler to a retort and was being watched closely in its more subtle mixtures. And it now resembled water. He explored the man curiously, but it was rather their meeting that he was contemplating, from the outside, as if he himself were a newcomer, and he thought it . . . picturesque. He saw himself, not without a thrill, painting an unexaggerated portrait of Ponche, and Ponche let the portrait be painted, painted one himself. His face, while he spoke, remained closed. The words did not emerge whole from his lips, they were peels of a kind, slippery things that one throws away when the fruit is in the mouth. Besides, no one heard, behind his flourlike mask, the hammering of the Word, its drunken and immodest assaults. Poor Ponche! My hearing rebelled against his words! Poor

Ponche, equal to all the dumb, and I equal to all the deaf! Speech would no longer arbitrate our hostile contact. Poor Ponche, who spoke without being listened to or heard! His mouth moves like seaweed in the sea, no, like the flowing of a broken egg on my sleeve . . . and it barely pierces the thick fog of my eyes which are still drowned by the tears plucked from me by all the idle conversations put up with in the course of twenty years of promiscuity and now summed up in a single feeling, a cry: "Wretches!" What could Ponche have said other than the innumerable things that launch nothing super-human or desperate in the consciousness of men? . . . Naught! naught! naught! He said nothing of any value. He said only certainties. We could not understand each other since he was not, like me, damned by doubt. Speech would thus be eternally humiliated in salivas. When it pretended to rise, it immediately fell back like furfura-ceous dust far from my stormy limits. How sweet it was to hatch a tremolo sarcasm in the quiet oratorio of my as-sembled dream! And while his lips engaged in labial eradications and his mask, livid and useless, collapsed into the hazy swallowing of my contempt, I sought again the means of checking that hatred which plunged its different and seething waves all the way to the last edge of my nails. That, no doubt, was what was called compassion! And it lasted a quarter of an hour and more during which time topmen were stabbed on the tall broken masts of scuttled reason, which strained and rocked in the secret squall of hatreds, here is the next-to-last gasp, the crimson one. Was Quinte going to turn on his heels, to flee in order to break with all that, or to rush forward and knock Ponche down? The latter's brain tract would inevitably burst on the machine tools. Or all that remained was to raise democratic nuances to the pitch of a limitless intolerance, or he had to give up his point by a degrading effort to understand.

Finally, Quinte realized that Ponche was inviting him to visit his barge. Quinte therefore began laughing nervously. He had thought the time had come to manifest his interest by a bit of feigned gaiety, and he had botched it. He answered "No." However, he was paralyzed by a doubt, as when one reads on a sign: "Ash Street." "Which ash?" one asks oneself. "The tree or the cinder?" One had to choose. But the doubt quickly returned to the charge. And Ponche, what was he? He imagined them both together in a night club ensnared in a jazz tune. A champagne glass turned indefinitely in his damp, pimply fingers. Suddenly a woman came and sat down, right between Ponche and him, straddling the table, with a thigh on a level with their chins, and threw them simultaneously into an animal hatred of each other, a hatred that savored of the taste and justification for killing. Her breasts cast a smell of death between them, they caressed her with one hand, with the other they sought a knife, or the hardest fist, that hurts too. When one does not use one's fists, they decompose and attack the entire limb. One thus acquires dangling, nauseating arms. They had been observing each other for years. Skeletally on guard, insensitive to the impartial moan of the woman, whom they both knew, having already seen her somewhere cross the sea of lusts and the desert of timidities.

Really, Ponche said nothing interesting, he did not talk to you about the necrocracy of the thirtieth century or the psychology of larvae, he did not carry you off in the toboggan of journeys on a woman's back across mountains on whose sides chained satyrs screamed their frightful desires, he did not quench your thirst with the wine of phantasmagoria, he did not make you spend the sleepless nights of the insane, he did not talk to you of calmness and purity as of something pestilential, he did not sharpen your thousand times too blunt hunger, he did not have a cobra instead of a tongue or rapiers instead of teeth, he seemed devoid of pride and insolence, and he was not a fanatic either, one of those people who can love and cause death with the same solemn and haughty rage, who can deliver themselves up entirely to an obsessive ignorance in the face of which any knowledge would be an enemy knowledge, and who can forcibly convert you to what they believe although they know very well that what they believe is incommunicable by nature; and Ponche was not a criminal under torture either, his corpse would not rot on Gemonies . . .

And yet that man existed, blindingly, and "so big that he surrounded me" . . . Was it a dream, a solid dream, a flesh-and-blood dream, or else the acceleration of a dream to the point of the illusion of reality? In any case, it was reality. And it was reality to cross long corridors, always the same, which resembled picture galleries without pictures. A big mural poverty gripped him, it was as if he were in search of an exit, but the corridors could not be fooled, they refused to end outside, on a sensorial shore, they were big, smooth, polished surfaces where kids would have liked to scratch obscene graffitti. Finally he came to a kind of waiting room adorned with a few hardy plants. From the windows with gilt casement bolts could be seen the ambiguous interiors of a few hotel rooms.

Thus he would never know the end of that story of Ponche's. Could it even have been written? He did not know. He thought of writers. Someone had said to him "to write is to be loved." And Quinte, stupefied, had nodded. He never wanted to see Ponche again. He stuck his left hand into his right sleeve. He looked like a conjurer who has forgotten how to proceed. He looked like a pear. He looked like the dog whose head he had smashed against the wall that same morning in a burst of love . . . He looked like . . . he looked like . . .

He made a vague gesture. Suddenly in the shadow of his big, twisted hands arose the unequal groan of great hand-to-hand fights. He dreamed that he was involved in a war whose only aim was the deliverance of a poisonous or somnolent art in the depths of man and that he was dying on that field of honor, in that uniform, yes that he was fighting against science in the name of human force . . . "Indeed," said Ponche, as if echoing. Ponche, always he, always that bushy, hairy obstacle of meaningless words, of all those who talk though they have nothing to say, their mouths in the form of an obstacle, their absences in the form of an obstacle, their venial little occupations in the form of an obstacle, their solicitude in the form of an obstacle, in the form of a grain of sand in your formidable mechanism, their limp and unbreakable bit lodged in the heart of your brutal thrusts. Listening to them say nothing, Quinte sometimes had the impression of living a better moment than all the others, but when they started talking again, it was like an aggression against his old treasures of adolescence. There are probably more than ten thousand ways of starting a dialogue. He seemed to have tried them all. With him, dialogues are either still-born in his imperishable solitude or else they crash and flow in colors on an intermediary stained-glass window that belongs to the history of stained-glass windows that were failures.

Such was the shop in its dismal strangeness. Such was the place where life lost one by one its reasons for roaring and where the few supremacies of the human soul, which were governed in their entirety by the demon of works, gradually returned to the vassal unison of animalcules. Such was the place where one felt like setting fire so that the rising flames guarantee the purification of the mediocre and resuscitate the wild recalcitrances of the body and the mind.

On the way, Quinte met some employees. They were haggard, some were trim and dapper, others were wearing old clothes, they were polite, even deferential. And they hurried along, with files under their arms or holding a simple sheet of paper, they were moved by mechanical thrusts that even Swiss mechanisms would have envied! Triviality, routine, it all hummed beneath their steps, along that inobservable rail that led them from door to door, from typewriter to filing cabinet, from behind-riveted-to-chair to column of figures in ink. They were instinct with inexistence, they exuded a premortal odor. They did not think of rising. Though they walked horizontally, they sank, they reached zones where breathing remains the only sign of life. They were almost nobody. And it was a miracle that the indictment of the great judges did not blow them out like candles! And a miracle too that they did not burst like bubbles under the lacerating gaze of artists!

He was in a room with white walls, on one of which

was the scowling photo of the founder of the firm and a photo of two blood-stained boxers who were hugging each other so as not to fall. Next to it, a drawing representing a runner looked like a holy image. The furniture was greenish. As for the lamp at the end of the wire, it was as if the ceiling were drooling. He wrote: "The game between the two teams was utterly sterile. Those rags were unworthy of what one is entitled to expect of sport. Playing without energy, they seemed basely anxious to maintain their position at the bottom of the league. They are no doubt very satisfied. Nevertheless, we required a frantic battle, an exasperated conquest, and we were presented with the spectacle of a barely agitated sleep, of a demonstration of human flabbiness based on the cult of security at all costs. Let us add that we left the stadium vomiting out every single one of our impressions and that we swore to wipe out that insult to our inextinguishable exigency . . ."

Quinte stopped writing. He had a desire to possess the sea, he saw it dancing a little, a bit hazy before his eyes, more beautiful than the reality of the sea, than "the" reality that plays surveyor around man and dictates to him his measures. But superimposed on that sea was the human sea, so much less likable than the other one . . . He saw his right hand which was falling in strips into the void, that hand of which he still expected, more than ever, a shattering act, which would half open the darkness of the sky, his right hand which had a good smell of blade and leather and which ran over the untuned piano of dark temptations. Perhaps there was a manner of weighing it; how much: a half-pound? Enough to slap the world, enough for a pulverizing of livid men.

Toward the Club

Quinte was sitting, with his legs crossed, on the terrace of the café sipping a sea-green drink, the table revolved about his glass, he had never seen so round a table and a glass placed as exactly as that in the middle of a table. He was not drinking. Not far from him, sitting at a square table, a black-haired old man was stuttering with anger as he told stories about kidnapping to a kind of grandson with blue eyes whom nothing frightened. The weather was good, but the surfaces were still beaded with rain, and they were supple and warm, like flesh. At the left, a military man was reading a newspaper which Quinte did not know and which was full of news that resembled no other. His face was coffee-colored, and his uniform was soft and brown like the skin of a mulatto. He made one think of those ne-groes who are a prey to a mysterious paleness. Only his hands, which emerged from sumptuous sleeves, were red, full of blood, as are all centers of pleasure. Quinte was not in the habit of going to cafés. He therefore felt ill at ease. The waiter frightened him with his big, dark movements that were shot through with white. He watched life flow by in the street at a speed that was not wild in itself but that nevertheless tightened the heart. He was not in that life. He was seated and jealous. A fellow went by with a bag on his back, his legs were trembling beneath the weight. "At least that one suffers. He has reason to think he exists." He took a cigarette, and, before putting it to his lips, smoothed it with his finger tips. There was a slope. A car went by. It was and was not disorder, it was blue, streamlined, its chro-mium plating shot fishlike flashes. "And me? Why am I sitting? Isn't there room for me in the car?" He thought of his thoughts, as intellectuals do. He could not help seeing his hands moving about his thighs, one would have thought they were looking for an opening. Dull blows shook his chest, a kind of gnome, a desire, he did not know what life to lead, he did not want a minor balance. Which was stronger, his senses or his mind? A woman went by, not a furtive shadow, not one of those supple, slender, wheat-colored animals, not one of those cereal healths that men's eyes bend and reap out of lust. His hands kept revolving wide open on his purple corduroy trousers, he seemed to be relearning an ancient movement. He remembered friends, men and women. Did he have any? It was perhaps they for whom he was waiting. They were going to come, to sit around the table, to encircle him. In any case, he would inform them that he was joining the Club. When one joins the Club, one tells one's friends, it's only natural. People went by, tight-lipped, at a military pace. Formerly, when his friends questioned him about his past, he would answer: "That's over, forgotten" or "You want to know too much." But they talked and talked. Their lips were jostled from within by a knowledge eager to be emitted. He felt sorry for them. They wanted to play at being men, remarkable men, but he felt incapable of noticing remarkable men, they were somewhere in the world, in prison. Nor did he know the addresses of the offices of all those swarming societies, of those innumerable mutual welfare associations which he was sick and tired of hearing about. It was particularly hard for him to believe in the existence of those gadgets. People also talked to him about saints, about martyrs, good God, where were they hiding, what had he done to them? Or else his whole life unfolded as if it were important that he know none of them. He did not understand. He called the waiter, a big shadow arrived and pocketed the money without a word. He walked away, through an odd reality, reality glided beneath his feet, into reality, there is always a crevice which suggests that underneath the real is something no less real; there is always a trap, an excrescence of falseness, the real was a layer which quite simply had the luck to be above others, he would have liked to take the deeper layers by surprise, to grab them, to reach out within them toward more remote ones. At the Club all these matters would be studied very closely, tomorrow, at six o'clock. After the customary formalities. At the Club he would engage in ardent suppositions. For everything is shifty, nothing around you can be used, like a mold, to offer you reality, you have to transfigure, create. He did not feel born, he lived, made efforts, in order to be born. But the world refused to be his belly, his entrails, he was constantly ejected, the world was abortive to itself. The world's thinking about him was like a continuous abortion, the world didn't want me, I was its accident. Nothing happened, nothing went on, he was somewhere, in a long, sad caravan, its melancholy ate all the horizons, one by one, and in that caravan itself people looked at him askance. Perhaps at the Club they would ask him to have more faith in words, in those which he did not utter, which were involved in muted periphrases in his heart of hearts, in those savage, smeared diarrheas of words, words that met, that were brought together for the first time in his head, and that immediately coupled, erotically, and that immediately gave birth, heroically, here checking abstract revolts, there exploding in the spleens. Perhaps, all things considered, at the Club it would be easier to converse. He stopped in front of a furniture store. In the middle of the window was a huge bluish bed that seemed to be awaiting the hollowing movements of two young women who were looking at it. Opposite, next to the bank, no, his eyes weren't deceiving him, he saw a structure with an opus incertum and extraordinary, cerulean bricks and a small, circular window, it was probably the headquarters, the Club. He had been told: the windows are Gothic, and in order to open the door there's a mask, a kind of frightful copper scarecrow, that was it, no doubt about it. Perhaps they were there at that hour, making powerful, necessary gestures. What were they like? Did they look like mountaineers, with black, shiny beards? He was so moved that he dared not approach, he was strictly drunk. Numbers flowed into his head like fifty degrees of alcohol, millions, millions of what, of whom? He did not yet know.

At the Club he would perhaps be asked to carry packages, valises, sheets of paper from one office to another, to sing in chorus, to kill. To kill. Oh, no, not that, not yet. Not right away, you understand? Initiation first. Quinte began singing nervously, with false notes. He thought of his gentle nature within him, he could almost run his hand over it to feel its gentleness. What was he thinking about? Suddenly he was shaken by a laugh that hurt his lips, he was still in the same street, it was walking with him, left and right were still the same houses, that one with its two thresholds that stuck out like boots, and that one, a little further on, invaded by the vine, and noon that pedaled in the light. Yes, the sun was furrowing the asphalt, people were taking refuge in the shade, but the shade itself burned, and it bronzed, as at the beach. And he, he was plunged in that golden imbroglio, he hobbled along, a black sweat stuck to his belly, he knew it was black, his belt bedded itself forcefully into his flesh like the vanguard of death. That was why he was shaken by a laugh that hurt his lips. He almost bumped into a pole which was striped like a cabin-boy's jersey. People kept going by, coated with cement, up against him, they were dreaming, were dreaming that they were dreaming, or that they could no longer dream, *that it was forbidden.* Bellies came and went, sleeping like babies, pushed like legs that gave the impression of not being theirs, the pot-bellied seemed to be squatting in their bellies. The air sparkled, and things spread in it like a water-color in the process of being painted, he tottered, he stumbled over the thorny gleam of laughter, over the oval flame of certain eyeballs, over the wind that sank like needles into his hard breathing. He heard queer conversations. He slowed down, picked up speed, weakened. There was, in the vicinity, the mouth, as it were, of a kind of toothless absence. Yet he was going somewhere, that was certain. With his nose against a window in which there were objects of piety, he counted the crucifixes. He stopped at ten. But the tenth was well made. It was as if he had gone all the way in order to look at it. He was feeling better, as when one finishes a pilgrimage: one subsides, one prays, one has a great whirling peace in one's bowels. Among all those crucified figures, the tenth was the best-looking. A good-looking fellow, a good-looking chap, a good-looking male. Never had he seen anyone so good-looking. Steel muscles, sallow flesh between the holes and gashes, and also that harmonious virility about which there was something exceptional. He must have been a man from the south, a sunny fighter who must have slammed lots of doors, cursed lots of slackers. Quinte could not quite make out the cross, what he saw was spread arms that isolated the torso wonderfully; a handsome man, really; he counted the ribs, one, two, three, four, etc. They looked like bows that were strung from within, you expected to be hit by an arrow at any moment. The man stretched, as after a painful sleep. His brownish, student's beard floated pensively at the base of the neck at the breastbone. Quinte walked away dreamily. He felt he was too mediocre to think about beauty. But when he read the poster for that concert, he could not help thinking about it a little. It's like music, it's like a divine thing which occupies only places where one does not bet, where one neither tells lies nor rots, those places which do not yet have a name. But Quinte was indeed a little afraid of art. He perhaps loved beauty, but art is doubtless something else, art was an undertaking, he did not quite know what to think of it. However, he envied artists. He wondered: "What *demon* inhabits them?" A pity that beauty is not always arranged. He saw it covering all inadequate objects, all plain-looking women, and causing obscure lapses in the souls of hangmen, lapses that inspired them with a taste for wandering in the hour of punishment. But it was only a dream. Nevertheless, perhaps hope is also beauty. His eyes blinked. He felt a big spot spreading in his head. He stopped again, but in such a way that he could think he had stopped beauty. It was not there. That tree was limp and scraggy. At the end of the street was a kind of industrial tumor that rose filthily to the sky, a sleeping legless cripple slobbered into his wooden bowl. What was there that was beautiful? Quinte had the humble impression that beauty is no longer what one looks at. It was perhaps a complicated, inhuman kind of matter that one gets involved in, beauty was the feeling of beauty, the feeling that the beautiful exists, that the foreboding of beauty exists, and that one must not despair of finding it. At the Club, there would obviously be discussion of beauty.

When beauty has fled, one is chased by animals. He was being chased. A kind of army of horrible statues was after him. It was perhaps the tranquillity of others. He made his way through a crowd of onlookers who were concerned with a corpse. The street smelled of blood. And nothing was left of the automobile; thin trickles of oil and gasoline took on interesting colors as they flowed in the gutter. Quinte waited until the two branches of that beautiful liquid met, then he walked away. He heard someone murmur "poor thing." He turned around briskly, realized that it was not he who was the subject of that warm remark, but the dead person. He was disappointed and in a way jealous. The thought of a flower seemed to invade him, it was pink as a rose without being a rose, and it bruised him as it bloomed: "I don't usually like flowers . . . I hate them, bah!" It was now four o'clock. He felt endless, propelled. His great being had no limit. Like a pin he pierced the flank of the sky, out there, on the horizon, he no longer knew where to take hold. He walked innocently, in the street, at four o'clock, listening to himself swarm. He felt the neckline of drunkenness quiver beneath one of his hands, he kept his lips shut with the other. It was a drunkenness for suffering a little more, for existing hard, it was barbed, it tore being by sinking into it, it betokened lucidity, wild lucidity. The pavement was hot, the heat shot up to his chin, sumptuous uppercuts swung a multitude of heads, he was suddenly surprised to see so many people, so much movement. The people who passed each other seemed dead in the center of their gay, bright-colored clothes. It was as if moving, processionary greenhouses were going off together to lay flowers on the graves of their horticulturists. Never had he seen them so old. He saw them aging, they were swooping to their death, they were road hogs without cars. Only the clothes seemed really to live and age reasonably. Their gazes remained in their eyes, their eyes wallowed in their sockets, they wobbled there, as if bereft of sight, without being blind to everything. Their darkness was the rare, the beautiful, the live. Within them, the equal clyster of the ugly, ready to squirt. A baby carriage, followed by the mother, emerged from a porch. He saw light-brown shoes from which a very young woman rose up. He followed on her heels. For once it was not desire. It was ... something else. Her flabby pink breasts in a blue smock, the melting expression of her features, on her forehead a red curl that resembled a cork, it all interested him, as did her arms stretched between herself and the handle bar. Perhaps she was going to the fair, in that direction. In the carriage, it screamed, it kicked to get out. He was hoping for a kind of reward. Her stockings had runs, her heels were worn, she often twisted her foot, and down her neck, like tobacco, very short hair. They reached a poor, deserted neighborhood. The wheels turned faster, he followed her, a vague feeling rose up in him, born of the comedy of living: a mad hope. He sported a limp, somewhat flabby smile. The street seemed to be running straight into heaths. But when they reached the cemetery, she suddenly slowed her pace and, turning obliquely to the left, entered the lane at the end of which was the calvary. However, she did not go as far as the graves. Without hesitating, as if it were going to rain, she entered the modest green structure that served vaguely as a waiting room. When she had opened the door, there had occurred, in the door frame, a swelling of heavy shadows, of stifled laughter, of belchlike sounds as in low dives. She sat down. Quinte took a seat not far from her, between a middle-aged woman who said nothing and another who was sleeping. He ran his surprised gaze over the faces.

The child stopped crying, for the mother had just offered it a round object. Quinte thought of Moussia, always her. A man laughed very loudly, he wore his cap over his eyes and a silk scarf around his neck. All one could see of his face was his teeth, which were as huge as a full sugar bowl. He was making broad gestures to explain a weakness. He said: "My weakness . . ." Children were playing war, there was real hatred in their eyes; that's always the actual weapon of a crime: what there is in the eyes, the hand obeys the eyes. In a corner, a woman had taken off her shoe and was tapping the floor with it. Another was tearing paper with her hands. Her peaked, greenish face made him think of bad wood that had been exposed to bad weather, something a little mossy, and her nose vibrated. She looked as if she were hanging, because of her gaping mouth, only the bond was lacking, for there were traces of strangulation on her neck and something shiny on her cheeks as if someone had spat in her face. At times, the movement of her lips formed a black, round little hole a quarter of an inch in diameter that was plugged up from time to time by the tip of her tongue. Quinte had a desire to cut it all out with a blowtorch. A pudding of jokes, of stories and war cries, made plop plop in his ears. The tombs stood out clearly in the dust of the windowpanes, they had clean angles. And as for the flowers, which cast a festive air over the stones, he had never seen such flowers, so full-blown, so plump. Quinte breathed with difficulty here. He would have liked to go and stretch out on a grave, to thrust his head into the mingled scents, to feel the hard obverse of the slab drive his flesh toward life, toward the sky, and the reverse side push that of the corpse deeper into death, deeper into the maggots; he would have liked to stretch out on it with the young mother and observe the palpitation of a nude in relation to an epitaph. "Three days at the sea!" shouted a stout woman to the young mother. The mother looked at her son who was sitting in his carriage, and agreed. The son started whimpering again. She laid him down, the sound of the lollipop could not be heard. Finally she told about the delivery of the child. There was the merest touch of emotion. The valetudinarian bowed her head, and when she raised it again, which she did abruptly, Quinte noticed that her lips were moist. The glances of a heavy girl, who had scratched her stomach several times, surveyed Reine's body homosexually. Quinte spread his fingers over his face, he was a bit discouraged. It began like a smutty story. All the men present seemed to be waiting for the episode of the caesarean. Each detail reeked of hospital flesh, steaming, damaged flesh, with cotton on it. In any case, everything had worked out all right, and he weighed ten pounds. An old maid with an unleavened stomach wiped the same tear away for the hundredth time. Quinte's finger tips were frozen, inanimate, his back was cold. What were they all waiting for? Nobody asked what time it was, they hardly had appointments. They smelled of fish, of dog bone. One day they would be where the graves were, my eyes popped. Quinte began to laugh. They thought it was at the joke in question. Reine wasn't bad. He saw pre-libidinous gleams misfire in her sockets. Her eyeballs needed tightening, they were loose. She had not stopped massaging her knees since her arrival, a soft, tobacco-colored light filtered from her legs; it was her stockings, which had a run in the back. The child tossed about in the carriage, he wanted to free himself from something absurd, such as the unconscious. Quinte tossed his head back. He thought about children. A little less about the mother, although . . . he would have liked to have her, but away from here, in the fields, when, nestling in the wheat, with his belly on the ground, his member digging into the humus, wild-looking, he would have suddenly seen her genetic curves rolling against the big blue sky and her removable dress beneath the big comic sun. She bent over the ten pounds, he felt her girdle get tight in back and loose in front. The event was now turning gray, it went deep into his mouth like a spoonful of cod-liver oil. Nevertheless, outside, all the vertical graves lit up at the corners, and it was beautiful. "Tomorrow at six o'clock," he said to himself. He didn't care. Not very much. "It's always the same thing. When beauty appears, I hang only by a thread to everything else." But the thread went deep into his head. The rape was within him in any case, something more than ecstasy. He looked at them all one last time. They had not changed, it was disgusting, all they wanted was to laugh, their heads moved slightly forward, toward each other, in little jerks, as when one does not know where to sniff, they inhaled the nauseating humor in the words that had been launched through everything, they searched them, like thorough little insects, like brisk, stocky customs officers, they sought matter for laughter in them, there was a sluggish bubbling in their guts. Rape was within him: "The act of abusing a girl or woman by violent means." He felt alive, menacing. When he had crossed the threshold, he heard the stout woman say: "And I assure you, it was as good as new." He shut the door violently, he had wanted to pinch that remark in the door jamb so as to

hurt it. He shrugged. Nothing was more insignificant
than those words, precisely those: "They taught me
nothing, they ought not to have been said . . ." It suddenly seemed to him that a whole life could stick to that:
to walk on the mined field of consciousness! To be a
constant bursting of words, of sensations, of sonorities!
And all that in silence, in terrible, uncajolable silence.

A boundless slackening, everything slackened, the
street, and all the contents of the street slackened, madly,
an infinite sigh, a relief that came from far away, from
very far away. Mixtures took place, bold, free, disen-
tangled, women's hair-nets and policemen's caps, motorcycles, newspaper stands, signboards, beacons and sheets
of paper, butter five francs a pound, sky, asphalt and flies,
garbage cans, a beauty mark, a cathedral, a dog's leash, a
ball, it all played in space, in the great approving triumph of all his senses flapping like banners in his chest,
an unbounded reconciliation, a cordial swarming, his
half-closed eyes swelled up, everything became convergent, congruent, a newspaper in hand, terrific headlines,
as things took shape, suddenly, it was enough to skim, to
let his attention glide over the black and white jumble of
news, one felt that one was a prey to the sea, one had the
impression of having understood everything, of having
drawn nearer to the dazzling beginning of man, it was a
huge present, peaceful and mute, perhaps one was condemned to forced love for life, people passed through
each other, and how easy it was to go there, to remain
here, to avoid that colossus whose arms were loaded with
bottles, to thrust one's hands into one's brilliantined hair
so that it would shine, to have an unperplexed look.
"Slackened," he thought. That big, impure title on a

movie poster, with that slit navel of the vamp that looked at you like an eye from China, like a slug's profile, all it needed was teeth to be a lewd smile, everything was slackening, just like that, without warning, morals, time; the mishap was no longer annoying, and that fellow was no longer poor. "One would think it gave me pleasure," a few feet away from him, to see the big head of a sex maniac, battered by vice, soaking libidinously in the milky photogeneticness of naked dolls, "my head is a sister of that one." "Slackened," that street noise, the style of the skirts, the gestures of lovers, and even that priest, he had a slackened face, his features, his disjointed hands, drifted, his cross drifted, his cassock, everything had a look of untied bonds, on page one of a weekly, nothing that was unknown about an intrigue was hidden, and the flabby, greedy, contemporary attention rubbed against it, catlike. It was like the discovery of a new, languorous, ironic order, it was like the slave's life of the living, the passers-by resisted nothing, nothing resisted them, at every step they gained in harmony what they lost in hardness, a broad, hospitable, patron-like wind blew, they could be seen softening inside it. A great ovation of whom and of what. And in the book stores there was a slack writing and ethics, Quinte exulted, he would have liked to open those books, but the miracle was that he did open them and that he verified the slackness, sentences hung on the lines like slightly dirty, abandoned, urinary linen, and there were thousands of the kind quivering without rules on the pages and in men's memories, all the works reeked of concession, of spiritual gangrene, of morbid, lymphatic doubt, and the toxic little bursts of the creative spirit dwelled in them, squeezed against each

71

other, that kind of perverted undulation that runs through the works, it's that, a kind of blind latitude that drags lightly from one man to another. Quinte. In his head flowed invitations to stretch out on the general sofa, to close his eyes so as to prevent nothing from happening. Deep in his belly, a little animal wags its tail, kicks, has its orgasm, says thank you, thank you, again, again thank you. It's the only thing in the world, dirty or sacred, as one likes, and we enjoy all the exquisite, base pleasure, as one likes, of its play, we enjoy that evil and that good scattered helter-skelter on the rug, like a big bag emptied by the obscene sky, that prick-made carpet of men which is the world, that big exhibition had to be seen in the street, inflated, drunken, pink masses that were under one's very nose, huge heads, loud colors, stands covered with books containing furious pictures, photos of naked women in a rain of feathers, heavy odors, neon lights, gaping and legitimately daring clothes, raucous music, and rouged cigarette butts in pretty garbage cans, mackled papers, rattles, papers with unfinished diagrams, an effervescent peace, prisons opened, the ex-convicts stepped into golden carriages that drove through a holiday-making city, there were no more culprits, the very notion of guilt had been eliminated, and by virtue of the fact that there was no more evil, people ran, they ran to a great, to an immense innocenting . . . Quinte, mad with joy, at last had a plausible notion of men's productivity, they produced much and more, never had so much been produced joyously and silkily as today, and the producers flooded men with their silky and joyous products, there were things everywhere, and among men, like easy cements, happy things straight out of happiness factories filled the streets, people's eyes, everyone stopped to read, to listen, to look at the big rounded, redundant, booming kinds of happiness, but there were also veiled, oblique kinds of happiness that tried by paleness or insinuation to be more concrete than the others. And everybody went off with treasures of hazy satiety, going from the shower of appeasement to the prospect of orgasms. Quinte felt it all, that opulence, that iridescent ventripotence of life, the fat, spongy accumulation of disorders, and he, he was a drowned man happy to be drowned, he wittingly swam badly, he sank down with all his might the better to feel that there was no wretchedness, no anguish, but only riches that did not find their rich. He finally sat down, wonder-struck, on a bench, amidst the precious din of the work yards and of the heavy trucks that entered the slaughter houses loaded with beef, a blast of fuel oil and rancidness made his nostrils quiver, gigantic billboards made green and yellow cracks in the highest gable of the city, an airplane skimmed the roof tops like the wild sperm of a god. He observed his hands, they moved forward, clenched, they were "gray, spotted with brown" as in the dictionary, they looked like hyenas' heads, they crawled to his battered knees like monkeys' skulls. "There's something beyond, a prey, a sexual world overflowing with life, and they'll close on them," he thought. But when they reached the edge, they fell. He caught them, disappointed. "What have I done with my hands?" They now reminded him of eroded things. He found them long after having lost them, and there they were, lying unusable on his thighs that snuggled against each other, they turned their backs like hands unwilling to pray, while

around him the sensual indifference of men started growing again in the light of lights. He plunged again into a
situation hostile to his will, the familiar little crystal of
hope sank into a black, hydrophobic padding, like the
very soul of pain. There remained one last resort: a
volatilization of everything, "but the state of things is not
volatile."

He was surrounded by the perverse, dazzling fair.
The merry-go-rounds were going. Why are so many
things going round and round today? First of all, he saw
an austere-looking man on a wooden horse. The rest was
merely flashes, colors, with little flourishes. Boys with
fierce eyes were showing off to girls who stuck a finger in
their mouth; one could hear the noise of smashed pipes.
Quinte stood against a post, with his back to the harsh
aroma of the electricity, to a garden full of sparks, the
colliding autos. On this side of the racket, he listened to
himself turning pale. The things he still had to say leaned
like a vast ram against his lungs, he perceived his fear of
having to die, which produced little white sounds in his
head. Soon he was outside the fair, that false, crackling
thing. Later, he would visit the hall of mirrors with a few
beautiful women, just to distort them. The only thing
that still attached him to the merry-making was a smell of
nougats, on his sleeves. He quickened his pace. He
walked by half-empty cafés, in the shadow he discerned
whites of eyes and of teeth, negroes no doubt, and the big
round lunaries of the mirrors. The music that came from
multicolored cases fell on his ears like jets of blood, they
were abattoir mouths, they were killed so that they sang,
they killed themselves singing. "It must be warm in the
dance halls." He went in to see. The couples were spin-

ning unavowed desires between their varnished steps, a knee became more incisive, almost pointed, the light went out, only a few red bulbs on the walls were a rampart against total and prancing darkness, patron of coitus, a dream of excision, a supple and gliding herpetologist's dream outlined its movement among the movements, everything was done unhealthily, with prefigurative languors, with half pressures, and embraces as if one were sailing toward a definite act, the kiss on the hair was a hardened breath, and the areas of flesh that the art of dressing exposed blazed quietly, even the rotations were scarlet, men laughed, the handsomest had Arab-like sets of teeth, luminous and cruel, the homeliest seemed to have stuck a fish bone on their mouths, but very near him, *who was not dancing,* two lines of lowered lashes fled like whole little fish. A fellow looks at a back that is being stroked by a fellow who looks at the back that the first one is stroking and they do not see each other. As for the women, they are beautiful in the arms where they are, all the pink arms have a sense of abandon inscribed on the elbows. "It smells of the abattoir," said Quinte to Vylinx, who had just gone up to him and who took him outside, not far from the most disreputable street in the region, with its miserly lamps and purple hotels where the town's sick and needy were in the habit of going to screw for a few francs. Around midnight, consumptives, the deaf, the unemployed, beggers, and even paralytics in their wheel chairs flocked to those places and the mutually penetrating cries of men flayed alive which their frightful destinies uttered went beyond the walls of the rooms and entered the fatigue of the night prowlers with such force that the latter took to flight, gasping as they went.

Vylinx obviously told about his sex life. They crossed the square where the slashed, bleeding dresses, the balloons burst by the turbulent children, and the spokes of the tricycles that turned and gleamed in the anarchy of the games made an exciting scene. A streetcar that had gone off its track rusted in the memory of the rains. Life, further off, was big and dancing. Vylinx looked at Quinte with indecent curiosity, even into his death, while he talked about his love affairs, about Reine, and about a certain M.

When he laughed, his head bounced on his shoulders like a ball, he looked both soluble and rounded, a kind of gauze floated on his green suit, his hands. As he went on talking about himself, Quinte had to beat down each unnamable wrath that pushed its vituperating crest into the brasses of his voice. It took place on the terrace of a café. Vylinx coughed, something that was hoisted up to his lips, then his face disappeared in the agitation of a big checked handkerchief which he had just drawn from his pocket like a conjurer. He looked at Quinte like someone about to say: "I'll pray for you a lot." But that's what it really was! A little boy approached with peanuts in his hands. Vylinx stroked his head. Quinte sighed, removed a fly from his glass. Vylinx was eating peanuts. In crunching them, he showed his teeth, two gold ones and the rest yellowish. His narration was reaching the supreme stage of turgidity and immorality. But he had mentioned a name, described curves, and whatever he was at any moment of the day he also was elsewhere, in others than himself. He knew the spots where he was possessed, he was situated. Quinte thought: "I'm incapable of taking my bearings, I have no history." Vylinx suddenly spoke to him about a party that was to take place the following day, at six o'clock, on Ponche's barge, and invited him to it. Quinte was about to refuse. But two women in mourning were running behind a half-undressed little girl, signals were waving in the soot of the lower depths. All of that was life, and he accepted. Vylinx snickered. A brief joy rumpled and then unpleated his jaundiced face, his dubiously caressed and hastily shaved skin. Drunk, dissolutely seated, with his legs spread, he had the impression of having a body that was entirely illuminated, like a gala evening at the opera. Quinte shook his hand. "It'll be gay," said the other, "horribly gay." People were no longer passing in the streets. And the sun had disappeared. They didn't hear a fly. The only remarkable thing was a flag, three different colors, at half-mast. Quinte was glad to have left Vylinx. He thought of Wasmes-Bô, of Wasmes-Bô's poisoned blood that meandered in his veins. Wasmes-Bô, that was better. He moved cautiously along uneven, sloping sidewalks. The passersby returned, as after a false alarm, so did the sun. He lengthened his stride. He imagined that behind him people were saying: but why has that man been walking so long, he's been walking for hours, walking fast. He doesn't know enough to go in somewhere, there's no shortage of houses, at least there, it'll change his outlook. It so happens that it's too easy to forget gloomy thoughts, to enter buildings, replied Quinte. He walked with his head down, he was looking into his inner life like a melancholy mechanic. "Where am I?" In the street. At the left, he saw cases of wood lined up against a moss-grown

77

wall, the bottom of which was covered with posters that had been discolored by micturations. At the right, little balloons for children were on sale. In front of him were men in rags, unemployed men who did not move from where they were, caked to the dirty pavement. He asked one of them where "the Club's headquarters" were. He got an unsatisfactory or unintelligible answer, he did not quite know. He therefore continued walking at random. But nobody knew the headquarters, they had never heard about it, they asked that he repeat the name, as if for the fun of hearing it. A woman in a kind of folk costume waved her hand toward the north, she said it ought to be out that way. As he still saw nothing, he asked a policeman. The latter listened to him without surprise and finally declared: "But sir, I think you're mistaken, it was last year." Quinte quickened his pace: the tiredness of his legs, the failure, the fever, it all pushed him in irremediable directions. "Stubborn, I'm stubborn." At last, at the turn of the street, trees appeared. His heart beat faster. The trees were a sign, there were similar ones in many neighborhoods which he knew. He counted them gratefully, then stared at the houses. He asked a little girl who was going by: "Mademoiselle, do you know where the Club is?" She did not seem at all frightened. On the contrary, without a word she offered him her hand. He shook it, not without realizing the uselessness of his question. He left her with a word of reproach: "Don't you know anything?" Jumping slowly from one odd number to the other, he reached 13. His eyes blinked, he couldn't get over it. It was a shabby structure, with two curtainless windows and no letterbox. It was there. Without hesitating, he rang the bell. While waiting for someone to open, he went to the first window to have a look. Rising on tiptoes, at first he saw only the griminess of the windows. Then he vaguely made out old couches, a crystal chandelier, etc. As there was very little noise inside, he went back to the threshold. He was happy to enter anywhere, at the Club. A huge old woman appeared. She was leaning on a broom, her violet smock fell like a hanging to her feet, which were covered with string. A smelly animal seemed to spring from her bogged-down collarbones and beat its wings beneath Quinte's nose, he stepped back. It was an odor in the form of an owl, it hooted. He announced confidently: "Good evening, madam, I'm invited to the meeting."

"What a nerve!" cried the woman. The door closed again. It all disappeared in the twinkling of an eye, the fibers of the broom, the folds of the hanging, a bloated, bibulous face of hatred beneath a shock of spiky hair. He had to lean against the wall, to breathe. The whole street became as yellow as a hissing hatred, the upside-down sun showed its dull ass. A few feet away, a movie camera was eating the face of a fellow filming a bow-legged woman who was stupidly clutching the door of a car with a folding hood. It was ghastly and throbbing. "Where is freedom?" It was neither in him nor in the others, it remained to be invented. He took a cigarette. "Perhaps that's what I ought to have done long ago? . . ." He lit it. "And that too." He took a drag. "And that too." He took a step, then two. One can learn to walk again in a few seconds. He thrust his hands into his pockets, which had holes in them, turned around for the last time to look at the house number, 13. He was suffering, he felt squeezed between the instant of a tempting freedom and that of a desired prison. That shadow on the ground and in time was himself, suddenly stretched from one point of the unknown to the other. It was a third instant, an instant of his, personal, all black, a sort of grim tragedy.

At the Office (II) and Leaving

He felt he was entering
for the last time, that he was going there to say good-by.
He was in the office of the editor-in-chief, a puny man,
and there, behind him, were photos of a weight-
lifting enthusiast pulverizing his fragility. When Quinte
saw him, the image of a crime filled his mind, and
the insistence of that image now assumed proportions
that verged on committing it. Quinte stared as one stares
at an animal lying on its back and moving its paws. He
realized vaguely that he was being reprimanded because
of the tenor of his last article and that he was being told
to be careful in the future. Very well, he promised, he
would be careful. That kind of situation would not recur.

He offered a cigarette to Monsieur Cuile, who accepted in a passion. It was very funny. When he had lit it and had said: "You know, sir, sports are important!" he stood up, walked a few yards, doubled up with his asthma, then collapsed on the floor like a foe of weight-lifting. Quinte could not keep from laughing heartily at the thought of Monsieur Cuile bathing in his blood. But his laughter was so powerful that it attracted the attention of all the editors, who came running. Quinte trembled with such joy that all his flesh, starting from his ankles, seemed to be giving his laughter a leg up in order to hoist it to his lips! The editors had just picked up Monsieur Cuile. Quinte looked daggers at them one by one (to look daggers, that is, to stab). It was like a revelation. He suddenly realized that the good relations which one maintains with colleagues are based primarily on the balance achieved between an undeclared hatred and an esteem that is slow in being born . . .

All that he thought of now was his goal. It came back to him, an aggressive diamond. Never had he seen himself so close to it. He was walking on it, in it, was pushing it, was drawing it to himself, he sensed the breath and gemma of it on his skin, along his blood. Suddenly, in a dazzled state, he seized the far edges of the table with both hands. He had just thought that what he was squeezing so hard with his iron grip was the goal. Alas, it was not! He would have to keep struggling, digging, thinking, to defeat adversaries within himself and outside himself, in the Club and outside the Club. And besides, it did not follow that the goal would be rough, like the edges of that table, that it would have those ridges, that it would be, in short, so small and hard. "It will be a surprise, a tremendous surprise."

At the end of the corridor, he bumped into a woman. It was Moussia, he was thinking of Reine. Vylinx had said to him: "You'll have Reine, I promise you." And he was already having a sculptor's dreams about that woman. He liked sculpture, which set up the multiform parapets of beauty between himself and the void.

Moussia apologized, he did too. But she was already running off, imperceptibly awkward. Her white hands were flapping in space, like tips of wings seeking their entire wing. Quinte had turned around, he watched her devourable, devouring fragility disappear. At times she seemed to stop being, then it was the turn of the stone of the walls to seem to stop being. She crossed things of her own, with which she exchanged her presences and absences, her strengths and weaknesses. Farther on, she slowed down. In the eyes of Quinte she seemed to be set on a slate pedestal where she vibrated as after a wild dance, she had borne her beauty from wave to wave, and now, exhausted, ultimate, she was filling herself with her statue, a flick of the thumb would perhaps have sufficed to make her dress fall, another three ounces on her might have been enough to break that heel, but her beauty lay precisely in her art of seeming always to graze such accidents . . . It seemed to Quinte that this was the last time the woman's purity was emptying her realm into his vision . . .

Quinte could not avoid Ponche, who was coming in the opposite direction through a passage lined with heavy implements. They stopped a few yards from a huge mass of filings that conjured up a scene in a barber shop somewhere in a dehumanized city of the thirtieth century, swarming with androids that had long zinc hair. Ponche's chuckles were high-pitched and like filaments. After crumbling something dry which he kept closed in his hand, he spoke up with a certain solemnity that disappeared with the acceleration of his delivery. He kept his forefinger pointing to the clock. The event had a blasting effect on Quinte. It was a little as if someone had knocked him three-quarters out and then thrown him into an itinerant jail drawn by wild horses at top speed over bad roads. It was even more impossible to communicate with Ponche, to tell him merely that he did not understand what he was talking about, since he was like the striking of a bell that rang in full peal against the iron, because all that fog and hullabaloo tended to pulverize Ponche's simple, clear, and hated vocabulary which was accessible to everyone. Quinte could not even lie to him, by virtue of that philosophical law which was increasingly strong within him: "To be is to change having, and in order to change having there is only the lie, which makes you leap from metamorphosis to metamorphosis ..."

"I don't understand, I don't understand!" screamed Quinte indefatigably while Ponche's lips, equally indefatigable, moved without reason or orison in the now raucous and super-deafening din of the machines. All that was lacking was thunder and that higher lack of silence, the wrath of heaven, to still the vile buzzing of the vain conversations. Quinte, unable to stand it any longer, advanced threateningly, like a constrictor, spitting his disgust into all the channels of madness, but Ponche was no longer there, he stood floppily in the

corner, amidst bars and barrels, and he continued talking, it seemed, saying that he did not understand what
had happened or how or why Quinte had looked at him
so long, so sternly, without ever stirring.

Quinte rushed toward a thicket of various metals, as
if he had heard cries there, but it was actually because he
thought he discerned silence and death there, and the
happiness of trucks, of barrels, of valves, of that world of
finished products which tirelessly inspired the men of the
century. Quinte was in the process of undergoing one of
those moments of struggle between consciousness and
unconsciousness in which consciousness has the upper
hand, but it was a sanguinary consciousness. A surging
demand could be heard within him. His instincts were
stamping, they were like horses which, in order to
carry him off, tried to pass beneath the spread legs of
a confused rider. He felt within him the "full speed
ahead," he heard his hounds demanding the act he had
promised them. He would have liked to toss some
hope to those starved beasts, to explain that all was
not lost, that there had been constant progress, that
there were a hundred thousand hours of waiting
squeezed against each other in his being, at the gates
of the final laceration, that it was like a river of glair
in spate. There was a cracking sound in his head like that
of an exhausted strap. Was it therefore true that the act
was arriving? "Stop!" he cried. He grazed the equivalent
walls, tried to leave. He feared that a hand might again
come down on his shoulder, that hand of others which
was meant for apprehending, which intervenes in your
dreams gratuitously, which destroys them with an ordinary hand's low realism. But there was only a worthless

panorama around a sign of life: I, who stretched out in exasperation to an ever-retreating world, yes the world is small to those who travel fast and far, but to those who think of it in terms of love and hatred, it never stops stretching, it's an immense refusal of all its dimensions for those who call it, oh to love, and to hate elsewhere and elsewhere than elsewhere! Perhaps that's what is called immortality: the ardent, flaming extension of an extraordinary unsuccess, not to achieve, to perpetuate the rage that this causes by hurling oneself to the following non-achievement.

Wasmes-Bô appeared. Merely to observe him gave one a poignant feeling of insecurity. Often, he did not move, he stood there, as if attached to a post by bonds that dug into his flesh, that pulled his arms backward though his hands did not completely disappear. On the contrary, veins stood out like bluish worms that coil up in a pisciform area fringed with dark, inert fingers, while higher up, his head made signs of denial and in the depths of his eyes drudged convicts' beauty-shattering dreams and while his only tooth, more threatening than a knife, rose up to you in a tremendous laugh from the abyss. It was enough for him to stand in front of you to break off sharply, but to your advantage, an inner symphony, to erode the deepest and hardest soil of your philosophy. He lived in the fractures, in the margin, of so-called accomplished things and beings. He seemed to be continually in the process of giving up an advantageous post in time and space, in the process of breaking chains and even the very opposite of chains, in the process of leaving, of going away, of separating himself, he had a tremendous power of breaking. He made you swallow the world's horror merely by making a gesture on the walls. When I met him that afternoon, I was still thinking of love, although that word had quite lost its power of seduction. My way of experiencing that feeling had begun to differ tremendously from the common practice and even the common malpractice. At times, that love rolled in my soul like animals in heat, at times it flowed like pus from my words, at other times it was as slender and obsessive as an evil flower. Yet it was still love, a love stronger than twaddle, stronger than all hymns and all sacrifices. It struck man in the face and forced him to feel the breath of life. Wasmes-Bô never sat down, but this time he leaned against a door. He looked at Ponche with what I knew was unmixed hatred. It had been going on for years. I was cold in that corridor full of geometric shadows and remnants of comings and goings. I tried to imagine what Wasmes-Bô hated about Ponche. It was no doubt *his balance.* For Ponche—it was a fact—boasted about his balance, he was nice and warm in his balance, he clucked his tongue with pleasure when he spoke about his balance, and he taught balance to his children. But to Wasmes-Bô that balance of patent-leather shoes and packages of caramels, that balance of restful reading and unswervingly pressed trousers, that balance of prejudices and best wishes, was something abominable. And Wasmes-Bô thought that trees too are balanced: they do not bother to go looking for birds, they wait for the birds to come, they do not move about in order to change their horizon, they always enjoy the same one, yes a tree is balanced, if you like. But man owed it to himself to loathe such castrating conceptions. To Wasmes-Bô, being balanced no doubt meant imperatively to regain one's

87

balance. The balance of the equilibrist was the art of going back to measure the golden mean after daring to go from one extreme of possibilities to the other. That was why Wasmes-Bô wanted to have done with Ponche. Perhaps he thought that if he killed him his gesture would have no more value than a simple flourish made by a child. But go try to explain that in court: that one cannot add death to death and that to kill a man who is willing to live dutifully is to toy with a corpse. In any case, Wasmes-Bô could not put up much longer with Ponche's presence at his side. He looked at me with unusual insistence, his eyes swayed in their sockets like sinister signboards, his rheum was as transparent as tears. He was chewing something gummy, perhaps that was his way of smiling today. He leaned toward me. He still had that same look of being cut off from common joys, of being beaten down by the stiff, inflexible winds of a mysterious ailment. At the tip of his breath, there was, how shall I put it, a homicidal aroma. He spat into a red-and-white-checked handkerchief while continuing to flash at me. That scene swelled my chest with an unhealthy, bacchic joy. I felt I was again being delivered up, little by little, to his ancient desires which were lost in the maze of the senses. In my wallet was the photo of my wife and daughter, and of my parents smiling and all dressed up. For a moment, my failure stopped dancing in my head, it remained suspended in my crucial consciousness. I saw the rash exuberate on his face and a kind of milk zigzag down from his mouth. What I saw was extraordinary, Wasmes-Bô handing me a knife! No I was not dreaming, it was a blade, a blade that with one stab could have killed the great hippopotamus of Africa Oh Africa! Before giving it to me definitively, he seemed to be judging me with all his might, all the vivisecting and trepanning might of his madman's stare. He did not look much relieved to see me put out my hand to accept that terrible gift. It was as if, as far as he was concerned, there was no problem. But was it really a gift? I had bought that knife, I remembered, several weeks before. I could see the coins and bank notes sticking to his damp hands. It was an inexplicable deal that had been concluded in a deserted place, without air or windows. He turned on his heels, walked a few yards. His back seemed to rise up, his legs to unscrew, from the orthopedic shoes, a lacerating cough, then nothing more, nothing but a bony, staggering puppet at which I felt like springing, out of neither hatred nor love, but out of complicity, even *out of identity*, in order to see all the parts of that carcass roll on the floor with mine. I felt the fatality of an act moving me in my depths. He and I were bound by a mysterious, tyrannical instinct. I was never to see him again.

Out of politeness, Quinte wanted to say good-by to everyone. He entered the big room with his head high, he saw them, their lively eyes, which were *full of greatly enlarged bacilli,* were watching him in an unprecedented way. He headed for the exit. That walk between tables which served as pedestals for white volumes that had been split by the abrupt fall of neckties sounded like a cigarette lighter, like crumpled paper. He pressed his weapon against his heart. He got up on a table and harangued them with his dear, new words. Something strange then happened, they turned around to him and began to contemplate him with ineffable amazement. He did not have the impression of being the object of their contempt or hatred. Confronted with their astonishment, he got stubborn. They were not laughing, they were mumbling without speaking. Then they moved away, though engaging in slight, inaudible palavers. He remained for a moment where he was in order to see white volumes on black stilts drift into a fog. He lowered his head. Then suddenly they came back, crowded together, they walked toward him with mincing steps, they seemed terribly serious, formal, despite the terebrant sound of boots they made as they advanced. He saw a line of fierce eyes looking at him and gleaming, he was already almost thrown against the rotting wall of their collective hatred, that mountain of dead cats glided toward him silently. He could not believe that they were putting him out. Why were they putting him out with such little consideration? He became frightened and he fled. In the lavatory, he frankly thought that he had a bullet in his flesh but that blood refused to flow, he had a terrible pain in his right side. "I want to achieve supreme originality before dying . . ." But it was not black, so it was not death. Posted on the back of his closed eyelids into which a violent wind infiltrated was the profile of a woman's face that floated with all its lacerated parts, and Quinte put the face to death on a slow flame. It would be a decease or a crime . . . *the autopsy gave no results* . . . That act was necessary in a world where one must love what one kills and kill what one loves if one wants to escape from the wretchedness of indifference . . . To be born must no longer be to be requisitioned for a certain death before the ultimate one . . . there must not be merely a difference of stiffness between the corpses of the living and those of the dead . . . Quinte put up a fight, he opened his eyes, they hadn't got

90

him yet, not this time, he smiled in the mirror; he saw only his smile, he believed only in himself. His face had disappeared. His finely parted lips made a red hole in the mirror, which pretended to bleed, he felt like performing a simple act. He turned the faucet, the water flowed, as expected, on his hands, the cold, pleasant water. He left. He kept going. On his way to the exit, he saw them all. No, he did not have what could be called false vision, they were assembled in the little glass room where the maintenance department usually stored its equipment. They looked as if they were conspiring, with their heads bent over a paper that occupied the middle of the table, which was violently lit by a huge lamp. Their hair gleamed at the ends of their yellow necks. They huddled together, as if in order not to be cold, but it was rather an effect of their animal solidarity. Finally they stood up as a single man and quickly put the table and paper out of sight, they all mingled until they seemed to be dancing slowly, then the atmosphere grew confused because of prodigious little shadows. At the end of a quarter of an hour of exercise, they noticed him, they turned toward him, toward the door, and he saw Hatred. At first they uttered a guttural cry, then they squeezed their elbows in an avaricious way. Hisses sizzled in the rear. They took a step back, then, at the order of a little gentleman, perhaps Monsieur Cuile, they walked slowly in his direction. Such restrained vociferation was impressive. He wanted to say good-by to them, but they did not give him time to; they advanced with their hands extended toward his mouth to shut it, to crush it. He ran away. He thought he heard a flock of eyes, of arms, of outraged souls pursuing him. He crossed the shop. Ponche was not there either.

He would never again see Ponche, the Man who talked too much; nor Wasmes-Bô, the Man who never talked. No one was left in the shop. Where were they all? He was unable to find his way. What with the shops and the administrative and editorial departments, there were lots of corridors which it was not easy to disentangle, which it was sometimes hard to get out of.

You headed for the shipping room with the intention of finding your way out. Doors that did not open marched by in the corridor. The quick, soft little tapping of typewriters could be heard. You were aware of almost reaching a temporary goal, that it was only a question of minutes, only the last door was still evading you. On the way, you said to yourself: "What I cannot imagine is what I'm doing . . ." Yet you could no more live without acts than anyone else. But your life did not resemble them. You failed to realize that you were acting, and even in what form and with what frequency your acts were being performed. It was as if that were a science you could never master, one that was more difficult than the science of science. At that moment, your act, for example, was not so much that of walking in search of a door, for, after all, anxious people have all had that experience, but rather a landscape where the olive trees that flank a road along which you are driving rapidly are epileptic and twisted in the big wrestling sun. For that too is an act: a field strewn with flashes where roots wild as lightning go deep down into inner inventions to touch the tip of the ineffable real . . . Alas, your body carries you here and there in given circles where little jobs are done which you forget the moment you finish them, and nothing seems to want to grow beneath the rubbing of your fingers or to flame beneath the excitation of your senses . . . But is it therefore true that you create nothing, absolutely true that you create absolutely nothing? It's not possible. You said a while ago that your words acted . . . In any case, you are going to create . . .

You said to yourself, "It's an obsession." And you wanted to perform an act, a great act, in order to get rid of that obsession, which was less dangerous, nevertheless, than recapturing memory. And you feared that that act might bring you back to your senses, right back to that vast memory in which one hears the bleating of the castrated powers of past time, and in which paradisiac faces from the time of your youth are ready to recite to you the long pity of their souls. Yet that prospective act smelled good, it aroused your appetite. You were sitting at the edge of action, with your back to the theoretical void. Little by little, you stop worrying about whether what you are going to commit is diabolical or kindly, provided it is this or that to the very end, totally. To pay for so many years of absence from the world, nothing is too excessively good and evil. One would think that the old armistice that had been painfully concluded between the law for everyone and your own inclinations were going to collapse and that the rolling impasse that your pig-headed head pushes in front of you were going to deflagrate. You will henceforth desire another world which is the same as this one plus the acuteness, in which one laughs and suffers *otherwise,* in which the energy is of a quality superior to what exists today, a world of action.

You go through streets but you do not see the streets, you go through people but you do not see the people, you are told long stories to which you listen with so listless an ear that it notes only the few words by which you can prove you were listening. Your entire life is indeed within you, your courts of justice, your crimes, your discontinuous saintliness, your long, incoherent and humble action, your smells, your degrees Fahrenheit, you have just laughed, you were thinking of their short-winded little acts. You yourself want something so much better. You are the soul of all that happens. You then began to laugh nervously in those corridors, it was frightful, thousands of javelins under your skull, you rose up against that incantatory action within you, your demon . . . Suddenly they returned to you, in all haste. Were they the editors or the workmen? In any case, they were gangs. But you were mistaken, once again. It was the sports editor, who was wearing his indestructible derby. He was slobbering, he was bent double. He greeted you and, handing you an envelope, said: "I'm sorry." You nodded, in your laudable way, and you put the envelope into your pocket. And of your mutual desire to go no further was born your brutal separation in that endless corridor. You again went through many rooms where everyone looked at you scornfully. He most definitely did not find his way. How many times did those corridors lead him back to the same point? None but himself could have said, but he did not know either. The walls went by, turned round and round, or crawled gleaming along that sort of speed between him and them. And the marble busts, the welcoming chairs, the smooth enameled doors, they all made gyratory movements around him and he lost his head and brayed with terror. Feeling them so ugly on his trail, he would have kissed the dazzling faces of the things were it not for their velocity and his very strong will to get away.

Finally he perceived a kind of exit in the distance, a slight opening in which the vapor of a boulevard trembled. He thought there would have been a guard to prevent him from leaving; but, on the contrary, the latter, the very old, hoary, patched one, who looked like an imitator of monkeys, pointed to the luxurious outside with his broken finger. It was a new street, full of the seeming-to-live of the passers-by and from which one discovered the depth of the city held in the mouth of evenfall by a jaw of sharp luminaries. Indeed, love of beauty is inseparable from the suspicion with which men view it. It seemed to him that they were following him, he heard behind him the sound of a limp chase, a wet effort, and he smelled the characteristic odor of venery. He immediately noticed that it was raining and he took shelter. Through a window of the shelter he contemplated the masterpiece of the rain. Drops were running down the glass, without grace and without limpidity, like the tears of a tortured face. Behind that, the world seemed to be cracking and about to destroy itself; it rather recalled the sudden mess that runs across the screen when the film becomes worthless, the autos were making the runny sound of urinals and all he saw of them was fleeting fissures. In comparison with all that, the water in his glass of water, for he was in a café, was . . . baptismal. A bird uglier than a pebble went by, and he saw people whom greed, much more than the blasts, seemed to bend toward the pavestones which had been enriched by the brilliance of the shower. People with their fundamental deviation, with their dirty, precise mugs, with what they know that he does not want to know, with their "continuity," their amazement at what is not continuous. It's astounding how imbued they are with continuity, they're always clamoring for it, they want *chance to be logical.*

He went out. All the possible toboggans took shape again as he walked, all the drunkenness of acting almost recaptured a certain bygone time, dear goal, dear freedom, dear something-or-other-that-transforms-me-and-carries-me-from-metamorphosis-to-metamorphosis-toward-a-being-absolutely-different-from-what-I-imagine . . . dear drunkenness . . . scaffolding of mists. Then it seemed to you that it was nearing you, getting bigger and bigger noiselessly like a train in the movies. But you hoped that once it was on you, a following scene would not come and take it from you, as in the movies. You would cling to the railway trucks and you would leave with it, in its whistling triumph and glowing steam, for a distant idea of a station . . . You uttered a cry and put out your hands, but in your supreme fingers there was still only the end of your polka-dot tie. A few yards from you was a fairly virgin poster, you could not even read the only word that was on it. He must have drawn very near it by God knows what sudden sense of curiosity and finally he was able to *see* NO. As if the letters were things laid side by side, he could not read the whole word but simply *see* it. He also saw raincoats struck by a rain of saliva, and green walls with broken ridges and bullet marks. It was the way to the stadium. With his knife pressed against his heart, he plunged into the terrible streets, which were full of men utterly foreign to his devilish itinerary.

In the Stadium

The game had not yet begun. There were many convexities in the sky; it was paved with the backs of apes, it was dark and hairy and suspended above a rain that was bent by the wind and did not seem to fall from a great height. The stadium was three-quarters surrounded with trees that twisted their slightest branches like dirty rags above the nearest heads. A capricious, almost tribal world pranced about a wretched lawn on which the first ghosts of its thousands of hopes were crawling. The blasts from the trees split the dark mass of hats which were turned down as if to put the birdless distances of the cold and fury on them. I headed for a godforsaken part of the grandstand, far from the press group where I saw frenzied pencils and cigars bristling in the confusion of cameras. "I must avoid their influence and preserve my judgment," I said to myself over and over.

As I went by, the smell of the wet turf entered me like that of a naked woman bathing. It was a particular odor, the odor of the flowering mystery of woman, the odor of *her* goose flesh, of her grainy brown skin sprinkled with blue water beneath the sun of creeks. I directed a few graceless gestures of my hand to that earth, which was beautiful in its dying wretchedness and shot through with a mild and rumbling excitement. It was just as I imagined it, absorbent and fertile. I then crossed, almost violently, huddled rows of people; I was slowed down somewhat only by the icy contacts of the raincoats and huge umbrellas which were lightened of their deposits of water by shaking. At a certain moment, it appeared to me that the rain was putting lots of things right, without my being able to tell exactly what things were involved. Finally I got to the grandstand, which was composed of shapeless, worm-eaten pillars undermined by the beatings of the winds. I shrugged my shoulders without lowering them immediately, just so as to nip my mean little smile in the bud. For the first time in my life, I felt a desire to have an intimate talk. Words reached me that suggested not so much the detective story as the castrating of bulls. Potent animals seemed to be at the basis of the collective emotion and even to inspire the people's yells; but actually their hoarse tones, which were permeated with rage, merely gave color to discourse insipid in itself which generally ended in a smile more neutral than the chipping of a cheap vase. An elegant woman, who was encircled by a half-dozen thundering giants, nodded her two-colored head (pink and black), which was invaded by fur, and kept taking from her bag oblong-shaped candies that she gave to children in order to keep them away from the group. What amused me was the first gestures, the first exaggerations of the body, that sly preparation of the surging and fury so perceptible through the grayness of ordinary movements. Hands blue with cold, taken out of pockets little by little, made a movement of flight, then another, before the brutal and vindictive tracing of arabesques in the vibrant space. But I still did not know that that row of figures shaken by beginnings of discussions, by gestures of window-cleaners, were the very ones that would be thrown on their neighbors by a scored goal as if they had been shot down. Finally, I smiled. Was it not, after all, a rare thing to be able to observe the birth of a true festival? And those people who had been torn from sleep were beginning to live another life! Another life!

Skulls shone in the rain. Extraordinary bald pates which gave the whole of the head the polish and ivory of things that are going to fall from their bases and roll to the abyss. Suddenly, at my side, a young girl, who was consulting her watch, made me feel uneasy. She was looking at the time as one looks at a painting. She was beautiful at that moment when I caught sight of her lowering her eyes, I who was sensitive to that movement which I had often seen save a woman's face from ugliness. But after the watch, her eyes turned gracelessly to the turf where the blades were panting, and from then on they seemed to me to be fighting against the hardly seductive whole of her person, as if they did not belong to her, as if they were those of a jealous rival who was looking at her. Their very sockets were too weak to contain them, and they tortured her. Actuated by savage anger, they must once have reddened her lashes which were red, red, which were red. A brown jet gushed from her mouth and fell, calmly, on her lower lip, a tongue full of chocolate. "Her name must be Barbara," I thought. At my left sat an unshaved man with warty cheeks whose ears were overflowing with wax. He was watching contemptuously the good twenty men lined up in the middle of the field. In the middle of the field were twenty men who bowed right and left. And he was contemplating them, as one contemplates a painting which at first is incomprehensible: with contempt. I counted them: ten in red and ten in yellow. (On the other hand, the shorts were green and the socks . . . the socks looked as if they had been drawn on their legs.) At first, I believed in the carnival with all my might, but later, when the men broke up, the colors shimmered like neon lights in ornamental lakes, and I changed my mind. The rain had become finer. At bottom, I pitied them. They were players. And thereupon things seemed to me simpler. In order not to get cold, for there were no hot toddies but a very fine rain, they kicked the ball at random. One would have thought they were dreaming, that they were in quest of their childhood, in the realm of clumsiness. They threw the ball against the sky. They were melancholy, a bit ridiculous too. The crowd now seemed gloomier. The rain stopped, and a big blond player, who was lying down, the only one who seemed to be there by chance, was swung by the wind like a hammock. The light of his socks contrasted with the earthy hue of his skin, but the luster of his hair in particular was remarkable. I first rooted for the reds, then for the yellows. Finally I sided with some vague clan, a kind of third force that was being set up amidst the disorder of the teams. People around me were yelling hurray for the yellows hurray for the reds hurray for the yellows hurray for the reds. The girl was reading an almanac, perhaps the horoscope. And the trees, in the wind that was dying in turn, as the rain had died, seemed to be foaming as after a long race. I felt incapable of choosing one side rather than the other. I was for good playing, for energy, for art.

Suddenly a plump little man ran over the field. Dressed in black, he seemed to be fleeing from a place where a practical joke had been played on him by shortening the breeches of his outfit. I could not see his physiognomy, but I knew enough about it: blond mustache, purplish skin. He bowed his head, as if he were praying, and blew a whistle. I thought he was going to fall, at least to kneel. Two players of different colors immediately rushed up to him, as if to help him. All three shook hands. Friendship is a fine thing. It was cold. I was shivering and I no longer smelled the odor of burning rubber rising up from the ground. I had forgotten my notebook. In the depths of my wallet I found a sheet of used, shriveled paper. Only one side of it, which was veined with red and yellow lines, was blank. On the other, I deciphered with much difficulty a phrase clumsily scrawled with a crayon, compact as a black-and-blue mark on a palish skin. It must have been a quotation in the style of: visible things have only time whereas the invisible are eternal. "Unfinished, unfinished!" I almost exclaimed. A pale gleam throbbed on the broken grass. It was a rift, a winsome effort of the earth and the roots to have pleasure again. Brushed aside for a moment by the passing of several black birds that skimmed the ground, it came together again as water comes together. Clouds were gliding noiselessly in the concave sky. I was fond of sports.

A small object, lusterless in the livid air, was tossed up down below. It must have been a button or a coin. Anxiety began to fill most of the people. They stretched their necks, serene brows were suddenly broken up by deep wrinkles, smiles disappeared into the gray anonymity of the heads. A player made a broad gesture toward the west, and the men of both sides started running in all directions, in a rare riot of soft colors that jumped about in the white rays of the sun. It lasted a few seconds, time enough for me to see them immobilized by unsuspected calculations in places where the general effect of their presence produced a strange harmony that seemed weighty with meaning.

The man with the whistle seemed invested with considerable power. I glanced at him with mingled envy and respect. Someone cried "Eric." And Eric replied with a wave of his hand. I was conscious of being present at what I had never seen, at *another game.* I remembered the long lines in front of the ticket windows. I was deeply moved. At each end of the field was a standing rectangle, a kind of hut, the roof and walls of which had been blown away by the storm. The frontage of these ruins was occupied by big, sad guardians who were rolled up in sweaters, one brown and the other dark brown, almost black (I would have liked to have one like that, for excursions). I almost blamed myself for not yet having distinguished these men from their teammates, those men who were more severely dressed than they. Suddenly my eyes re-

membered two crushed, vertical shadows . . . in the . . .
moving . . . blood and gold . . . wall . . . of the players who
were lined up. The blast of a whistle suddenly issued
from the umpire. He, thick-set, powerful, like a big wild
animal on the defensive, taurine. And his signal, shrill,
slight, like a solo in a little bird-symphony. No sun above,
but chalk, like the stable plane of plenitude. I was moved
. . . how shall I put it? Moved by that idiotic profession.
But I was considered the best sports *critic* in the region!
On each side of the field where the crowd was longest,
two men attracted no attention at all. They were trotting,
they did not seem proud, did not seem partial, they were
holding a piece of wood at the end of which was a color-
less rag. I was almost sure they had a role to play in the
affair.

And the whole grandstand seemed to pitch, everyone
was being offered a real chance to get away from himself,
the essential thing was at the meeting of tigers, we were
going to incorporate ourselves by means of tension and
joy into an external disorder having all the appearances
of our untamable dream. I noted vaguely that something
round and juicy was rolling on the grass. The grass was
thick. Round, juicy, and dirty, like the idea of evil perhaps. It was happening in that big vat with swordlike
flashes where the bright intervals resembled a generous
legacy from the rain. My soul was wet with pleasure. I
greatly appreciated that choral passion of the crowd. It
was strange and beautiful, as if all men together had finally realized the necessity of getting away from themselves, as if they had suddenly stood up to asseverate the
desperate impatience of their flesh, of their treasures of
avidity, or an anxiety, or even their personal conception

of the meaning of life and death. Even those who said nothing, who were not fluttering, I noticed not only that they were not indifferent, but that they had lost in a way the secret of the indifference which they could not fail to display elsewhere, in the meshes, for example, of daily living. I squeezed my pencil in my fingers. It was not professional duty; but it was that nevertheless: the necessity of writing, and of looking at handwriting as the exact shadow of the emotions. Yet I knew that I would not write, that it would seem to me useless and incongruous, that I would fling away my pencil because of the fever, because of the triumph of life.

The judge had just given the signal for the start of hostilities. A pitiless cry went up from the crowd. It was a cry of neither love nor hatred, nor of joy, but of anguish. It was a screamed hope, contracted in its means of expression. The supporters of the reds were more numerous than the supporters of the yellows. But no doubt that was only an impression, for many people seemed to be concealing their inner preference, many people were there to rail at everything and nothing, many people were there to be in at the illusory death. At times, the supporters fought among themselves. As for the game, it developed disagreeably. It could have been a fine spectacle, because of the colors and in spite of the corpse of the rain in the sky. The wind was not a wind that mowed down and that bent. It was cold and lots of collars were pulled up. Supporters fought among themselves, as if to get warm. The game developed in an utterly incomprehensible way. At times, a man kept the ball at his feet, as if to admire it. Another offered it with a certain formality to his enemy, who did not much appreciate the godsend. Some seemed to avoid touching it for fear of offending someone, in that case they asked the opinion of a friend or even of an enemy. Furthermore, the orientation which the ball was to be given was not always very clearly apparent from the will of the players, and the guards were bored in their huts, and when they were not bored it was because they passed the time looking at the girls who were waving to them. The men out in front seemed perfectly aware of this state of affairs, but did not protest. When the ball came to them, one had the impression that they wanted to make a hole in it or take it in their hands, which was forbidden. The men in back were obviously less radiant than all the others, one would have thought that the meaning of the game escaped them completely. As for the umpire, he whistled without a stop, adding the brake of his frequent interventions to the slow, absurd, and affected character of the game. As soon as he detected some imaginary fault, he punished the imaginary culprit then and there, without even investigating, without worrying about what people would say. Expeditious justice is a fine thing. At times too a man would slide and fall, while the ball rose very high into the sky. The judge's assistants looked a little like stool pigeons when they gave a piece of information. The public was confused, disappointed, embittered. It did not know what decision to make, what direction to impart to the violence that welled up from everywhere and that it was no longer possible or desirable to check, to reincarcerate. The grass seemed to have been spat out by the earth, it was no longer green, it was gurgling, it was like a swamp. A spot of water on a raincoat resembled a saw. There was a host of gazes. They went up and down the shadows of the players, they got fidgety, it was all very busy. Night was falling, and the rain, harder and harder. The game was less and less visible, one could barely make out the ball, a dark round thing, here, no, there. It would disappear into the earth, it would not be found immediately, one had to nose about, or else some big fellow would hide it behind his back and bring it into play again only after everyone had given him a nice smile. A few players left the field lying on stretchers with enormous bells. The stretcher-bearers, intimidated by the crowd, ran with their heads down. There was comment all around, people consulted each other furiously, haughtily. In the grandstands, one could see empty bottles flying, packages which were still tied up. To tell the truth, the displeasure was very great, all chests were dilated by cries that would not come out, by a passing impotence; gestures were discordant, rose up against something imprecise, but the imprecision of which decreased. On the field, the men ran into each other softly with their arms out. The ball had completely disappeared. From time to time, a black made a show of pursuing a spectral sphere, as if he were the victim of a mirage, of touching it with his foot and jumping for joy as if this time he had really done it. But the guards, who had their backs to the players, continued to make appointments with the girls and to give autographs despite the crisis. Actually, the scoreboard indicated nothing; people were not falling on each other as if they had been shot, while the blacks persisted, as did the blacks, in turning their legs or projecting them forward to give the illusion of a match. The umpire kept blowing his whistle, as if haunted by infractions. He constantly kept his hand in front of his eyes. Impressionable people who go to see horror films are somewhat of the same ilk, so are dazzled people. He was dazzled by the shadow. By the shadow of evil, I thought. Everybody watched his movements. It was an indefinable gaze, on the borderline of doubt and anthropophagy. The girl next to me let out a scream, a fellow was amusing himself by sticking her in the behind with a long knitting needle, another extinguished his cigarette in her hair without anyone's paying much attention to the scene. She went down the tiers and fell near a big dog that started licking her. The darkness was little by little nibbling away those of the players' movements which were still perceptible. The blacks engaged in a limed, exhausted, desperate orchesis at the four corners of the field. Their limbs made their way through the chaos, dubious forms that went from the huge twisted hose to the thin ringed wire that seemed to have fallen from the immense, enraged pubes of the sky and the night. Barbara had not come back. I would have liked to make a play for her.

I thought that perhaps I did not know enough about that game, and it bothered me. I sat down on the stone, and from the depth of my sadness I observed the ghastly half-belt in front of me. My neighbor with the wax in his ears was muttering insults in a language I did not understand. He often put his hand on the inner pocket of his jacket as if to make certain that a weapon was there. He lit his cigarettes with matches which he first stuck into his ears. The flame sputtered.

Each spectator was brooding over a terrible revenge. Public anger now knew no limits. Before going home to die, everyone wanted to be paid for his pains in the form of some igniferous eruption that sprang from the annihilation of all idea of pity. Those men suddenly believed in a kind of efficacy of Evil. It mattered little to them that what is desired is eternal and that what is possessed is mortal. They had to have something horrible, damnable, immediately.

A weather-beaten brightness collapsed on the foliage of the trees. It was funereal and lightning-like.

I thought of my own game, of my inner duels, not between my flesh and my spirit, but between my flesh and my flesh, between my spirit and my spirit, between me and me. What is called God and what is called Devil dwelled in me without being enemies. They coexisted. They played. Sometimes they opposed each other, but only as athletes, without hatred. It was only a match in which they engaged, after shaking hands. They vied for the best place in my being, where I could become their son. But what could I do to break that sequence of embraces, antagonisms and inseminations? I was the field, judge, spectator, and Lord knows what else except the stake, which was the only thing I would have liked to embody. I was now in a grievous night. I no longer knew the meaning of the little intrigues in which their crawling and infinite presences were engaging.

Someone said to me: "The game doesn't seem to interest you." "But it does, it does," I replied. I added: "Are the blacks, the blacks . . . sick?" He exclaimed: "They are, but so are the blacks!" He tried unsuccessfully to say something with the help of powerful field glasses. On the grass there was a stirring of thick mud from which some indistinguishable mass, endowed with a certain life and fed by the rain with increasing abundance and ferocity, seemed to be trying to extract itself. And an invisible stick was stirring it all with gruesome delight! The guards were pawing girls under their huge umbrellas. The crowd's malice harmonized with the jagged fury of the trees which were swept from within by a torrent of sap. All was a mass of jeering and booing. All was hatred in the urticating arena of uncomputed time.

I saw an extraordinary sight, I saw the thought of a crime run from soul to soul like a password. I saw hands at the ends of arms twist and close and make terrifying clubs of them, I saw the crowd change in a flash from man to wolf, I saw an extraordinary sight: human rage. Thousands of furies issuing from necks, issuing from veins of necks, like black spouts of ancient Cainian blood, nebulous collections of instruments of torture creeking as they escaped from the frightful scowls of the faces. I saw a wave flow over the field, a wave of giants with bronze biceps and little shrimps with flax muscles, all of them spurred to the marrow of their souls by the tireless jockey of hell.

I did not understand. What I wanted was to get material for a nice little article and then leave.

His Honor the Judge tried to flee. He evidently lacked the leisure to do so. He was caught, thousands of arms, too many for all of them to fall on him, fell on each other. I approached. I swam across the darkness which was a flood of ink. That was part of my job. I had to see everything, tell everything, unflinchingly. I heard a cry, a kind of isolated pain, which the din of the persecution failed to drown. Does that mean, I would write in tomorrow's paper, that a cry of terror is louder than a thousand cries of terrorism? I could tell that many faces were pressed against that of his Honor the Judge and that the privileged ones were biting it. That too I would write. There was one that was going at his nose and another at his mustache. It was as if they were trying to obtain his death's head, then and there and not in stages. He disappeared beneath the stack of the pack. His black socks and the blue skin of his calves had glidingly sunk under swarming clothes covered with stains. I thought I would never see him again. The judge's assistants illuminated the work of the necrophagous by means of powerful flashlights, the beams of which revealed, in particular, each obscene or unwonted detail of the scuffle, such as that white male leg standing beneath a huge green boot or that female behind bared by a bold old man buried beside it who spat out run-proof pieces between bites.

A few yards away, the smiling players stood in an arc and applauded. I no longer understood what it was all about. I was ill with I don't know what sickness. I wanted to go away, and I did. Besides, everything was over. The stadium emptied. When I was very young, my father often told me that I would suffer as a result of my not understanding things and human beings. I would have liked what he said to be true and to suffer as a result of not understanding. But that did not even help me suffer, I was always beside the question, but beside that question was another and I was inside the latter because I could not avoid it. The only thing I could avoid was to answer it. But if I did not answer, it threw me out and I then fell into the neighboring question. Whether I gave a false answer or none at all amounted to the same thing, the same absurd fatality that stretched all around me like a big lake. Someday perhaps I shall give true answers to questions that will be false and I shall be the kind of little hoodlum that the streets are full of.

I cast a last glance at the field. I saw a pyramid of fanatics and I must have turned pale, and I certainly shuddered. Outside, black smoke from a chimney ran along a huge beech tree as nimbly as a monkey. The sky was hard, muscular. It seemed to be bending the monstrous bow of a terrible menace in the direction of the earth, and the line of the house tops trembled on its taut horizon. Before fleeing, I had the strength to write the word "pyramid" at the bottom of my paper.

I dragged myself outside. My face was torn by men's delirium, by those abstract voices of the deep, individual humanity of each of them which launched in space the breedless crossing of the machine and the animal.

In the Theater

I felt ransacked but ag-
grandized, destroyed but stronger. I did not quite forget
that I had a knife. Here was the street and there a non-
pathetic cripple on a threshold, ready to ask me why all
that yelling. I thought I would suddenly emerge into the
brilliance that all things which restore your solitude usually have. But I was mistaken, for, at a certain moment,
in any inexorable march to death, Life, which modifies its
meaning, intervenes. Someone yelled something ominous
at me. So I turned around, I don't know what time it was,
at the corner of the boulevard that leads straight to the
law court and of that which goes to the zoo. He was a tall,
thin fellow wearing a beret, his chin shone darkly, the

straightness of his wrinkles was remarkable, but I could not see his eyes because of the needed thickness of his glasses. He greeted me with distinction. He told me a story of reminiscences, soon we talked in unison. Without a word, like a prisoner, I followed him. What was the use of resisting, I thought, I have only one chance of escaping them and that is to go to meet them, courteously, with the desire to laugh as tired horses laugh when they show their yellow teeth.

He did not ask me, as so many others do: "How are you?" but he seemed to be thinking about that question angrily. "After so many years," he said simply. Suddenly I was struck by the day's violence, my eyelids were shattered. We entered that establishment. Why? I don't know. We crossed a big, light room. A vaguely oriental face hovered over the bar. Wherever you looked, there were mirrors, things that gleamed, like the varnish of the tables and chairs, like the liquor in the glasses, and the empty glasses. We came to a smaller room. As soon as I set foot in it, it seemed to me that I changed, in the sense that whatever was foreign in me was transformed into familiarity. "Where have you taken me?" I asked him gratefully. He replied: "You'll soon find out." He added, scratching his face, "It's not that people here are brothers, but, in a certain way and out of habit, they assume that relationship . . . At times they play at imagining that they're running through a dress rehearsal of one of the finest roles in life. They dress up in man's oldest dream, they kiss, and it all seems to spread outside, like wildfire. Oh stupidity!" I decided to let things follow their course. What did I have to lose? Sweeping aside my last fears, Oswald said to me, "You're going to see the

Bearded Man, he presides at the meetings, he mustn't even make an attempt to impose his ideas. They're accepted in advance, simply because they're *the modulation of the true* . . ." There were a rostrum, a kind of enormous flag transformed into a curtain, about fifty or a hundred shaky chairs, and an apparently abandoned record-player at the front of the stage. The walls were smooth and had been carefully whitened. Behind the rostrum one could not help seeing the portrait of a great leader (no doubt a very great leader), "the father of the proprietor of the café," Oswald whispered to me. I wondered what was going to happen. It was as if a former feeling of confidence had come over me. Everything had been going well for some moments, and even better and better, my body slackened its own slowness under the influence of the rarest things which were being offered to its expectation. My heart was thumping, I tried to conceal my odd emotion from Oswald. Wasn't it true that that life was going to stop refusing obstinately to let me be the protagonist of something or other? There was a look of spiritual famine on all those faces. I could see Oswald very well on the rostrum, fascinating the crowd with his somewhat hoarse voice, with the graceful vehemence of his gestures, with his arrogance that was broken by long spells of gentleness, with what spiritualized the most hackneyed words, for a trivial remark in the mouth of anyone else blossomed on his lips supernaturally. We sat down at the back of the room. "Are they believers?" He looked at me curiously, smiled without parting his lips, and said, "Why not?" Then, leaning toward my ear, he whispered the following words: "They think they're on the track of something great." I shrugged. What did it matter to me?

I then noticed that the men and women were reading the same newspaper, while the same spoken dream, amazingly identical statements, buzzed in my ears. I mentioned this to him, and he replied, in a confidential tone, "They came here to sow communion, but it's collectivity that they're reaping, or, if you prefer, striking resemblance. Wouldn't you think they cancel each other out? There's an air of decrepitude that prevails here." I seated myself more comfortably, my curling-up was interesting, yes, yes, and closing my eyes I listened with delight to that strange tumult which was born in the rarefaction of differences, that russet autumn of dead souls. Oswald touched my arm. He was asking me, with a movement of his head, to examine a scene. A few yards away from us, a girl was sitting in the lap of a white-haired man. "Her name is . . ." The name, which seemed to me to be composed of only one syllable, was lost in the scraping of the chairs that were being pushed forward. "It's a cabaret show," he added. They kissed, I heard people whisper that they were engaging in the long-kiss contest. What was it all about? I had never seen such a thing, never. No one explained anything to me, I was sad, I wanted to protest, but I did nothing of the kind, for at bottom something within me was not against it. "It's a matter of breath," said Oswald, whose eyes were shining fixedly. "It's like foot-racing . . ." Their cheeks grew enflamed, their fingers spread, then came down, the women's under the armpits, the men's on the breasts. At times they seemed to have difficulty in maneuvering, their movements grew slow, jerky, as if they were going down a flight of tiers one by one. Tics quickened their rhythm or were absorbed in opposite tics. But what characterized that strange struggle was the quasi-immobility of the bodies; the heads were disheveled as if by miracle, without moving, it was as if the hair dropped down by itself, as if the game were emptying it of its force from within. And it was at that moment in which contortion declined and in which the absence of victory was going to make statues of the two winners that everyone breathed out in little gasps.

Suddenly they separated with a cry, as if something had burst between their mouths. People stared at them, questioned each other, thought there had been a bite, one would never know the truth . . . It was over, I rose up again from a camphorated abyss . . . All around me were eyes strewn with dreams, a sullen languor. Oswald had disappeared. Where was he? Someone who had taken his place asked me, "What do you think of those stained-glass windows?"

"Stained-glass windows?" I asked, somewhat surprised. But immediately I saw them, cutting amber and crimson designs into the walls. Thanks to them, the shadows in the room evoked colloquies of people in mourning, gatherings of voices from beyond the grave. "It's in order to relearn silence, decorum, austerity," the stranger suddenly declared . . . "It's excellent for communion . . . You understand? All rooms in which men meet should be provided with stained-glass windows . . ."

There the matter rested. Besides, I could not make out his features. His words emerged from a big black sphere in a state of imbalance between two shoulders.

Suddenly the course of the hubbub seemed to alter. I noticed that a bearded little man was taking hold of a huge microphone, the existence of which I had not noted. And to think that Oswald had left me without shaking hands. It seemed to me that I would never see him again. I was tormented. I now saw my neighbor a little more distinctly, he was a kind of gnome dressed as a tourist, and I moved away from that eager, yellow face. The audience did not calm down completely despite the gentle authority that emanated from the bearded man. The three taps that he made with some object or other against some other object took the crowd's feigned indiscipline by surprise. He waved the microphone, uttered a guttural cry, and finally decided to speak. I cocked my ear. I think he spoke of the necessity of tightening bonds. But what bonds? It would have been hard for me to say. I listened to him in my own way. All I could hear was the hoarseness of his speech, its unexpected haste, its variations, which bordered on the musical, but particularly an incomparable ring of truth that dissolved the veracious matter of the words and kept only the soul, the soul of truth probably. "He'd make lead twitter," I said to myself. My ear welcomed words that it could transform however it wished and in accordance with its taste by stripping them of their reality, of their intention. By removing their essential precision, I had the agreeable impression of de-individualizing the very person who was uttering them. What escaped from that rostrum had the horizontal intensity of the simple passions. Or the upward flapping of prophecies. I suddenly had the sensation that we were all playing a lottery of words. I heard amidst a slight din the following distinct sound: "Disordered and divergent intelligence is bound to succumb to the blows of organized and convergent intelligence." And other more sibylline sounds. I was now almost sure of having noted what the man had not said, much better than what he had said; after all, what he had transmitted to me was what he had suppressed most fiercely, either because he had not had time not to suppress it or because he lacked the art of doing so. I had clasped my hands, no doubt unconsciously, they were long and pure, like those of one who prays. "Would you like a rosary?" someone nearby whispered. Much annoyed, I took a handkerchief from my pocket and wiped my nose briskly. The bearded man then withdrew, and a wave of applause hailed his departure. Complete darkness and silence then prevailed, and I immediately felt myself bathed in those two blended things. Three taps were sounded and the curtain went up, to my great surprise. I first saw a kind of gutted chapel flooded with light, its walls (those that were still standing) were papered with calendars. A kind of ivy crawled along the plinths insidiously and in the middle of a hodge-podge of wobbly chairs and ridiculously blue pedestal tables, I saw rising from the earth, like a tree, a broad, gleaming saber topped by a birdless nest abundantly drowned by a lighting, the source of which I could not locate. It was only then that I noticed a human shape stretched out at the foot of a pile of hoops. It did not move an inch and really seemed to be no longer of this world. My heart contracted when I recognized the frightfully pale face of my friend Oswald. It was turned to the audience and looked as if it were covered with flour. His eyes were bulging with a fixed stare, they looked as if death had just laid them in those tight holes like a pair of eggs, and his clenched hands, which looked like stumps, were frightful. I wanted to protest, but as nobody flinched and as we were no doubt in the . . . I controlled my emotion. Suddenly a thumping step broke the silence and a man appeared. He was tall and strong but distinguished-looking, he was smiling sternly and balancing a whip at the end of two fingers. His entrance was hailed by an ovation which he seemed not to notice. He walked around the ruins rapidly and finally stopped near the dead man, whom he began to look at with contempt. His legs quivered nervously, then they grew still. This lasted a few minutes, during which time we held almost all our breath. Finally, a shiny boot pierced our waiting and rose up slowly, and a foot was placed without any formality on Oswald's chest. From the way in which that foot disappeared intermittently from my sight, I imagined, of course, that it was digging into my friend's movable body, and that hurt me. But nobody around me was upset. I therefore had to bear the scene alone.

"Get up if you dare," the man suddenly screamed.

Oswald did not even quiver. He continued being dead, with the same dead passion. From the whispers that rubbed at my ears, I could tell that they were waiting, that everyone was waiting, not, like me, that Oswald stand up and avenge himself, but, on the contrary, that the master get more violent and even whip him. But by some miracle his whip remained fruitlessly hanging from his numb fingers. Many minutes went by in that way, during which time we heard the master repeat: "Varlet, get up if you dare!" But the varlet did not make the slightest move. He slept, in his stonelike fatigue, and perhaps none of us knew what to think of his rigidity. I began to feel that nothing more would be got out of that man. "I know him too well . . . ," I said to myself. And yet some solution was necessary. It was necessary for our nerves. I thought I saw the tyrant's impotence slacken within him, spread, purge, his complexion turned green, he trembled with an intrigued, heavy, disheartened rage that, by loose blinking, dislocated and quietly unsettled his eyes and the gleam of their cruelty which flowed down his nose like retractile tears hanging from a thread; he looked about him, hunted down by a pack of eyes eager for action. We could see his foot vainly scraping his victim's bare chest, we could hear a groan crawling toward us and then teeth chattering. People around me were getting impatient, and I, who did not know what I was involved in, hesitated, I dared not take sides, did I even have a right to? Did Oswald have to stand up and accept the monster's challenge? That seemed to me a great risk, but on the other hand it would have been unbearable if things did not take another turn. I had had enough of it, I too, of that filthy uncertainty, and a rumbling which started in a corner of the hall fed the confused fears that I felt. Murmurs, like particles of sounds fallen from God's thundering, ran, faded away, resurged like half-screams along my row, along all the others, while on the stage the same light of Asia paralyzed two persons, one of whom iterated for the nth time: "Get up if you dare!" and the other his silence. The blows, which kept secretly raising their bid, pissed phlegm and lymph-sweat on the barbarian's detrital face. The spectators rolled up their sleeves, unbuttoned their shirts, some of them took off their shoes, and the women, the terrible women, had their hair in their eyes and their nails were sharp, their mouths liquid, and there was a sound of innumerable whinnying, hands were making lightning gestures in space, heads were thrown back as if for infirm ripples of laughter, to say nothing of hiccoughs that shook three quarters of the chests, or of knees that knocked together with helmet-like resonance. And I, what kind of calm could I still maintain? The man with the whip was spitting on Oswald, to no effect. An exasperated spectator screamed "kill him," two words that were immediately taken up in chorus by the crowd. It was like a signal, projectiles started raining down on the stage and, as if everyone were a crack marksman, they all fell on Oswald. They must have been heavy, for they fell with a noise, the noise of a storm and of iron-smelting. The born-bully was now using his whip, as if he had been waiting for the spectators' support to be really himself, and he lashed so hard that black sparks seemed to be flying. As for me, I was outraged that such extreme measures were adopted but I remained dreadfully seated amidst the fury. Through the blur I saw a young man in the first row stand up higher than the others. He was facing the audience, and his voice, which, I had no doubt, was trying to re-establish order and peace in men's hearts, was heard above the tumult. Surprised for a moment, the spectators suspended their hatred; in fact, a kind of shudder ran through them in all directions. It was purely a gesture of opposition. He was a tall, orange-colored young man, not at all good-looking or distinguished, and was wearing a filthy, mottled jacket. His trembling voice was saying things that seemed to make lots of people turn pale. And I was already supporting him inwardly simply because he was responsible for breaking up the atmosphere. His apostrophe reached me only in bits and pieces but I realized its importance, and, had I been able to, I would have made every effort to retain in my memory, even if I could not have restored them until later, as many mutilated words as possible.

Never had I anticipated such mental agility. The curtain had come down. "You don't impress me!" cried that blunt hero. "I'm telling you that you don't impress me! You're not free men!" At these words the crowd's impatience knew no bounds, and I became a witness of evil. Why was I not with him? A trifle would have sufficed, I who was all aspiration minus that trifle . . . People stood up amidst a din of displaced chairs and imprecations and rushed forward to the first row. With my bedimmed eyes, I saw fists rain down on a single, ugly, reddish face and a beastlike behavior become manifest in a compact group of individuals who were awaiting their turn. I could no longer bear it, I left in all haste. I was afraid, no doubt I was fleeing, I walked through the café like a guilty man, hardly seeing the surprise that appeared on the faces of the peaceful customers with cigars between their lips or fingers. I took a few hesitant steps in the eternal street, I bumped into a garbage can, then tottered on my way. All I wanted was to lean on something solid, and then, a few yards farther on, I became aware of the proximity of a wall . . . "Free man . . . free man!" I repeated to myself.

When I touched the first bricks with my fingertips a surge of fear immediately threw me back so that I stumbled. Not far from me I saw a sign of life, black and high, like a shadow wavering in a fixed shadow. A man was standing there, near a crevice. I approached. He was dressed in brand-new livery. With his head bowed and a milky, gold-ringed hand resting on the dark wall, where it shone like a gob of spit, and holding a cane in the other, he seemed to be dreaming. Too motionless to be drunk, too vertical to be dead, he ended by really intriguing me and I took a few more steps to examine him better.

The man was quite simply vomiting, but the act was so discreet and the trickle of vomit so slight and weak that one would have thought, not that he was trying to hold back, but that he was performing the act with great elegance, at the cost of a great effort, as was attested by his bearing, which remained noble . . . I turned my head away in disgust. And yet that sight seemed to me not entirely ineffectual. For a fraction of a second, life gave me the impression of being clear and easy. A softening of my whole being took place, as if I were being caressed with ineffable pity. Then nuances emerged, though they could not alter a dominating impression composed of grace, of austere pleasure. A smartly dressed man vomiting with studied elegance, it was nothing, it was everything. "How odd it is," I said to myself. It seems to me that because I just saw that man conduct himself as he did and against the wall which I coveted, I have now attained a fullness similar to the memorable joy of suddenly feeling that one has no duties and no rights . . . But what is that joy which resembles sadness, which resembles a liquid, shimmering melancholy? I haven't the faintest idea. Furthermore, the barking which I hear in the distance, the tongue which I turn in my mouth a hundred times, they keep adding to it . . . This is the very first time I have attained this ease . . . this sovereign ease . . . which even follows me in the very thought of this ease . . . Could it be a counterfeit of well-being? Oh! no question . . . which is not already an irrefutable answer . . . the very death of that question . . . My skin, my bones, are full of trivial objects, of interstitial, unctuous objects, like that door knob sparkling on the dark façade, that dachshund lifting its paw, that unused lamppost . . . Tears came to my eyes, I would have liked to be attuned forever to that absurd, fragile peace, to those deliquescent surroundings which sweetened me, which so pacified my peace itself as to take from me the memory of all that had happened in the theater (?) a few moments earlier. To pile peace on peace, to eternalize their fragile total, the formulating of that desire was very sweet to me and exempt from contrition.

I crossed the street. Every step I took hoisted a bit more of that unwonted happiness into the upper volume of my legs. The reverberation of the pavement seemed, as far as I could see it, to offer itself to my walk like a crumbly delight, careful of the orientation of its brightness toward my own person. Everything seemed to be a piece of happy news, something to know absolutely . . . Suddenly a bent and staggering human shadow whisked by beneath my nose. I was startled and I stopped, I watched it drop down on a bench some distance away. It was groaning. I went over to it, and when I was right against it, I grasped by the hair, but not brusquely, of course, that head which was buried in blood-stained or mud-stained arms and I turned it to the light. I recognized Oswald. At the back of that swollen face stretched that of Oswald, his lips were beaten to a pulp and a kind of dye was flowing from his hair, which was divided into twisted locks. Upon examining it, I saw it was blood. I felt that everything which had enabled me to stop thinking was fleeing from me: the bruises of happiness, the gurglings of ecstasy. I took a handkerchief from my pocket and wiped his face. Without ceasing to groan, he shot a glance at me, the gentleness of which emerged from a disorder and a cesspool that made it even gentler.

"They got you," I said to him in a hollow voice.

"Not so much . . . I'll never forget what you've done for me."

"So little," I answered.

"Had it not been for you . . . But why did you do it? It was dangerous. They might have slaughtered you . . ."

I realized that he took me for the tall, orange-colored fellow. Actually I had the same build as he but the resemblance between us stopped there . . . Besides, I also resembled Oswald, in every particular. I tried to protest, to re-establish, if possible, a sort of truth, but he did not give me time . . .

"I heard you cry: 'You don't impress me!' "

It embarrassed me to hear words that were not mine, and yet I did not mind playing at being the one who had uttered them, I was almost flattered to hear that praise. Yes, I was suddenly being honored, and neither a feeling of usurpation nor of cowardice perverted my joy . . .

"Are you able to walk?" I asked.

"Of course," he said, cheering up.

I lifted him by the arm and, with a flick of my thumb, set his tie perpendicular again. We undertook to leave together.

"They're not bastards," he said.

On the way, we were passed by a man in a hurry who was walking almost without bending his knees and who was twirling his cane. He was richly dressed. "That's he," I thought, without quite knowing what I meant by that.

"Let me treat you to a drink," I said. "That'll buck you up . . ."

"In this state?"

"We'll pick a café where there are no customers. There are lots of them in these streets."

And as my companion said nothing, I mentioned the fact that my name was Quinte.

"Delighted," he said. He kicked aside a tin can.

We entered a dimly lit saloon. An old woman was standing in a corner. She had a hooked nose, her bulky gray hair was falling over her face in strips. Perhaps she was smiling at memories of an orgy, anyway it was a frightful grin, her lips formed a kind of turd, a kind of cancerous blossoming, they swayed like a stinking, faded flower on the invisible stem of a tradition of extinguished revels and preserved vices. Her eyes floundered noiselessly in enormous sockets. The only color they still had was, if one may say so, their blinking itself, something like color devoured by movement . . . I dreaded the idea of seeing them fall, recoverable, to the bottom of a bowl, like whites of eggs, but fortunately she did not lower her head. We sat down at a table. He kept my handkerchief pressed against his lips, which were still bleeding or which were no longer bleeding. A servile little man brought the two cognacs we had ordered.

I tried to find words. Too many in me, none.

"It's awful here."

"Not very, look, that dirty calendar. It could be even dirtier, and that photo of a vamp or of the Virgin, I can't tell very well from here, on which you can see grease spots left by fingers. Well, it could be even filthier."

Shrugging my shoulders, I offered him a cigarette. He refused it, pointing to his bleeding lips.

"It'll be a woman's cigarette," I said.

He shook his head. And yet he drank the cognac, which burned.

"I want to thank you again."

I made a casual gesture, which seemed to please him. In his case, words were a prosperous and delicate industry.

"To come back to that photo, that calendar . . . When you find yourself judging human beings, you mustn't forget that they could be worse . . . To be worse is, for example, to start a war . . . to exterminate a race, to have too much power . . . I sometimes feel happy amidst so many men who have only an individual's ideas . . . For example, a criminal, a simple criminal, someone capable of killing only one man at a time, well, I feel sorry for him, I feel almost grateful. Sometimes, when I think of war, I wouldn't refuse to shake hands with him. Any criminal becomes likable in apocalyptic moments! He becomes precious to us, he seems almost to be a defender of our lives, of the lives of all of us. Unfortunately, there's always that collectivity, that terrible collectivity. We know individually that we could be worse. Worse but never better, for being better means not being worse . . . I don't think you follow me. . . . The awful thing, you see, is that though each man is unable to be a demon, they're all able to be one collectively . . . because of an idea, a little idea that succeeds in collectivizing. A community of innocent people isn't far from being a demoniacal community. And we have no recourse against a people that has one idea, no attack is possible against a people that has an accepted, cultivated idea. The leader, or rather the inventor of the idea, must overcome three obstacles: the people's resistance to that idea; the people's resistance to the resignation it feels as a result of the propagation of that idea; and the people's resistance to the enthusiasm to which it's driven by that idea, which is intended to drive them to it. The third phase is what's awful. At the present time, the mass *ideal* is triumphing in all its forms where the individual has committed suicide: it's a tyrant for each individual and God for all of them, and all of them do everything for that tyrant and for that God. You see what I'm getting at: at that kind of gregarious preponderance that can engender only creatures that will resemble it . . . There are no arrestable murderers. Actually there are only innocents about whom the only thing you can hate is what links them to each other, that absence of warm flesh, that idea . . . And there will never be a court to judge the clever, victorious uniformity . . . or the defeated diversity . . . The modern enemies of the spirit are inaccessible . . ."

I had kept looking the fanatic in the eyes, I had admired their fire, somewhat as a beggarwoman admires that of jewels in shop windows at night. I had always dreamed that my own passion would shine through my face, but all I ever saw in the mirror was *my* face, my ordinary, photographable face. This time I was subjugated.

"But my conversation bores you, doesn't it," he said. "What can one say that doesn't seem like a demonstration, like a sloppy thesis? In the present age, the conversation of serious people in this mad world resembles the defense of a thesis by lunatics. The wise man escapes only insofar as the psychiatrist escapes his madmen and madness . . ."

"You don't bore me . . ."

"Do *you* have problems?" he asked me point-blank.

"No!" I cried (but I think I was lying).

"How do you manage?" he asked, keenly interested.

I did not reply. His gaze had been resting for some minutes on the face of the old woman, who had the hiccoughs. It withdrew from her, clouded over, as if all it had seen there was coprolites by the hundred.

"Why didn't you accept your master's challenge a while ago, you could have stood up and smashed his head . . ."

"That wasn't what the crowd was waiting for . . . And besides, I'd had enough . . . I've been in the theater for five years . . . always playing the role of servant . . . I couldn't stand it any more, so I rebelled . . ."

"You call that a rebellion?"

"Of course. I ought to have stood up so as to be beaten and battered even more. I didn't. I just lay there. I betrayed the work, but I don't care. Nothing is a betrayal when it's a matter of becoming a man . . ."

I sat there pensive. Was that an act? A rebellion?

"Are you really convinced that you acted right," I insisted, "that you acted at all?"

He tried to smile. I saw his head nod.

"Have you been in the theater long?"

"I've just told you, five years . . ."

"Is it . . . interesting?"

"It is . . ."

"Is it true," I asked eagerly, "that there's a way . . . of being someone else?"

"Not on your life! When I was very young, I dreamed of multiple existences. The fact is, there's only one that I've ever had: my own. When I went on the stage, I had an aim: to become lots of other people . . ."

He slapped his chest.

"There's too much going on in there. I think that that's what's called personality . . ."

He slapped his chest harder.

"You can't eliminate yourself, not even for a second . . ."

"Then what's the point in being an actor?"

"To act well. But to act well, I grant you, is to express, with talent, the desire you have to be someone else. And the actor is the man who has the least illusions about the matter. The spectator goes to the theater so as to get away from himself, and the actor so as to get into himself. Do you get it? It's when you're not an actor that you imagine yourself most easily to be living another life. I've often heard so-called sophisticated people say: I'm multiple. Outside the theater, it's a common thing to have inner conflicts that one is eager to take for other presences. But what one actually experiences is man's natural tendency to think that he changes his being. There are no inner conflicts, there are only different or divergent ways of remaining oneself . . . Those are things that the theater unites by sublimating them in the actor's heart. Nothing is easier than to have conflicting feelings when they depart from their state of filth, except when they're acted . . . There's nothing foreign left in you. I am what it's possible to be, that is, one's self first of all . . . The theater is, in a way, the illumination in the actor of all the little opposing and preconceived ideas that are current everywhere . . . No less than that . . . And all the actor has to do is to let himself roll up to himself . . . You're completely the edge of a circle from which you lean out on what's called a character. And you pull back entirely, dragging it with you to the center. There you come back to yourself. *That's* the duration of a role. What, to the spectator, is an act, is, to the author, a retroact..."

I found these words . . . rousing. I had heard the theater spoken about in other terms, more pleasant terms, more ambitious ones too. And yet this man adored his profession. We were in the heart of poetry.

"I still don't understand your attitude on stage."

"I'm coming to that . . . For some time, I had stopped feeling my . . . my . . . my essence . . . To me, acting no longer meant 'being armed with a character and going in search of what one is oneself' . . . I took leave of my character on the way . . . and I didn't return to *myself* . . . So I got scared. I thought it had happened, that we coincided, all the servants and I, that we were set in our resemblance . . . I snapped out of it like a free man . . . I think that if we could really become someone else, we'd refuse. Man does want to be someone else, but he doesn't want to go through with it . . . To change, to put oneself into other people's boots, very well, but then . . . to order them around!"

"And what are you going to do now? They won't forgive you . . ."

"I'll look for work elsewhere. I already have a name . . ."

"Would you like the role of a master . . ."

I saw his eyes light up.

His only answer was: "I like my profession."

He opened his jacket, and I could judge of the prodigality of his blood. It was all over his shirt, on his tie, on the edges of his belt. He continued:

"You see . . . it's in the street, in the office, at home, when you're exposed to influences and fashions which you haven't chosen, that you'd like to feel yourself moving toward an existence that's not your own, toward hope in that existence . . ."

"I understand . . . You want to stop being the person who loves or hates because he's taught to."

We had two drinks, one after the other, without saying anything. We were like the scales of a mad balance on each side of the table. We were looking at each other, and that seemed to me very risky. And I think we both looked as if we knew a great deal, much more than we managed to say. I saw him as something that I had already been. Standing between two flaming wings that carry him off to an exile where total invention reigns, for the last time he plows the soil of the true, the land of taught lures, with his hatred and contempt. But how hard it is to soar . . .

Suddenly he began to laugh. His pupils had a weird brightness. His hands clawed the table.

("And what if we were in the theater?" I wondered.)

"Look here," he cried. "I don't believe in God or in hope in God. Or in hope on earth. I'm on the stage in order to lose all hope. As long as hope continues there'll be mediocrity. Hope is a prison in which one waters artificial flowers instead of breaking stones. That means there's an intelligent, fruitful despair, something dynamic, a despair that impels man to overcome it by another despair which can be called, for example, art . . . If that could happen . . . we would live a great tragic epoch in a society of artists . . ."

I was frightened . . . I was no doubt livid . . . I felt that I understood . . .

"I'm like a sieve that can't be filled . . . Hope's a

filthy invention. If it's been possible to uproot freedom from the minds of so many men, it's because their minds could be planted with wild hopes . . . After killing God, man made himself an astounding promise. A final target was created in his own image, but in order that he not be discouraged by the distance, a multitude of other targets, various stages, were placed between this present and the completed future. But stages that don't bring you nearer to anything, false, brilliant intermediary stages . . . You get it? . . . What I like about despair is the will . . . the will to make hope exist . . . The will . . . to defy evident nothingness . . ." He drew himself up, expanded his chest as if to take in a bowl of air. The old woman snickered. Whereas he, with his anachronistically chaste face . . .

He continued:

"I sometimes hope, just for the fun of it. I trust in things that I know are vain . . . I'm afraid of Fulfillment . . . I adore rough drafts . . . outlines . . . whatever is built and perishes in desire, or the rapid encircling of a dream . . . Obviously that's an actor's game. For example, mankind. Have you ever amused yourself by saying the words 'I love mankind' in a labyrinth where the echoes keep rolling back and forth? You haven't? Well, take my word for it, it's comical, perhaps the most comical thing in the world . . . Then, when you've had a good laugh, you remain dumfounded, you wonder whether your ears have deceived you, whether those were the words you cried out and how it's possible that those were the ones you chose to launch for repercussion. You say to yourself, 'But it's impossible' . . . But the curled shavings of a diamond are also impossible . . ."

He folded and unfolded his arms. The proprietor

was watching us from behind the bar . . . Those shifty, stuttering eyes. The bar was long and gray like a row of houses belonging to the State.

"If it was possible to love, to struggle without hope . . . But it's hard, isn't it, and you get tired. That fixed little animal is present wherever there's consciousness, let's say that it's the witness of our falls into error . . . So long as the noises of the heart drown out the bored sighs of the mind, things keep going. But then what? It's simple and tragic to realize suddenly that you've committed the irreparable in the name of the greatest hope."

He drained his glass, rubbed his hands slowly, while I took advantage of the pause to relax by inverting the crossing of my legs and clearing my throat, somewhat as people listening to music do between two movements. He was darkness itself, and yet I *felt* bright within him, within myself. He was the purest inventory of night. There was only one thing I did not know: the weather.

"I, too, loved too much all at once. It happened in the past, when I still didn't know that the theater could be all that love. I was at the age when certain privileged persons discover the total keyboard of living. The soul, the heart, the senses, the mind, it was all given to me, all at once, and each with its voluptuous power of loving an incalculable number of love-objects by drawing them from sleep. Yes, I tried to abandon myself to everything by every possible means, I plunged through a thousand different sensations toward a single moaning frenzy that would crown the colossal plural of delights. But the more of them I looked for, the more I had to find. At times I stopped at the hugged light, and I would dream of a sacred treasure house of intoxications, the blue ones, red ones, spherical, angular, ancient and recent . . . An event occurred that upset this euphoric order . . . A flashing event, like a sudden awakening by thunder. It suddenly seemed to me that huge tanks were parading by. It went on for days and days. There was no end to it . . . They crushed everything as they rolled by, flowers, stones, bushes, little animals. They crushed everything that was small and humble, and also whatever smelled good and had a certain nobility . . . The procession was, of course, an impressive sight. It displayed great force, extraordinary self-assurance . . . But I felt that those caterpillars were destroying some eternal value which I could not yet name and that an appeal was being launched by its surroundings, by its environment (for it dared not, or could not, defend itself, it was ashamed of having to defend itself), an appeal which I couldn't hear. Then, by some miracle of my manliness, I threw myself in front of those steel monsters to pick up something where they were due to pass. What my hands brought back taught me nothing worth the trouble of being saved, I was filled with doubt, had my intuition been correct? Even now I sometimes ponder the patent truth that tinkled for me amidst the overwhelming din of the caterpillars . . . But what's that thing called, don't *you* know? All *I* know is that it is, that it exists . . . Perhaps it's *mystery?* . . .

"And what were the tanks?"

"Oh, they were the very opposite of a mystery, and rather what crushes it: an unbounded assertion, a huge, tyrannical simplification of noise, of anger, of logical laughter . . ."

He became solemn, then biting.

"Man who is elusive. When I don't see him, when I

escape from him, when he's not under my very nose. That's how I like him, if I may say so. But don't tell me about man, I beg you, you'd be doing me the worst possible service! Besides, whatever one may say, art is meant for keeping men at a distance, art is first of all a distance, a sculpted, painted, written and other kinds of distance, not a bond . . . I'm quite aware that when I get on with man it's because I don't get the hang of him. There's always an expression of himself in which it's impossible for me not to hate him, and though it may not be revealed, nevertheless how could I bear to live in its presence, knowing that it's hiding from me and that I'm being deluded? The theater makes you love men in the right way, that is, insofar as it abstracts them from you and puts their intensities in their place . . . They're indefinable, unfinished . . . Can we dream of more exquisite impurities? . . . Man's grandeur is due to his obscure intemperance, to a battle within him between similarly strong opposites, it's when his violence and his mildness are equaled only by the might of the mixtures with which he opposes any definitive avowal of his being . . . I had a friend who was built that way, I lost him. He wanted to be a stable enigma as well as a mobile clarity, he died as a result of fulfilling his wish, but what a beautiful death! At the present time, men die and cause others to die in the name of a fixation of ideas, for a future of analogies. Frightful!"

"It's odd," I stammered. "I feel that you're talking to me about things which concern me . . ."

I saw his chin go up like a shiny ball. His head thrown back, absently, and that long, distended, grainy neck, hairy in spots, what a sickly smile it all was . . .

A drop of blood rolled down his forehead, which he had wounded again with a scratch of his nail.

I made a vague remark.

"You'll never get away from it."

"But that's what life is: not getting away from it, not getting away from it . . . Oh, I realize that I'm a barren animal and that the sight of me would make the multitude roar with laughter, or that at least it would pity me if it made my acquaintance . . . But it will never make my acquaintance! That's what reassures and hurts me at the same time . . . I'm more or less free to be alone . . ."

"But what do you know about me?" (He was talking to me about my plans, about my childhood.)

He ran a very long hand over his forehead. He was perspiring. I had a headache. (But it seems to me that it's my thoughts that hurt. Each seems more wounded than the other and to be waiting for treatment that will never come. They are perhaps former thoughts which are not used to a new being, their own riot, and the repression that follows.)

"What we both lack," he continued, "is the power to rest . . . In my condition, I no longer feel fatigue the way others do. This absurd fatigue. This fatigue that doesn't even build a future enigma . . . It's almost monstrous to talk about fatigue when one is young . . . And yet . . . It's certainly within me, as present as my veins, but so much more alive than they . . . It occupies me, of course, but I don't let it force me to rest. I want it to remain what it is. The ideal thing is not to succumb to it, without wanting to overcome it . . . It's rather odd, moreover, to want to live on good terms with it. That leads to surprises. Bear one thing in mind: relief itself is a yielding to error. And error is a daughter of hope."

"May I?" I took a piece of paper from my inner pocket and jotted something down.

He went on:

"It's nice out. Take a look. Night is floating at the windows . . ."

"Not at all, it's daytime," I retorted. He smiled banteringly. He dominated me with a strange poetry. I saw his eyes staring at the old woman and then at the proprietor. There could be no doubt about it, he hated them. It lasted a few minutes, time enough for an evil thought to be born and become a promise of an act. I would have sworn that he wanted to kill them and that I was the only obstacle in his way. The heavy unrest of all his limbs issued from a dull pain, and the energy of desire exposed his standing face to the wounds. Finally he whispered to me: "I hate them." Then, all at once, I was relieved. Words are always less criminal than the silence that covers them. He stood up. It was as if he stood up over a mad, radiant set of eggs. Yet the seat was dirty, filthy. His gaze wandered slowly about the café. The old woman yawned, her specter trickled about her black, open, meat-guzzling mouth.

"Come," he said. But he hesitated. He gave me the impression of being unable to choose between the pursuit of a theoretical conversation and the grip of a stern force. I felt ready to follow him very far. The event I was awaiting could come only from him. In any case, I was prepared to commit in turn the act that he would commit, whatever it might be, or to help him commit it.

"Be careful, you're quite pale," I said.

"You're right . . . The paleness of deep truths . . . It's a pain in the head . . . A memory . . . I now look like a traitor, don't I? Listen. My father used to say: 'I am what I believe only insofar as it's still too soon to prejudge what that means for man . . .' My father was a humanist. He had a foreboding of the possibility of a social and spiritual masterpiece . . . And he set to work on it. 'I'm devoting all my poor strength,' he would say to me, 'to the idea of a fine overwhelming of man. But cautiously . . .' But as for me, I see it's not toward that man that we're going . . . My father would no doubt have had the courage to stop at the first perceptible perversions of the work, to fabricate repentance for himself. My mother was more fervent than he. But her face displayed an anxious goodness. She was fraternal, as few women can be. Women are amorous or maternal and always on the point of toppling over into one or the other of those extremisms. If they're neither this nor that, then they're simply hard, for it's up to man to be friendly or fraternal . . . But let's drop that. Penitentiary death has purified them of their wager; it has slipped into their ideal the only moment of truth and certainty they were entitled to expect . . ."

His eyes grew hard and cold. I saw a frost of tears.

"Who will put an end to the crimes they denounced, they who proclaimed loud and clear that man must not be the death of man in the name of a conception of man!"

Then he became fervent. He seemed to be reviewing a train of thought which I could not see.

"What they wanted was not men who thirst for justice, for thirst deranges, it drives you mad, but men who are just . . . They also taught me that the ideal thing for a militant would be to multiply and complicate the ideas concerning man and his condition, for it seemed obvious to them that it's the inordinate attachment to a few simple and supposedly clear notions that makes political murderers and victims . . . Humanism, said my father, is more a groping than a finding . . . I think that they too would have defended the mystery in man and in things, I even think that that's what they were defending, without illusions . . . Certitude . . . Servitude . . . A frightfully rich rhyme . . .

"You're lucky to have had parents like that," I said.

He wanted to move forward, with his hand out. His wide-open eyes were mastering something or other, tears or rancor. But I, strangely, made him sit down again. I suddenly realized that he was relatively ugly, but only with regard to his physique, for elsewhere, somewhere beyond his uncomeliness, he was not without a certain fluid handsomeness.

"What are you going to do?" I asked him.

"I'm going to change my fight or my fatigue, do you understand?"

I stood up. And we left. I saw him scrutinize once again, with a dark gleam on his entire face, the old woman and the proprietor, the walls. The old woman had fallen asleep, with her head on the windowsill, as if waiting for an ax; fringes of hair were steeping in her glass. The proprietor. He was no longer there. His hideousness floated over the bar. It was he. In the street, we lulled ourselves with the women's faces. How sweet it is to the eye to pluck them when crowds are milling. Even if you merely look straight ahead, it's possible, they are like hesitant little balloons that have lost altitude. It's delightful. At times their eyes remind me of empty, hypersensitive beaches quivering like cats in the sun, and sensual. He talked to me about them, awakening memories. But certain memories rise up only to consecrate a forgetting. I noticed his metamorphosis. A new passion was dislocating the features that had contained and guided the other, the preceding one; invisible switches must have been functioning beneath that tight texture of the physiognomy and modifying the direction of the exchanges, of the emanations, of the tics. His face was cleansed of its blood. Beside me was no longer a kind of tragedian who had strayed into extra-theatrical reality, but a completely bodily being, astonishingly sensual, shaken without perversity by the deep conflict of desire . . . His voice was searching a thing stuck on his mouth. It was warm and incisive.

"We must love women, though they don't pay us for philosophical disappointment since they themselves are the reduction of this world which we don't understand. . . Between women and mankind there's only a difference of quantity. All the insoluble problems, all the meaninglessness of the world, are in them: impossible unity, realizable domesticity, the never total gift, dictatorship, freedom, ingratitude, morbid hope, *savoir-défaire,* corruption, stupidity, genius. And who hasn't been cuckolded by the world?"

The notion of woman entered me like the idea of a revolution of bodies, parallel to the exaltations of the mind. Oswald's words made a tremendous impression on me. What he said about woman was true. And yet there was a difference between her and the world, we could lay our head on that microcosm, our human will could make it cry out, with our ear pressed against that complicated breast we could listen to the dark rumination of the Unknown and destroy it out of impatience.

Oswald was silent! And I had not noticed it! His silence made me think, against my will, about sexuality, which was so important that it triumphed in the most official faces of life, so crafty that it could infiltrate into the least corruptible natures. We were walking so straight, so resolutely, that the dense mob opened as we went along, we entered it like a sex organ piercing the rot of a divided piece of fruit that has burst as a result of some acute emphysema. We went through kingdoms of bare downy skin and nails attacked by love.

The act. That Act. To dare imagine, some night, that the pleasure of that lightning will be prolonged, that you will feel yourself "a cathedral of drunkenness" with all that the expression implies: duration, grandeur, and matchless gifts being built up within you, concisely, by means of the orgasm. But if that were possible a single time, it would be the last, all men would let themselves die on the spot, none would dream of struggling against death. Who has never felt that to stop coming is certainly to jump off a runaway train, destination Death, but not to jump off it voluntarily, and that the ghastly peace which then comes over us is not the return of Life but a state which precedes it, worse than death: an absence of desire. But one can also think, as Oswald did, that it is this kind of unavowable and pre-sleeping failure that magnifies us, that increases our heroic and tragic knowledge of love, failure, that is, the natural brevity of happiness. It hisses in us like a lash of a whip, then, that's all, a kind of luminous bitterness follows it without which, this time too, we would be ugly and abject . . . Lovers are serious people, often grave, tense, simply because the hope of prolonging what they are going to undertake does not dwell in them, they are convinced that they are building what will have to be begun over immediately, that they are storming what is forever overflowing their embrace . . . But they persist because they have a taste for what has been lived and an infinitely keen consciousness of what is lived . . . The near and the possible interest them to the highest degree, and, when it is a matter of pleasure, doubly, for pleasure seems to them to be both the duty—performed—of feeling that one exists superabundantly here and of feeling that one is dying superabundantly elsewhere, in the devouring desire of the other. And I, how I kept dreaming, pounding that pavement, among suspect destinies! I was for woman . . . but also for some feeble plot against woman. As we crossed the square, we passed a marble reproduction of the most beautiful woman in the world. Oswald was saying that physical love is only a love of art that has rushed down the magic and perilous path of the senses. I agreed. He continued, a walker choked by emotion, hollowing out step by step steep visions that threw him from sordid contacts to taciturn drives as if really he were made only for a desire, that knotty, violet desire that opens beneath our steps like a tomb of flesh, like the supple, pink, and tapering grave of their flesh. "I knew a tiny little woman who disappeared under my belly," he was saying, "I too," she was not more human than a butterfly living in a closed hand, no sooner could I wrest such retractable confessions from her that it was as when one questions the world and the world answers: "Something-or-Other" listlessly or very loudly so that you stop pestering it, said Oswald, but everyone knows, I said, that you pay a great deal, far too much, for the confessions that women do not retract; her name was Pelouse, when I knotted her hair around my wrist and pulled her face down, it was more naked than marble, but her eyes survived her, they had the slow surge of the memory of a wake on lakes with swans, Oswald said: nothing but a marvelous surface on which could be read a bit of fright, and a traveling dream that slipped into the folds, along the nostrils, which rowed in the blood of the lips and threatened to break up into spirals of pleasure in our gold-washing eyeballs, the sureness and dubiousness of love closely mingled, closely absent; I said, she had small fingers, great adroitness, have you ever seen fingers bubbling in a hand, or better still, a hand bubbling with all its fingers, no I've never seen anything more beautiful, repeated Oswald, we were telling each other, Oswald and I, that when she was naked, the first thing I wanted to kiss was a spot on her hip, a spot whose configuration corresponded exactly to that of our country, and that when, disturbed by the analogy, I verified it in the dictionary, which I laid cold on her burning left breast, she had begun to laugh, but not when Oswald stuck her on the place of her native village, lost in the mists, for she then uttered a little scream at the sight of the drop of blood that beaded at the end of that erotico-geographical little session, a sexual dream, a religious dream, a piety set up around any god except the one whose name is written with the capital letter that was stolen almost two thousand years ago from the word "desire,"* said Oswald, full of that rustic incontinence of mythologies. The exceptionally clement temperature prompted us to say yes, we said yes yes yes, yes to that uproar of drunkards emerging from a street, with a woman, a man, then others, pressed against each other, yes a heap of clowns. We walked a hundred yards, all of them motley. We chatted, our individual words recognized each other, coincided in the heart of our emotion, perhaps we were already friends, because of this absolutely non-realistic dialogue. Non-realistic. Oswald participated in the noise, in the speed of the world, formidably, with his own weapons: art, sensuality. He had just been talking about the body, talking so well that my nose was still beaten by fragrances of damp leather and hairs stuck on it, he jumped from the prevailing quality of the body to that of the mind, not as one goes from the cock to the bull, but as one goes from the cock to the cock: "the body and the mind: not two swords that cross, but two parallel swords, but a single sword, pointing toward the shadow" . . . "but there is no sovereign body and the body culminates in joys only when licked by a flame in which the obsessional winds of the mind wave the sparks of beauty," yes, something lyrical, Oswald, yes . . . And while we quickened our tormented walk toward some dark destination, we imagined together the fluorescent pleasures of the city developed to the point of debauchery, we already saw ourselves sitting on chariots full of naked girls and liquor, we rolled ourselves up, possessed, in question marks, "will she come?" "will she open the

---

* The French words for *God* and *desire* begin with the letter *D.*—Trans.

door for me with nothing on but a dressing gown?" "how many of us will there be on the barge?" and in conclusion Oswald said to me and do you know what an exclamation point is, it's a question mark with a hard-on, just that, yes, yes, we said yes, because of the exceptionally clement temperature.

Everything was a rolling-mill including the very high birds' nests, everything was forged, beaten, dented on the expiatory anvil of the sexes, but the sky opened and deflagrated above us, for the challenging of instincts is stronger than beatitudes. I was sitting on a bench, and I took out the blood-stained handkerchief, which was like a little flag unable to float, and ran it over my face. A good smell of blood. We said yes, yes, that body like a shot, those punches I gave myself in the belly, sitting on a bench, next to a very dark woman with rings in her ears who is not reading, who does nothing but not look at me, why does she struggle and utter piercing screams that nobody will hear since everything is a rolling-mill including the very high birds' nests, everything was forged, beaten, dented on the expiatory anvil of the sexes, I writhed with cruel delectation in a briar, but after a short struggle she disappeared, leaving me only time enough to see her open her bodice and her hair, which was like epileptic snakes. Oswald and I walked side by side, we said yes; my panting produced a dense, dancing vapor, he removed mucus from his nose with the end of his tie, his long steps ground huge lemon peels beneath the sun.

The Artist at Home

"Yes, I paint," he said to me.

It was he, Oswald. His flabby lips rolled over the bottom of his face, red as the first flow of blood from a sudden wound. We were not yet at his home but had stopped in front of a museum as if we had planned to enter it. He said I paint, he surprised me.

"I paint without being a painter. I'm not a painter, I play at being a painter . . . You get it? Play well and you stop being a player, you become real . . . And to think that I had decided to paint in order to forget about the theater." I had the impression of being involved in his labyrinth and that there was no way out. It was a haunted path which echoed with the great grief of owls and specters, but where the habit of roaming finally foretokened the luxurious violence of a day of glory. My silence sat down in one corner of the ring, and his in the opposite corner. They confronted each other without hatred or disgust, they were awaiting the signal of the word. Who can know the truth about Oswald? Between us, between our deathly silences, voices rise up and proliferate, voices that care not a rap about the concordance of versions; they describe a being in which there are his story and mine, and that being is created as a result of being described, and we vie for its autonomous life. He has traveled a great deal, he has trafficked. His hands, which have been yellowed by China, hang down along a black jacket. At night, he paints in the unstable room and fragile setting of a suburban basement.

I would like to say a word about his individualism. His hatred of association is exacerbated at the thought that he himself is the product of that historical manufacturing of the living and the dead which impotence gathers together without respite and mingles wrongly in a tremendous plot against life. A swarming of base interests thus builds, with discreet laws and imperceptible wiles, the part of being in which one recognizes that one is good or odious without having the consolation of being in any way responsible oneself. He was furious at not being able to seize the multiple authors of his variation itself and at feeling that he had been invaded and conquered by the blind action of groups. Therefore, when he attempted to become reconciled with men, it could be only with all the solitaries of this world, only with all the exiles, only with all those who are driven out of communities because of their unfitness for belonging. And even with regard to objects, it was in their isolation that he enjoyed them most, when they were a black nakedness in the shadow or a unique thrust toward the sun.

In his eyes, there was no innocent meeting, there were only inner failures drowned in a number and in a kind to which there inevitably corresponded, far away in time, criminal collusions. The unbounded quest for protection and help was both the veritable motive and veritable nature of human movements. He thought that most men who always and everywhere proclaim themselves free are fascinated, sucked in, by the mob and by the very idea of solidarity which makes it possible to pool one's weaknesses. That the interest of dying alone at the bottom of a mine was less in the eyes of many people than that of dying there with a hundred others; and that with regard to happiness, man finally consents to its being manufactured for him and for its being involved in that of others. There is no need to seek elsewhere the proof of the individual's surreptitious stubbornness in falsifying the courage of his solitude, and solitude itself. He said of all those who have faith in something: "All those idealists are right in saying that their ideal is the finest, that it is the purest and the only true one . . . But how is it that they do not discover that from the moment they have fellow fighters the enemies of that ideal are amongst them, amongst all those who fight mistakenly or for the pleasure of fighting or destroying what is, of replacing what is by what might be, and that henceforth what they must conquer marches in the same direction as they, at the same pace, similarly armed, lulled by common agreements, that the enemy is thus in the gathering which they have joined, that it is the gathering itself. Nothing makes me flee from church or party more than the idea that it is a family in which an individual's purest ideas about love wither and die." He dreamed of a love without bonds and of free fraternity more than of free love, the kind he envisaged as existing between proud men, beyond dependency and duration. Rebellion was nothing if not a transfer of servitude. The quality he tried to arouse in himself and to recognize exasperatedly in others was men's resistance. He believed in the attempt to resist, not in that to destroy. To resist everything in one-self that tends toward a wasting of existence, to resist every barren way and every turning off of every way, to resist the weakening of the acute consciousness of being (being meant, in his thinking, giving and receiving, on condition that giving meant throwing out being as one throws out ballast, *in order to rise,* and that receiving meant receiving only what one is free to choose for one-self). Resistance, as he saw it, was, moreover, not opposed to action. It gave rise to action precisely insofar as it was rich and passionate and as the renunciation which it im-posed merged with an increase of richness and passion. But for the temptation of acting, which, according to him, could only lead from rebellion to repression by way of drunkenness of triumph, he substituted, for himself, that of reacting, which word in itself covered precise knowledge of adversity, the act of opposition, and the limit of victory. His past tallied marvelously with the idea of resistance. Excited even by the memory of his youth, he reflected back to it a willful and somewhat haughty self-image in which a calculated excess of soli-tude fed on preferences brutally discarded between what must and must not be retained of what had been accumulated by the heart and the mind. Acting was blind, reacting was a reward of wakefulness. To raise one's individuality to a self-sufficient sovereignty was a dream that might be realized by a simple elimination joined to the gesture of welcoming. The thing that counted was the meaning of the choice, the perception of what makes man greater. "To resist what is mediocre: evasion, futility, the enrollment of human beings, the thousand sordid things that bind a soul to pettiness without exception and without light." If he had had to preach to men, there is no doubt but that he would have spoken to them in those terms and only those terms. But he did not preach to men, because he loved them only in his own way. And besides, to live alone confers upon the solitary not the opposite of an ethic but an incommunicable ethic. He hardly spoke. He derived from his resisting life a kind of bubbling discretion. His rages were brief and smothered, always on the point, it seemed, of splitting him in two and scattering him to the wind in sparks.

What impressed him most, after Will, was accident. Man and matter bathed indivisibly in accident. It was born of created things and remained attached to them: that was what freedom was, a tremendous ambush for everyone, maleficent or beneficent, neutral too. We were cast into this world for infinite collisions. As for death, it seemed to him intolerable only insofar as man had got rid of the idea of living in the jungle. "Yet what is human life if not the cruel condition of a jungle slowed down by civilization?" There was really nothing outrageous about dying killed or dying of exhaustion, that higher form of accident. He perceived, with strange lucidity, all the shades of fear, the porcelain which one is afraid may break in one's hands, and one's self when one feels one is porcelain in the surrounding hands of life. But he liked to fight against fear, against the very consciousness of accident. He multiplied life within the minutes that made him live it. It was impossible to be both more alive than he and more knowing about death. Pain, solitude, and risk emphasized the value of everything that was not men, and evasion could not have given him so intense a feeling of being present because it is dangerous (but also thrilling) to be there. He was not a person who braces himself against death by muffling himself up in the habit of doing only what has to be done, but rather one who goes to meet the crafty pressure of dramas on human beings. Sunk in a frightful earth, we had to love it as it was and constantly seek, by means of art, reasons for loving it. And it was a question of life and honor to resist the oppression of the herds and the underhand will of the gregarious to standardize the world and take from it the deep and mysterious disparity of its destinies. He wanted not only not to fear accidents, which for a brief moment or definitively resemble death, but also to invite them, to provoke them himself—for himself—by a sacred effort of being toward its highest spiritual condition, toward an inner weight unequalably heavy with all beauties. To be was to want to be a statue in a sublime bewilderment of body and soul, but it was also, in a certain direction, to occasion for oneself the boldness that calls into question the sense of limits and the ordinary meaning of life . . .

Though he might feel wretched himself, eat little, and suffer from cold in winter, his wretchedness then had the luxuriance and strangeness of what soars intensely at the height of the Spirit. "I sometimes love the world as it is. At times, when I look at it with true loving desire, I see it as a sun that no longer casts a shadow. When I think about it with my eyes closed, its beauty prevails over its ugliness. I therefore have reasons for mistrusting what people want it to become . . ."

He was experiencing implacable solitude. And in a man's solitude, especially if it is sharp, there is at first his unique hope of incarnating God . . . the only great illusory role of life and the only illusion that cannot survive a great role. He was alone, not because he loved men too much or turned away from them too knowingly, but because he wanted to attain and occupy in dream that point of heaven's indifference where silence descends upon men who are eager for voices. But what did he obtain from his high mountain pride, from that raging need to have neither friends nor brothers, from that endlessly repeated pretense at the approach of strangers whom he saw everywhere coming to him from everywhere? He said he had gained a new power of the eye from this non-humanist diversion ("I don't see far but I see ardently, in the light, the things that I see at close range: I see the lenses of my glasses before I see the object I look at and before I see the lenses I see my eyes themselves") and had obtained inner landscapes that broke the classifications of the world in their jaws of light. In the brilliance of that unleashed solitude, everything visible on earth acquired an adornment and an essence hitherto unknown, which were tragic, of course, but fertile and hospitable. Trivial words and gestures themselves were no longer words and gestures, but things which surprised consciousness as things that cut surprise the flesh.

He sometimes had the impression that he knew the secret of a true poetic life: it was the transmuting of non-values, the changing of insignificance into a sign. Encouraged by the inventions that this second world revealed to him, he had wanted to transcend himself: to create without a public, without admirers, not to try to sell anything, to keep everything for himself, in defiance of the basic motives of the demiurgic. This complement of solitude had soon appeared to him to be similar to a solitude multiplied by itself many times, like a savage rush of that solitude toward its realm . . .

"Do you think it right that creatures of art be prevented from living in the sight of men?"

"No," I replied.

He explained to me that his works seemed to him to be growing pale, anemic.

"What they no doubt lack," he said to me with a snicker, "is not the food of my eyes, of my mind, but the eyes and mind of the largest possible number of admirers. Art probably unfolds at that price."

But, I asked myself, is he a painter or an actor? I no longer knew.

Pulling me by the sleeve, he made me retrace my steps for a few seconds. Then he changed his mind and we went forward again. The museum stood before us one last time, fabulously calm, closed to our hustling wretchedness. "The museum closes at six o'clock," I read on a notice. We turned our backs to it. We threaded our way through an alley where the griminess of the gables and the crooked eaves were hardly in keeping with the pure flight of the sky. But our harrowing laughter was at times in keeping with a piece of rubbish, at times with a wavering wall. Sounds of pots, successive leaps of two black cats miming a kind of sexual terror, a child with fixed, fawn-colored pupils, whose legs hummed with impatience all the way to us, waiting to get rid of that imbecilic presence of strangers who were preventing it from crushing a broken ball on the leaf of the shutter opposite, all of that fed our somber prescience. The daylight, with the exit in view, seemed to us to be the light from the sky based for a moment, in the manner of big white aircraft, on an immense plain. When we reached that avenue, our eyes blinked and we saw a few proud-looking trees oscillating in the indecipherable mirror of the windows. Then, again, there was a street without light in the middle of which I realized that we had said nothing to each other for at least five minutes and that we both seemed guided by a presentiment much more than by the destination which Oswald must have chosen and of which he must have been only very vaguely conscious. But I mechanically followed that man who was certain he was being followed and who was walking rather fast with both hands in his torn pockets. From time to time, an effusion of melancholy broke the rhythm that was imposed on him from without, but actually what it did was to make him walk faster again. We reached the shore of the river where the water glided through motionless shadows, which, eventually, it gave the impression of rusting. From a deserted, dilapidated barge rose fine, impressive spirals of smoke which were quite vital because of their exaggerated suggesting that there was human life inside. And despite the monotony of the movement, it was surprising to discover great varieties of motifs in it.

Blue masts and strengthless ropes broke the tension of the distant sky against which birds seemed to strike and then drop down again to the earth to die. He stopped me by jabbing his elbow in my chest. I thought he was going to say something long, interminable.

"It's silly," he said simply. Then he shrugged.

We continued our senseless walk.

"I don't think," he said, "that apart from an artistic action, a professional ambition, or a will to revenge, there can be men who are sincerely concerned with the fate of others . . ."

I remained silent. Speeches of joy crumpled in my throat. I was almost sure that he was taking me to the goal, that I could rely on him. I was no longer alone.

"I entered the harshest existence," he declared. "My reason for living is an active indifference which results in short-lived works and in fixed passions, which wilt. And die on themselves, shriveled up . . .

I heard him address me with the familiar *tu*. For me it was a kind of grace.

"Do you think about the meaning of life?"

I nodded vaguely between yes and no.

He seemed reassured. I enjoyed following, like a big, castrated animal, that tyrant whose voice resounded in the evil night and who, like a furious docker, piled up mysterious loads in my soul.

Oswald, a tall fellow, concave everywhere, whose head gushed up livid from a respectable height of shabby clothes. But it was mostly in his face that the force of pains dug obscure signs. His skin stretched across more bones than man usually possesses, but his lips were exceptionally fleshy, as if the flesh lacking elsewhere had gathered in them, with all its blood. "The head of a madman, of a man who can kill at the most precious and most exquisite moment of his victim's life." I trembled a little at the sight of him, less with fear than with uneasiness, at the thought of what he must have ravaged for years inside and outside of himself. That old jacket, that fatigued walk, each of his movements disjointed the whole menace of the world in the aluminum light exchanged by the river and the sky. With the will of asses, I followed him. And my head bowed slightly toward the ground.

"If I knew the meaning of my works, I would thereby know that of my life . . . But here I am back at the idea that men must gather around them so that their meaning comes to life, unfurls . . . What's the good of my strict solitude if the work it begets withers in solitary confinement? Two eyes alone make everything die, nothing is immortal for two eyes alone . . . Many are needed, a long chain, which from transmission to transmission and then to conservatory yield eternity."

He seemed perplexed, on the verge of sadness.

"I'm obsessed by that question, by that publicity . . . that nutritive publicity. In order for a work to throb in space, in flowing time, men must look at it and be thrilled. A pity . . . I knew a heroic painter. He meditated in solitude, but with an innate sense of artistic despair, on what he thought to be an immaculate order of things in which the white symbols and holy forms were patterned by the light of heaven. So much for the initial project, for the will. Now listen to this miracle: without even a change in his state of mind, imagine, he saw the inverse sign of the soul gradually expressed as the work went along, he saw stunted demons infiltrate into the body of the work and impart to it their ways of being and seeming putrid, a life of dregs on a spree, he saw a powerful rush of greenish tones take possession of the sleep of the themes and flood it with orgies. Tormented by the lugubrious seethings of art, the man envenoms his work, the work envenoms its man. They're tortured by a magic that's relentless and beyond law . . . One day, however, he visited the cellar where he had stored his paintings. He realized that they had weakened, had *receded*. The characters had lost the mingled force which had given birth to them. They were bloodless and shaky, there was nothing around so languishing and livid as they. He realized confusedly that all of that was himself, the end of his energy; he had suddenly lost all power to give life to what needs it. Instead of going back to his white symbols and holy forms, he thought he had no talent and committed suicide. Later, people thought about it and decreed that he actually had had no talent, that he had done the right thing in not trying to sell . . . What do you think of it?"

That absurd story had depressed me. One of the rivers suddenly grew silent. And we did too, but there were still disheveled voices between us. A certain emotion weighed on our footsteps, the loudness of which spread far off toward the ends of the dock. He kept an unavowable tumult behind his pressed lips.

Indeed.

I was in the same boat as he. I had his build, his spiritual dimensions, and that big fist held out toward man. There was a blaze in his shadowy sockets, and he nudged me with his elbow, while with his left hand he pushed back locks of hair which were like cigar stubs. I followed the fire of his gaze, the tips of which sparkled on a very young girl who was walking some distance away. She was not thin, and the harmonious thrusts of her body dilated her woolen dress as far as it could go without tearing, she was one of those superb, blond, quietly laughing girls whom one imagines to be consumed in their muffled opulence by a desire to be kneaded unceremoniously. "Do you see?" asked Oswald. "I do."

He seemed to be munching something very peppery, he pressed his hands together as if to break walnuts. He said, "In a bed . . . You know, I paint streetwalkers as beautiful as that girl . . . yes, as that girl." I mumbled "Oh." I smelled something stale. But it was the odor of the river, the memory of the odor of the river. We felt at that moment a kind of extreme sensation of having once shared the same joys, the same hardships . . . He said, "I see love as a big obscene ball, as a big physical carting." His irony doubled the volume of his lips. He slapped his left forearm with the flat of his hand. Oswald headed for the door of the café in which the girl had just been swallowed up. His gaze was swollen by a kind of cruel lust. Waves of gleams seemed to be lifting his pupils. His teeth ventured out of his mouth. He turned to me frankly. I thought he was going to ask me whether I was married. But he didn't. "Women," I said in a tone that must have been . . . extraordinary, judging from the way he started. "What other love than that?" he asked in a grave voice. But just as there are evil joys, so there are evil enthusiasms. His feeling of love, at this juncture, was precisely that: an evil enthusiasm.

He spoke. His words rolled around those which I did not say, his narrations were not separate from my dream, our "friendship" was the pooling of our disorder. At times, when he spoke slowly, his words took on a rare consistency. They held on to his lips, like leeches, then they fell with meatlike sounds. It was as if he were cutting up his sensuality, his teeth were full of blood. We arrived at the small port. I realized that what I saw there was merchandise, dockers, and boats which were joined together by cables and wood threading their way in a big mass of fixed clouds . . . the smells were as percussive as clashes, the clashes as penetrating as smells.

"I can imagine your solitude," I said to him. "It's certainly . . . very pure." I wanted to know more about his models. He was furious, but not for that reason.

"You can't understand either solitude or purity . . . Nothing is as pure as the fact of being alone, or as that of being with someone else, for pleasure!"

"You're not happy," I shot back at him triumphantly (I felt like bursting the straps, like stopping the mad pulleys in my head).

"I'm lonely!" he screamed. "Do you think that's a state in which you can know whether you're happy or unhappy! You live, and all the rest is a matter of weakness, even and particularly the feeling of happiness."

Was he lying? He was seized with the vertigo of a man who has lost patience, that's it, that's it, he was like a person who feels he has indulged in an excess of confidence without having been understood. I imagined that wrinkled forehead to be flat, and I almost counted the racing pulsation of those temples. I said "obstructed by women." I heard a singular story, told with preciosity, a story that welcomed mine in its bosom, and that meaningful mixture zigzagged between us like a hybrid and malevolent turbulence.

What he retained of his early loves was not some romantic image of a kind that inspires one with nostalgia, but a simple conception that was bound to have developments faithful to itself: eroticism. He liked women, but they peopled not so much his life as his bed. He liked them sarcastically, without flowers, without his soul. What he consented to spend with them was moments of abyss, of agglutination. "What I find between a woman's thighs is not some slimy sprite, but the paroxysm of my solitude." After love-making, he found himself so alone that he thought he had got rid of himself at the same time as of her and of all others. He therefore did not want them to chatter or murmur before making love. He preferred to hear them cry out as soon as possible and, so he preferred, inhumanly (cries of tortured women), since nothing outside the human left him indifferent. Love was thus sexual love, the elementary stiffening: a rage of joy burns out in an unforgettable and, of course, always forgotten minute which is lived on the ivory reverse of pain. To be sure, he adored them, but always at the end of a skeletal desire already obsessed by its future famine. He could not do without them and they came to his room in large numbers to listen to and undergo a passion freed from its million enigmas, with its twofold aspect of revenge and male will. All that he asked of love was an acute pleasure and the proof in few details that the girls who lay beneath his body were not really of the kind who make one feel that one is no longer alone in life. To love was to wrest from the hardest, most bulging forms in his hooked fingers the almost precise sense of not dealing with any human being, and the greatest confession he expected of them was not for them to make but for him to find, to find it where the semblance of total abandon

actually protects the flight of the eternal part which re-
sists. To love was to require simultaneously the shamming of a violent attachment and the promise of an
irreversible departure. And he did not mind the fact that
all those chamber deliriums were, when all was said and
done, loaned by death, as if for try-outs, to an excess of
life. His caresses, which were marked by a roughness that
the woman liked, were nothing other than the deep outline of a vision in which sham and semblance are enriched by all the promises of vanquished duration.
Oswald rarely left them the illusion of invading his heart,
and he sometimes amused himself by making them feel
that they were quite simply robbing him of an additional
opportunity not to love. Yes, they could keep what they
had and what they were, the non-prostitutes, since what
they could give was chiefly the innumerable stitches that
make up the dreams of happiness they deposit in men's
depths by means of intoxication. They knew how to es-
tablish bonds, to prolong the mad germ of any adventure,
to shatter a solitude. As for the others, those of the streets,
he went through them, provided they were clean, as one
goes through the freedom of the wind, and what they
restored to the reality of broad daylight, after pleasure,
was a man who remained free, a man who could leave
without turning around. He preferred to give himself as
an animal, without repenting, without the dubitative
manner of healthy men, and with the independence of
movement cultivated by the broad gestures that reply to
beggars at church doors. No doubt he was not happy, but
that was how he meant to live. To be sure, loving—
whether the word signified vice of loving or love of vice—
could suffice to cloud the pure quality of solitude, but the

dark force that drove him to debauchery was equaled by his resistance to the temptation of being loved. He knew that a time would come when he would need, like others, to win hearts, but first he had to pursue the experience of vertigo and fury, of vitality and haughtiness, *of lack of support in this world*. He said: "I feel myself moving little by little into an exquisite singularity. It seems to me that what I say was never thought of by anyone before me, and people therefore call me a madman. The fact is that for me the world is no longer the same and, in a way, I've left it. What I'm afraid of, unfortunately, is the return . . . I'm like an astronaut who has succeeded in fleeing from his earth and who, as a result of learning to do without it in flight, is afraid of ever having to walk on it again. That man would have only one desire: to die up there and to take with him to his grave of worthless stars the secret of what he has seen."

At that moment, for me to remember someone was like borrowing his image from another memory . . . There were only Oswald, the Man who spoke to the point, and I. I was his past, his cadence, and my most unexpected rediscovery. Perhaps he saw some difficulty on my face, for he stopped. But I said nothing, and I had the impression of answering without being called upon, and of hearing words that had been loaned by me to a voice that succeeded in passing itself off as mine. In addition, I had the sensation of being canceled by the extreme identity of two "me's," of being the mirror of a mirror . . . We turned our backs to all the boats that were going to leave, I was already imagining the dark dots of their successful escape on the horizon. We walked through deserted alleys where the windows opened, inanimately, on the opposite walls. Eaves with holes, like flutes, filled the space with the mournful song of worn water. We talked about despair and wasted efforts.

"There are no wasted efforts, there are no lost girls. There are efforts that do good and others that do harm. Revolution makes more efforts that do harm than efforts that do good. The solitary man makes efforts whose terrible richness eludes the men from whom he remains apart. From whom he remains apart on one side so as the better to enter by the other, where they don't like to be seen."

"You don't want to be alone, you want to be unique."

He pulled at his lower lip as if it were a piece of chewing gum, and when he turned to me, who had not said that to blame him, but as if in order to give myself a warning, when, as I said, he turned to me, I could see his eyes . . . running . . . over his face like . . . gay rabbits . . . "He's still thinking about that woman we met," I said to myself. Finally, his pace slowed down. And I heard him talk in a whisper. His chin dug into the knot of his tie, and I could see traces of scratches on his open neck. "What are you saying?" I asked with interest. His only reply was to look as if he were strangling himself with his tie.

(Where was it all leading me? Uncertainty was climbing into my head like a tribe of apelike shadows . . . in a forest of shadows of trees . . .) He plunged straight ahead, like a nihilistic pilgrim drunk with all horrors still to be committed, on the way to some anti-holy city where disorder and decomposition reign and where one wallows in blasphemy. And yet he seemed to me a force that could have been broken not by other, more gigantic forces, but by the weaknesses that are called: "beautiful alexandrine," "child's gaze," "adagio." Why did he make that violent gesture? I had the impression that it made him suffer to hear me talk about all that.

We were now walking comfortably, side by side, with our eyes turned upward, like two poets captivated by the sky.

"I don't want to die alive, I don't want to *yield,* that's why I drive so many things to the limit, things that are unprepared for the task of being 'objects of passion.' There are, to be sure, vulgar passions. But there is also an art of being passionate that kills the object's vulgarity. Obsession during the day, insomnia at night, I'm sometimes gripped with such a desire to be alive that a trifle would flame up if I so wished. I seem to be a sentinel to myself, to be on the alert, threatened by what dies."

I saw him as a somnambulist glowing with fever.

"Why do you look at me like that?"

"Nothing, nothing," I hastened to answer. He had almost burst out crying. His hands flung away the end of his tie, with which he had been playing, as if it were a crumpled paper. Who was he?

We came to a halt in the very middle of the bridge. On each side of the river stood courts of law, huge and black, whose powerful windows shot flashes of triumph and warning to all the fearful city. It was not hard to imagine that what went on in their labyrinthine guts of rare marble, through the sumptuous connivance of the styles and the pomp among themselves, that what went on there: the inquisitive delights, the unrevealable states of mind, the sudden coalition of all the mental reservations, the most sinisterly juridical rumblings and hiccoughs, that all of that together composed externally the impossible face of avenged society. Of course, as a result of being accused we felt guilty, but among those imposing dwellings the ample, discreet, and limitless ablution of the waters seemed to cleanse us of all suspicion, us, the bandits going by, and the others.

"What we call a judgment is most often only the development of a prior condemnation," he said in a gloomy voice. Suddenly the word *acquittal* came to our lips. We looked at each other in astonishment, even with incredulity. "What's got into you?" I said. His only reply was to take an envelope from his pocket. It contained, he explained, a copy of a letter that he claimed to have sent "to all the judges," though this term did not seem clear to me and in keeping with our remarks. I read the following:

"Gentlemen:

I thought that you would come to drink at my rotted generosity, at the bar of my black mirages, that you would come to kneel in my eye, where the weight of dreams grows heavier daily! That you would come to rub yourselves to the point of total desquamation against my torments, against my humble and painful omnipotence. I would have shown you my soul, the supple and granite-like stratum of my soul, which closely parallels my mysterious maneuvers, which staggers and leaps with me in sufferings and crises, and which I exploit with dumb rage!

An ineffable fright paralyzes the sky's gestures

. . . I possess God's great decease! His name suppurates in my reminiscences, but I have struck that silence so often to make it cry out that my fists hurt! What does it matter, henceforth . . . Immodest art quivers in the depths of the earth all the way to the constellations! A new passion is going to submerge men, whom a lucid, dreamlike force will drive to the sun of the higher communions! Soon the great viscous fatigue of the sated will have no more existence in my sight than the increasing impulse of uniformities or the pyramids of filth raised by cowards to the memory of swine! From the great Art born of the necessary and desirable solitudes and conflicts will spring unsurpassable reasons for living!

Yes, I thought you would have come to scent all that in my prison of fire. But you did not dare, and you were right! Your skulls would not resist the scalping fulmination of my blasts! And while I write to you, I burst at every moment with the frightful, sickly laugh that reveals my big teeth which have been struck by the sun's barbaric light!

Asininelikely yours,
Oswald"

"Where are we going?" I asked in a choked voice.
"We're there."
We entered a quite ordinary house that passed unnoticed in the succession of the others, though the whole street itself seemed to be composed of unremarkable things, like a plain of things set up in brick. Perhaps it was already the suburbs, for we had walked a long time and felt tremendously tired. The disturbance I felt was

replaced by the surprise of being there so suddenly. I had only to cross the threshold and go down a few steps to feel myself shut in by the *opposite* of that outside world which I was accustomed to breathe. It was a cell and, in addition, what, closing my eyes, I did not yet see, a shininess, a very dense region streaked with fine pallors, but no, no they were not huge X-rays. I did not know what attitude to assume, and standing in that room, I smelled the frayed odor of paint, of oil of turpentine, wafting toward me.

"It's a beautiful poem, isn't it?"

I gave a start. Through the oblong opening of my half-closed eyelids, which were as cutting and icy as razor blades, something was vaguely alive, was oozing furtively in a lacunose setting. Mostly painting, lots of big splashes on the floor where they had spread their deformity like pounded entrails. Haggard nudes, streaming with mercury, seemed to emerge from the walls, they stopped in bewilderment on the threshold of a possible existence among creatures of flesh and blood. Wretched corpses seen in the Orient, treeless and skyless landscapes, found in the depths of the earth, seemed to defy the eye to find a single semblance of life in them. And yet they rather gave the impression of being poised on the moldings as if the will to be born and a germ of hope awkwardly dwelled in them. It was a coming-and-going of grays and purples inhaling and exhaling unusual shades more or less everywhere, and there were also, raised by cracked, obese gobs, notched horizontal lines and fibrous intricacies in the center of which stirred a spot. I thought I knew nothing about painting, and yet in the presence of that supple incompleteness of everything, I felt as if I were a connoisseur. Soft flashes, falsely coiled in still-lifes which I dared not examine too closely, suggested the stretching of lizards, a woman's purplish gazes in an ancient night. A lean sun wandered beneath the heaps of stone of an excreted landscape and in the depths of a joyless texture the sky's fingernails obstinately sought the conditions for a . . . break-through.

"It's not completely negative."

I noticed that the painter had his back to me and that his head was bowed. I heard him declaim: "One can learn to paint, but one can't learn the talent to paint. Talent, in all things, creates a morality and a spirituality that suffice for it. Even the talent to be immoralistic, even the talent to be anti-spiritual . . ."

Was he suffering from that great new boldness that made him show his works? Perhaps. Putting myself in his place, I thought it an unparalleled immodesty. But I did not have to put myself in his place. I was the kind of privileged person who receives everything because he begins himself over.

I dared not sit down. My blond reason undulated in my head. In my ears were the distant roars of the meaningless. Besides, where were the seats? Nowhere, except that couch which I could see in a corner and which must have smelled of woman. No furniture on which to lean, but a crucifix on the wall resembled a fanatical young Slav of the past century.

"Why did you bring me here?" I finally asked.

"For no reason, to put an end to it . . ."

"To put an end to what?"

"A habit . . ."

And the heat that . . . continuously . . . swelled up

the place did not come from any stove but . . . from the incomplete death of the things and beings that hung . . . from nails or were standing in their torpor. I mopped my brow, I felt I was going to faint. No question of thinking about anything but Moussia . . . *Never would I have thought Moussia capable of that.* At first, I thought I was annihilated, or struck with extravagance. But no, it was indeed she who was dazing me a few steps away with her forced or voluntary sensuality that lay pale pink on garnet-red cloths . . . The framework collapsed around her, and those exhausted limits opened the way for the full and fragile radiance of the flesh, but its suggestions of murmuring and pleasure were snapped up and absorbed by the neighboring works. Was it witchcraft? *There were no angles there.* And it was Moussia, it was she, I recognized her, not by the beauty of the body, which, moreover, I could only imagine and which at the present moment I thought I was seeing again, but by those eyes which were carved in children's dreams, by that intelligence which was rooted in the darkness of the face, and by that hair . . . in which one would have thought that the madness of the senses and the bouquet of modesty . . . each in turn . . . had taken refuge . . . and by . . . and by . . .

(. . . She was not pure, she had been looked at. I now realized how much I had counted on her as a desert island for my exiles. I had even displayed great patience with her. I had gazed fondly at her from afar, and I had liked knowing that she was there, not far from me, draped in the indisputable reputation that she had among men and even women. I remembered the day when she had crossed the shop, in all her wild, frail, intact beauty, devoured by the eyes of the men, who, as she went by, yapped and stood like tall, impure hedges that were all dark as a result of having "lived.")

"Who is it?" I asked painfully, pointing to her.

He began to laugh, but his gaiety was not communicative. His teeth hardly shone in that color of the air in which everything that was lusterless was asked not to gleam.

(It was that day that I had thought for the first time of a preserved woman, of an integral isle of Honor. The spectacle of that . . . of that intactness . . . had seemed to me exquisite. I could not take my eyes off her, she sat enthroned in the digressions I sought for myself. I saw her everywhere, not as a woman, but as the path of a pure refuge . . .)

"Well?" I said.

"It's a drunken girl I picked up in the street . . ."

"That's not true," I screamed. I grabbed him violently by the arm, and I think I pinched him. He pushed me away . . . Nevertheless he seemed ashamed, and apologetic . . .

"I wanted to paint her as she was. I had never painted a drunken woman."

And I saw arms, mine, returning along my body. I calmed down, more quickly than I would have thought. My lips were simply dry and broken, they alone seemed to be still communicating with my subsiding anger, which bogged down. What sweetness . . . what colorful embarrassment . . .

"And after that . . . ," I said blandly.

"After that, don't worry, I cheered her up . . . She wasn't angry with me, not quite. But she wasn't the girl I thought she was . . . She had fainted. A disappointment in love . . . She'd been drinking."

I turned my head away.

"Do you know her? She's not your wife, I suppose?"

I must have made a movement which he took for a yes, for he was very upset.

"I'm terribly sorry," he said. "Obviously I didn't know. But I swear to you, nothing happened between us . . ."

(She was not my wife, but she was one of the women in everyone's wife. In the presence of a too accessible, too possessed body, I brood over some idea of regeneration, for instead of being thoroughly totalized before my eyes, some part of itself, from before my memory, refuses to rise up and flees instead. I don't know which part, exactly what its name is. And it slips away, as if it feared me, I vainly put out my hand to take back the former part, with each possession it moves further away, but in fact nearer to what, to what origin? Though I put out my hand, it garners only clusters that have been learned by heart, only the subscription of the same sighs to the same lips, only the usual talcum. There is something inaccessible about the woman who has been married for some years and the authentic virgin, and about the woman who has been married a long time and the virgin who ceases to be one. There is something about them that I cannot have, toward which there is even no point in my moving, and it is not the maidenhead. It is even simpler than that, a simple thing lost in their being and in time and which they themselves are unable to enjoy, even to remember, and it is like Moussia, like my wife . . . Like that woman in my wife, both unknown to each other and hand in hand and it is . . . perhaps the dissolved opportunity for happiness. Or else? Hypotheses! Hypotheses! Why are you swarming?)

"I've always been a coward, I wanted a drunken woman, with a foul breath, and credulous flesh obedient to everything and nothing . . . arms that I would have spread V-shaped, like those of conquerors, or in the form of a cross. But that one there, your wife, I swear to you, it wasn't that at all, I had no desire to . . . She was like a corpse . . ."

He seemed to be begging me to believe him. My passive face emboldened him to tell everything, but in an apologetic tone. I was not in the least angry with him. I entered fully into his anti-system . . .

"She didn't shudder a single time. When she opened her eyelids, I saw that she had the eyes I had given her on the canvas. I was happy, that was all I wanted . . . She was a gentle, a faltering woman, and I'm afraid of gentle, faltering women because I'm afraid of the great love that can come to me only from them . . . Come now, I see that she's not your wife, stop fooling me . . . You wouldn't be friendly if it were your wife . . ."

I made a gesture that indicated saturation, the need to hear about something else.

"So I gently sent her away, but before I did, I dressed her, at her request . . ."

I shuddered. It was as if my back were being dusted. With a feather duster. I no longer believed in Moussia's chastity. The path was free, cleared. I could plunge forward, with that sharp, virile, renewed gallop. What man has never dreamed of ravaging purity that has been abolished by its first lapse (simply because he regarded that force as *his* force) while at the same time he venerated in the brothel marketable impurities deducted from increasing stocks? Who forgives the incorruptible for becoming *all at once* pasturable!

"A question . . . Is it out of preference that she's not . . . purple like the others?"

He did not answer immediately. He picked up a brush by the hairs and the blue paint came off on his fingers. I went over to smell Moussia, with my eyes closed and my nose on top of her, I deeply inhaled her dark armpits, her deep wine, I wept, I laughed at feeling my tongue tickling her side, at running my fingertips over the huge, pink garlic of the outspread charms, I thought of the color as if it were magic, as if it were God. "I had a pink spot in front of my eyes," said Oswald about another canvas. I was unable to tear myself away from my contemplation, none of the details, which were enlarged by concupiscence, escaped me. It was not quite Moussia. It was the difference that there was between Moussia and another woman. Oswald was humming: ". . . a true love, something fragile, a bit silent, in a simple dress . . ." Oswald said to me: "There's something in the eyes of young lovers that's unknown to me, a kind of film forbidden to me alone . . . it all eludes me, it does without me, as if I didn't exist. I'm neither expected nor expecting. Why does one stop being young when one lives alone? . . . One is immediately mature but one doesn't age . . . So you're married?" "Yes." "Why did you get married?" I ran my hand lightly over my forehead, as if to forestall a memory, or to draw it out. My eyes gave me the impression of disappearing backwards, into their holes, and I had a feeling that this time my past was over, that I would never again have a hold on clear, minute images of my past. "What an odd question," I said. And I added idiotically, "Not for the sake of vice." He laughed. "Nobody gets married for the sake of vice . . ."

(As if Quinte did not know that . . . No more than one prostitutes oneself for the sake of vice . . . Anything that resembles a habit, a commitment, a function differs from vice. Vice is, to be sure, a morbid calculation, but also a combined operation of the body and the intelligence to save love from its subjection to failure, to the habit of failure . . . What does vice offer to welcome the disparity of woman and of the world, to decipher pleasure, to sabotage the rocket of happiness that it sends into bellies, from one universe to the other, rapturous flights whose course it cannot check and whose landing it cannot enjoy? An indirect way. And that is all. But marriage is quite a different thing, it may be the only curiosity not worth being satisfied, to marry may be to abjure a plenitude of little peculiarities and to launch into a long habit. As a result of marriage, most often, resignation, man's instinct of resignation, by giving itself free rein, drives him into the refuge for souls. If ever a time comes when man's ideal is to get out of the habit of habit, marriage will no longer be marriage, there will no longer be a woman at your side to accustom you to the idea that you are insignificant, that happiness is everything, and that the resources you seem to feel within you are only the rumblings of metabolism. It is not possible to be a tractable husband, if, while being a husband, you continue to believe in yourself. But about whom was I talking at that moment? And besides, wasn't I a slave of my vices? It's a thing one often hears said, but what a slandering of a conscious, thinking man . . . How can one be the subordinate of what one dominates, on the edge of instinct, and of what one sees in oneself with such clarity and sometimes such disgust? It's true that I used the word "vice" to mean something spiritual rather than merely physical, that I found in it a strange, transcending virtue which freed me from the prisons of immanence . . . And I thought that only fine sentiments could catch man in the act of transcending himself and take him where all the vanquished want him to go, in a state of humiliation.)

Something inexplicable happened. I had cried out: "Do you believe in God?" and he had answered: "God doesn't bother me when it's a question of art, and even when it's not . . . They say that God is dead. What a mistake! He's simply continuing His greatest absence . . . He's spending His vacation in hell, and that's why things are so bad on earth . . . But He'll come back when we'll have become interesting again, when we'll have become supermen again . . . God is an artist who has lost his models . . ."

He had nevertheless assured me that he did not believe in Him. But I could not rely on my memories. I saw his mystic's head shudder between the flesh and the darkness in the room. He was the kind of man who rejects everything and dreams of the absolute, why didn't he shoot himself, what was he waiting for? Perhaps he had believed in the people, or in Man, he was the kind of man to have believed in man. For the people is not man, it is almost the opposite. And now he deeply hated both man and the people, with a hatred that came from a great love. His hideous, crablike fists hammered the walls. He was so ugly that he seemed to be plotting against poetry itself. It was his solitude, a torturing thing, a bloodless combat, in which one takes prisoners only for the pleasure of releasing them. I was trembling, I was sitting on a shaky chair which shook because I was trembling. He asked me what was wrong and I answered: "I'm changing." He guffawed. He said: "Nothing is so degrading as immobility." I answered: "But moving is sometimes equivalent to fleeing, to killing." He retorted brutally: "That's not the mobility which I'm defending . . ." He meant the creative movement, I was sure he did . . .

"It's the dead who now bewail the living."

We threw ourselves across an unexpected solitude of drugged smiles. The paintings around us were pissing a cheerless and friendly matter. It was a less difficult moment. I stood up. It was as if the way my legs were quaking kept me on my feet despite a terrible fatigue. Oswald came over and dragged me forcibly to the right. He ran his finger, with a certain hesitation, along the frame of a picture swollen with women and gray fruit. Then he looked at me as if asking that I approve his gesture. He turned his face to me fully. The black knots of his eyes, which were blocked in a setting of high bones, gave it a strange spirituality. "Why does nothing happen to us?" he suddenly asked, even more somberly. "Yes, why?" We shook hands. He repeated: "Why does nothing happen to us?" "Nothing," I said mournfully. I would have liked to be able to yawn for a very long time so that everything would be annulled. There were lots of sounds from outside: the voice of a negro, many high heels, the braking of a bicycle, but they bore witness mainly to the icy persistency of the world, even when they rose up in me in scansion and suffocated in a kind of makeshift strain. A luminous ball drifted silently, very fast, very fast, very fast, it was only a dot in the now desolate landscape of my being, a depraved willow resisted the collapse of all the madness of its branches which bristled skyward, I now know what free despair is, I felt only vaguely attached by my heart to the last convulsions of a social ghost, but that heart had stopped beating, it was odd, odd; and all alone, as if lost in my vociferating forest of nerves, that need—which, moreover, was annoying—to come, but what miraculous negress would, at that moment and no other, have attuned my clamor to her prancings, what ringing and sweating negress?

And the superiorities of existence continue to sway softly in the extreme rejection and the extreme unknown of fate. What he said accumulated in my own voice, and it had already been said, and it was repeated sumptuously in my griefs, there is adventure and non-adventure, there are those who base their presence in the world on insecurity, and there are those whose quasi-mystical search for comfort dispenses them from existing; there are those who run alive from misery to joy and from joy to misery, and there are the paralytics without paralysis who suck a morsel of life while waiting for death, but there are also those who take an adventure for the Adventure and are said to lead a double life, actually they lead only two half-lives and that's little. Oswald pulled at his long, unruly hair with the force of a bell-ringer, and those repetitions, those litanies, were uttered in an increasingly loud voice, in a voice that moves toward the gulfs, as if I were hard of hearing. But no, Oswald, believe me, I understand, I understand that stability is a pettiness that's always starting over and that there's no great conquest without the rejection of a certain peace, and I understand that if you do not conceive God as both a terrible exigency and as the very doubt that He can exist, you would not believe in Him, nor in that art of living which He shows us. Oh! I was somewhat upset at the way he conceived God. But he was an actor, a painter, and many other things as well were allowed him by some creative miracle or other. The fact is, I was unwilling to forgive him his solitude. He could no longer keep raving within four walls, it was a silly wager, he was meant for screaming his ideas at men, for dancing his acts in the dazed crowd. "Go out!" I cried. "Plunge into the multitude, dazzle it!" He seemed staggered by my words. There was something of the oscillograph in the dream of his gaze.

He quietly took a knife from his pocket.

I did not think he would murder me.

And I was right not to think that.

He simply went over to the painting in which Moussia seemed to be dying of pleasure and calmly, like a butcher, slashed it to pieces. That lasted a few minutes. When the devastation was at its height, I uttered a strident cry, but it was a cry of relief.

"As long as I have the courage to destroy what I think is the most beautiful thing I've done, it means that it still wasn't beautiful enough . . ."

"You're mad! It was a . . . a masterpiece!"

"Not enough . . ."

"But, you're crying!"

He was crying, with his head buried in the shreds of the canvas and his feet fleeing obliquely along the floor. And I, who was more and more happy that this tragedy had occurred, moved toward him, for, regardless of what one says, it is always baneful and pathetic to see a man cry. But it is fair to say that other reasons impelled me to make some gesture on his behalf, I was being sucked in by that existence, and besides, a vague female odor was prowling about, below the windows, near the sofa. His mysterious life was beating wildly even in my own veins. "I'm no longer bored." I saw his long limbs try to embrace the destroyed work and a ray of light flit over his back like a white butterfly. A composed drunkenness was coming over me; the heat and the colors shook my closed eyelids strangely. To fall or to fly, the minute to be lived is summed up in this dilemma. To fall and to fly at the same time. The painting came off the wall and Oswald flattened himself on the floor. Once again I understood perfectly that a breed of men wanted to live otherwise than in accordance with groups and plans, otherwise than in accordance with the dull, unsupple multitude. I bent over the painter with the eager sadness of people preparing to discover the truth of death. I heard words, for the river kept rolling, fulminating, between the monologues and the dialogues, between our flesh and our spirit, between our individual and what may be superior to the individual. And the Vanquished Man was already standing up. I made a broad, weary gesture as if to assure myself of the "presence" of the silence around us. He pushed aside the locks of hair that obstructed his sight. His eyes settled again in their red rings, with the brilliance of expression that cries the highest leap. His clenched fists framed his temples, which was a sign that he had recovered his resistance. A mellow light was now filtering into the room and invincibly guiding mills of black dust toward Christ's face. Sheets of brightness were trembling here and there on the patched flesh of the paintings, and a panel of shadow, engraved with phosphorescent bars, seemed to be imprisoning a mass that had been driven into the angle of two walls. My gaze wandered around a hodge-podge of rags, pots of glue, and shells in the process of dramatizing a corner of the room. He came closer to me, he smelled of boat, of storeroom, of clandestinity. I saw his features little by little release friendship and even a certain gentleness. But the imminent revelation of a secret seemed to be bolting heavy shadows within me. I thought to myself: "That man has only one master, God. But it's because he doesn't believe in Him . . ." His burst of laughter pierced big sections of stone. He had been drinking, that was obvious. I hadn't noticed it . . . I anxiously looked about for a bottle that had been drained to the last drop, for a glass shattered by rage. But there was nothing, nothing but that decayed soliloquizing voice by which words that vied in incoherence and truth were rising up like rats into my gnawable skull. I thought he was going to collapse, but he clung desperately to his jacket, and with his eyes, which were without the white and without anything that replaced the white, with his eyes that were all darkened by derision, he dared not look at me! "It's not true that I'm absolutely alone, that I have no master, every week he buys my paintings at a high price, preferably the nudes, in fact only those, that's why I paint so many, the fellow is gifted with extraordinary flair, his fingers run over the bodies of the painted women without ever going beyond them, he has a white cane, he leans on it, swooning with happiness, sometimes he stops a finger on a cardinal point of the flesh which he then names with real pleasure, I'd like to blind that flair, those other eyes, why isn't a man ever totally blind, I hate him because I need him, but he may die, I see him dead in my nightmares, and I like him murdered that way, but who'll replace him, a frightful question, an old crank, it's awful, isn't it, that ripped canvas was for him, he had reserved it, that girl is his mistress, they were both drunk and I didn't know whether it was the blind man who was leaning on the girl or the girl who was leaning on the blind man, it was more or less he or she whom I wanted to kill, it's written that our gestures and words can't get out of the circle of symbols, we'll never be able to have a real cause to kill a real man or save a real life, it's dangerous to play with a knife in his presence, I might make a mistake and take him for an old bag with which to paint, with blood, absolute solitude, why didn't it occur to me, at present one would think that those untamed works were asking for daylight, that they were no longer satisfied with my presence alone and with the life I thought I gave them by calling them by their names, my offering them a blind man to see them is a mockery, they move, do you realize, they move like girls who've been in an orphan asylum, they want air, ocular solar light, honors, alas, and the name of all that, damn it, of all that germination, is thirst, ah ah ah one can't do without men bah bah ah ah ah."

He laughed so freshly, like a child. After a few swerves, the laughter became adult and then bizarre. It came from his whole face and his whole neck, a laughter that sawed the knotted space, while his hands, which were raised above his head, crossed violently, tormented by the most mechanical union of madness and negation. His whole being entered my slashed vision like a long convulsion, then it was a rhythmic, sabbatic flight. When he returned, he tried to hold a cigarette between his fingers. His pellucid nails quivered about it finely, like elytrons. But he had to drop it. He didn't ask me whether I wanted one. I was thinking of the strange destiny of Moussia, that exceptional woman who was looked at without being possessed and possessed without being seen. What was she escaping thereby? I abhorred her. Someday I would find her again, I was sure of it.

Oswald seemed to have finished dressing, as after a terrible match.

"Tell me something that astounds me more than what I've just said."

I had absolutely nothing to say, nothing to add.

He motioned to me to leave. It was not a matter of bad manners. As for me, I wanted to flee and to stay. To go out? But what was the weather like? It must have been nasty, a materialistic or pseudo-religious weather not fit for a vibrant dog . . . *Our weather*. I wanted to flee, but also to walk a bit more with him, with his power over things, over events. I wanted to flee because I felt that he had not told me everything and that the rest was untenable. I reached the door. I had a terrible pain in my legs. And behind me that great fertile fury was casting rough seeds, they sank into space like nails pursued by a gleaming hammer. And his husky, inaudible voice, full of obscenities and appeals to God!

When I reached the threshold, I heard him yell: "Hey, Quinte, come back! Quinte, come back! Quinte . . . I forgot to tell you that I'm a musician! Quinte! Come I'll play you a violin piece, Quinte!"

That was too much.

I started running.

The weather was what I expected. A hard wind, blowing from east to west and strangely horizontal, was pressing me to choose. All around me was what a strange conception of reality had often concealed from me: spots, those on walls, pavement broken in places, rare cars, and aerials . . . And between the spots were others, just like my eyes which were drowned in my ivory head, and bulging. On the right, where I leisurely jumbled high houses, and on the left, in that street, lies, vice, all the treacheries of current things were going to start plashing unexpectedly, like the awful liquids of streams . . . And I kept walking, in astonishment. It seemed to me that a delight was groping aimlessly in the depths of my flesh. And I almost, either through carelessness or in desperation, followed a priest whose red woolen socks rebounded silently on the black pavement, like a signaling created for me alone. He was walking with long strides toward a church, the belfry of which was, fundamentally, not comparable to anything.

Two Ways in the Night

As he hurried out of the church, frightened as he was by the aisle where coldness prevailed and where gigantic columns and sullen totems loomed up, disgorging gold in a dungeon-like semidarkness, he looked about him, and he had to make a violent effort not to express aloud the interest he suddenly took in the multiple appearances of the street, though he really perceived only the violet brick of the houses and the last rays of the sun striking the tips of wet leaves in the garden of the presbytery opposite. And this time the street resembled a desperate stab inflicted by the daylight upon the emerging evening. The beardless pavestones were dark and puffy, like negroes' cheeks.

He had an imperturbable dream: stiff, yellow gnomes and sandstone statues looked each other in the eye for a long long time like china dogs, without making a movement or saying a word, while a wind full of whips came down on them, whistling an air of hatred. And its metamorphosis was like those interrupted games in which a silence seems to continue to play, despite the uproar, with another silence.

It was almost six o'clock. He knew it without having recourse to a watch or a public clock. It was a matter of flair and rapport between him and the undertone. He suddenly felt slightly cruel, a certain cynicism stirred in his mouth as if to open a half-smile of supreme disdain. Suddenly, scruples, what were they? He felt infinitely supple, unexpected muscles unknotted in his skin; he was even aware of swaying his hips as he walked. What is that wheel that makes its nest in the stomach, and that turns, and that brutally quickens its speed, and what is that blood that rises fluvially through the flesh to the far shores where one dances nude? His hand met his unshaved chin, and it seemed to him that he was rolling that skin in bread crumbs. He took off his wedding band and put it around his second finger merely to have an impression of tightness that did him a lot of good. Suddenly, as if springing up from the misty epiphany of the streets, the world's cries, laughter, and tears made a circle around him, a circle of breath that smelled of garlic. The arena in which he moved about like a clown who decides to laugh instead of making others laugh was as alive beneath his feet as a face. He wanted to fight and even to be forced to fight, otherwise that night which had been chopped up with doubts and stern ideas would end at dawn with a flower bed lacking corpses and cartridges, as shameful as the one face of all his inabilities. And there would then be no question of committing suicide. It would be like *running a sword through his body in the water.* Fortunately, everything aroused his curiosity. The visible almost had the devil's face. And the invisible was a confidence of things, to be grasped between the eye and the hearing. Coming from a world of ideas, he has just arrived on this too earthly earth, he is its first tourist. His fingers stagger on the small objects they encounter, they drum in the air, panic-stricken, as if those objects had just been invented by means of manual wings. He had to be initiated in humble manipulations in a universe that had become spontaneous. He was solitary, not in the manner of those who bear witness to solitude, but in the manner of those who, abandoned by everyone, attain a freedom which they know nothing about, and nothing yet about the way they will use it. He dared not look at his big, unoccupied hands. But his jubilation was keen. He felt like his father, mistrustful of everything that has no body, fond of touching, reaching out tirelessly toward the most superbly hard foods. His father. What would he have thought of Moussia? He would have laughed at her as he himself now laughed at her. Moussia whom he was now becoming free to curse, Moussia was wallowing in his head. For he could do with her whatever came into his head. He could, for example, do endless cross-word puzzles with the definitions of the girl Moussia, with each definition inscribed in Moussia's flesh. My father would have liked Moussia, overpopulated Moussia, Moussia bolted to the sun, the oiled rolling of her bosom and hips, the visible division of her buttocks, her unimpeachable hands. He could very well see his father pressing her against the wall, weighing lightly on the fertile spring of her belly, and, before she had time to open her mouth, gulping down both her lips together . . . grilling his eyes in the chaste anger of hers . . . Then he had a pain in the groin, a whirlwind, a sudden aridity that called for diluvian rains of something or other . . . temptations clattered vertically like bloodthirsty orders given by a dictator confined to bed . . . And other memories . . . that nude beach . . . That dressed couple denuding themselves on that nude beach . . . That beach wearing the clothes of the couple who had denuded themselves . . . And he, behind a sharp rock, was drying himself with his inner fire, with the torrid fixity of his gaze . . . He took handfuls of flesh from his belly to throw them on the breathing beach . . . But his flesh remained with him, and he had to smooth his thighs, along which ran a light, dancing breeze, in order to recapture the dark peace of his suffering . . . Suddenly the beach detached itself and began to navigate on the sea . . . The sun fitted their bodies with copper . . . He will weep in vain . . . Why had he had the misfortune to be born during the night? Beneath that pot-bottomed sky, at the foot of the grim caricature of a pyramid, in the non-truculent tribe of brooding souls . . . For the sun that the males of his land made shine within themselves, in their senses, could not bronze their skin. They remained white . . . They shook their darkness off on women, but that was not enough for the sun to loom up between the women and them, like the reciprocal bite of eternity . . . It was a night of close bonds formed among men, poverty, and rain . . . He could no longer distinguish one from the other, and that reminded him of the famous battle of the negroes en-shrouded in the tunnel . . . But there was the unblacken-able whites of their eyes . . . And besides, we were not really black, ebony black, for then at least we would have been handsome . . .

We too would have liked to run half naked in alleys decked with slips and motley handkerchiefs and cries of birds and flowers at the end of which one falls in whirls on chalky spaces scented with anise and brine, and with the sea . . . But we could not, neither in our youth nor afterward. It was cold, the rain froze the pavement, the walls cut the fingers that sought a resistance and a reverse to disgust with life. All that remained for us was to dream of the unbuttoned women of the shores whose bronze thighs opened to oblique lights that glide like bobsleds from the common slope of the sky and sea, loaded with salt and flakes and that accumulate like strange ingots in their bellies; all that remained was to dream of big widows whose laughs are heaps of fire from the tops of white balconies . . .

And through the frightful reconstructions of the crime of living, namely his memories, words recaptured him and they were stronger than the surrounding hair shirt, than that huge blackboard of life against which mil-lions of men were going to hurl themselves like hastily effaceable chalk strokes. At times words were his whole consciousness on the defensive, with its back leaning against treasures of uncreated things, at times they rolled out of him, danced before his eyes. The pleasure then lay in watching them as one watches women, in undressing them mentally, with artful slowness, in being a prey to such operations of the mind that what was most turbid in virility shared in them. And suddenly, as a result of combined despair and sun, the road was alive, it had the sighs, curves, and plasticity of women. To sleep with words, that was what dreaming meant. And tirelessly, the fact of reconsidering the word, of redefining it, of making it die and bringing it to life again on a low flame, to be faithful to it every moment, not by not deceiving it, but by reinventing it in others, these notions forced themselves upon him like tasks of a couple. He also said to himself: not to believe that one knows them by virtue of the fact that one uses them, that one associates with them, that one enjoys them, not to believe that there are right words, above all not to imagine that by grazing their reality, that by forcing them to confess, one can learn how they live and have lived and what they are in the daily mystery of saying and hearsaying. And Quinte had a feeling that he was exercising a kind of voyeur's talent at their expense, when, with his eyes glued to soft and mobile orifices, he caught sight of their dubious and shamming privacy, or their conspicuous integrity. And a thought of rape calmly permeated him, an aptitude for sullying them or sinking into their abundant, tepid meanings, the words, like charms, fertile, fragrant, full of active wombs. And he also said to himself: to botch words is to botch their intensity, and thereby our own. And finally he said to himself: really, there is no great future for a poverty of words . . . And at the bottom of the hard, firm river of constraints, sitting on the big millstone which perpetually drowns them, one can see, by leaning forward a little, the mouths of poets opening on a last crystal verse.

The street continued to fall into his arms, like excessive gifts. Miasmas of port and fishing dug salted rivets into his nostrils, which also pocketed other smells as one pockets a tip. "Oh," he suddenly exclaimed. Nausea pushed yellow burdens everywhere into his throat. As regards sensation, it is as if the flesh were rotting visibly, one feels like having an orgasm promptly on a litter before exhaling one's hatred of the world for the last time. But that vaguely ending flesh was the right one; thanks to it, his true dimensions, the passional, greedy ones, seemed to be overflowing the street, to be spreading far, far far beyond appearances. When he had lost sight of the crossroad, where cars were making big chrome-plated signs to all poor devils, he took a long, unpretentious street and the only thing he noticed as soon as he turned the corner was a slightly luminous air hole from which there floated music that was harnessed with kettle drums and fifes but muffled, it seemed, by blankets, he began to hum it, but in that particular way of humming that thickened his lips, swelled his cheeks, etc. The music also had a smell, the smell of a mildewed couch worn away by various rubbings. At that very moment, the image of the knife flashed across his mind accompanied by a fanfare, then another image, a silent one, of a man and a grim-looking woman in the act of crashing like tall trees struck by lightning, uprooted at the very spot where their desires had knotted, closely twisted, and into which they had dug like roots into their living soil, then again the image of a knife. And it seemed to him that they repeated the maneuver several times, it consisted in crashing down on the couch which was more unstitched than ever and they seemed to be struggling with an effort exceeding the ordinary powers of a human being, they seemed to be diametrically naked, to have enormous knives between their teeth. He continued on his way, with his own means. He was so excited that there was no counting the things that went by beneath his nose. And he staggered, pathetically. He passed a blind man and his dog, thought of what he would do if they started dying in front of him, without warning. He laughed. The fact of having to cleave those rudimentary mists, of being able to feel them open before him like a curtain on all the monochrome, silent scenes here below confirmed, by the absurdity of it, that he was actually going toward her, who was no longer waiting for him resting on her elbows by the window that looked out on the park, the very park from which he was chased by the statues and emerged at first bottle green, then jade green, hardly mobile between the gates, under the lamppost at the exit, on other days. He sometimes stumbled against a tree, rubbed his face against the udder of nightfall, which suckled his chimeras. Was it autumn? Was it the city, or other places which are not called the city? He did not care in the least. There was his jacket floating to prove a thousand things to him and, inside, the famous knife standing, with the point down, against the putrescently fat bellies of unmaternal females, who screamed rape, and since there was the matter of points, there was also that of his patent-leather shoes, which at times threw out a spark, when, for example, he fell into a trap of venal illuminations.

There was the passion of what was happening! Although manifestly nothing was happening, neither for nor against him! An approximate reality shook up his chest, but explosions of joy made the taverns tremble.

And he was afraid to put his hand on his heart, which was broken by the fluxion of savage emotions!

He leaned against a tree that was hard as iron, torsions were exerted on that ex-soul which he had nevertheless set up like a pentelican column toward *a* sky, not others! An anger with neither gesture nor cry now made him scowl and bend as he pleased in the bordering nothingness. His arms stretched out, not in order to touch nothing this time, but to prevent the fainting of any prey. A miserly and fundless fervor immobilized him in front of the many all-powerful stations with their departures every five minutes!

Little stones rolled under his feet. In comparison with the barren, grayish slabs that pivoted slowly in his head, they gave him a tremendous impression of vitality. A human shadow padded, without moving, the corner of a door a few feet away from him, human because the pellet which he saw reddening and fading in turn was a cigarette that cast vague, dramatizing flashes on a real untortured face. And, as if elected by the moonlight, two legs alone shone in the sordid-making street, and the light, ragged though it was, slackened all the marble figures toward him. He did not yet see it, but he sensed that it was big, brownish, perfect, and that it had vast eyes in which there wandered lithely a vice impossible to define but which was there, watchful as a lookout, and which was interested in him. That gaze was an isolated lick of the tongue in the darkness, but of such importance in that invisible face that the existence of the whole body seemed to depend on it, and the flesh, so probably hard and curved under the silk sheath, that flesh descended from the eyes, hung from it, attuning its rhythm to theirs.

She said "hello" to him. And that voice was a whole call, a reminder, a reminder of what, of some other voice, of some other idea of a voice, emerging painfully from a former nest of vile, knotty, erectile dialogues interlaced in the underground memory. She looked at him with odd curiosity, *satisfied curiosity,* she must have had wide experience of curiosity, of the way men were to be looked at. She said words to him that smelled of wool and sofa. He did not quite understand the meaning of her question, but he shook his head negatively. He might just as well have said yes, for his immediate answers were always the result of a race between two conflicting reactions. He turned around and stupidly looked back in the lunar slant, which softly purified the girl's legs, he said a few absurd words to her. This encounter did not surprise him beyond measure. How close he felt to that opulence, to that blood from behind the floodgates, and to the gliding sweep of those big fields of hair; and to the back of that dark, tongueable mouth which only dentists light up, and to those breasts which were more than two and which will not be easily detached from the trunk, however rotted they be! It even seemed to him that he was on familiar terms with it all. Higher up, at the other end of his pain, a mystic, convulsed thought tossed about, it was his dead faith. The roll of a drum was heard, louder than those which had thus far given rhythm to his impatience, and suddenly he no longer felt like hesitating.

He was almost willing to plunge without turning back into one or the other excess of which the woman, owing to the singularity of her condition, offered him the most direct, disillusory image possible. Her too-penetrating perfume limed the zone of air in which their heads dangled, and he was aware that adventure or any important act of life emits that odor without which there would be no sudden courage in cowards or sudden energy in weaklings. Desire laid out painful furrows in him which gaped at pleasure. But he did not want to, not yet. He walked around the woman twice, the first time as if he were looking for the place where, like dogs, he would piss, and the second as if he were going to attempt an act of force, the desperate hope of achieving an exit through that belly and back via so many secret entrails, that hope intoxicated him, and he drooled. But instead of going to that something at last supreme, to that crime, he went away, and the circles he had walked around her accompanied him and began to proliferate, like emptiness, in the fleeting axis of his footsteps. He saw them stretch more and more, they became millions, billions. They gave him the impression of not advancing while he approached by means of faked shadows to shores more and more remote. He now existed only by virtue of the sensation of being at the center of a polar area, pale as death and without seals, but from which he received the privilege of masking multitude and his unity with a great extinguished desire. And he had to strike hard in order to break that last image of his iciness in this world.

But in his head were the wild tom-toms . . . of Eskimos! Sounds climbed to the highest din and descended to the weightiest silence, and so forth. He zigzagged through rectilinear crowds which were amazed to see him eccentric! The street was full of realists, it's not bad, at times, to see realists swarming, he said to himself: "reality for the realists" and other such slogans went through his mind. A show given by realists was a comforting thing . . . In the century of speed, in a present filled with the abolition of the past, they were practically the only ones who remained level-headed and believed in the virtues of progress. But the sadness that invaded him had nothing to do with the realists, to hell with the realists, he preferred to bound like a deranged drunkard in a coma, astride a poetic meteor more deranged than he. He was sad about having left Moussia. For his flesh remembered what he would have done with her in bed, the things he remembered seemed to him in a hurry to be born; at times he even remembered things which had never existed for him, but the memory of which tortured him, he did not have what might be called a reconstituent memory, but an inventive memory. The world's confusion must have thrown itself entirely in his face one day and brutally given him a choice between a submersion of what was and the living future. He could now discover in the distance the frightening forms of his future, which was pregnant with all his negations, all his late joyous and intrepid faith.

The last good whites of the day prowled over him. He could not yet get rid of them, could not tear himself away from all the secretory souls that engulfed him. Yet it was no longer a flame that was in him, but an inflammation. His skin was making demands. The black, distant musicians were striking his bones, were blowing a song of the world into his veins, his flesh had never made so much noise, had never shuddered so much as today. In that hermetic night, a sensuality without a past and without a precedent hollowed out a giant mouth for him to kiss the earth. It was as if soon nothing would be left but an obese sun, its rays are already falling like blue entrails into his entrails, the color of which he does not know, and it was also as if it were all silently taking root in his gaze. It is the night.

He was near his home, why, why? He recognized the little light in their bedroom. He took a few anxious steps. The night had stopped reassuring. It was a night of crime and madness, a night full of terrible and merged destinies. He was blind in it, but it was his real homeland, the real homeland, the homeland of solitaries, of drunkards, of the obsessed, of all those who want to live more at midnight than it is possible to live at noon. But for the first time that disquieting, savage night was receiving him in its bosom, he no longer felt outlawed, rejected even between its dark, opaque, warm thighs. It was the terrible night of Oswald and Wasmes-Bô. But he was dead tired, and his clothes reeked of drunkenness, of doings in low dives.

He was near his home, opposite the café. Something happened while he looked up at the lighted skylight, something happened like those tears, the kind of tears that do not fall, that turn and burn in the corners of the eyes, that remain where they are to feed an idea of suicide. Tiny landscapes came crashing on his consciousness, like flies on the windshields of cars. He had to face something, he was in the process of undergoing consequences without an origin, without their act. And it all resembled an end. A dog rushed between his legs, an animal whose hairy skeletality and foaming mouth were all that could be seen in the darkness. He swore. He felt the animal vanishing in the distance and thought: "You lousy dog, I'd kill you like a man!" It was not, strictly speaking, a spoonerism, it was a temptation. He was no longer at all sure, there is being, seeming, para-being, but there is also disappearing, and as for him, he perhaps was not, he perhaps did not seem, he had perhaps disappeared, and perhaps he had just been sought, even in his disappearance, in order to be forced to perform an act that was not his.

He was at last going to real unhappiness. It was not a joke this time, not a performance without an actor. It was no longer a kind of play that is played only with prompters, before an empty house. It was his unhappiness. The unhappiness that men had willed, conceived, and fabricated specially for him, it was present. Not in the distance but within him, and it upset everything. It was a real weight which he carried on his heart, a real volume which he could almost touch with his finger, the polyhedron of the cruelty of fate. And nothing burned, nothing caused such disaster as did that truth, nothing dug a knife that has time into the flesh as that truth did. Luckily that in order to kill the truth there is always a quite other truth, which itself is already lost, the truth was a future of truths without a future, continually that truth. But while waiting, he groaned, because of that real unhappiness, he would have liked to slow it down, to slow it down for centuries, because he was, in a way, imprisoned in what he knew of that unhappiness, which was like a *wickedness of values*. No publicity, no, it would not be known, the new one was of the kind that does not cross more than two or three thresholds of consciousness. He was near his home, and the whole street suddenly took on an air of flight without a fugitive.

He imagined himself returning home. He entered, tense, wary. The door opened wider than usual on a brighter light. J. smiled at him. T. rushed at his legs. T. was more childlike than usual. J. was more beautiful than on other days (but what other days, those which had existed for him or those which they had given back to nothingness?). He took a step back, dazzled, scared, a step charged with symbols and inaccessible myths, a very simple step. "Hello," said J. He did not answer. T. cried "Daddy." Quinte was modest. He did not realize that he was the object of all that solicitude. It was also too great an honor. They crowded around him as if asking for an autograph. He was not really expecting that, after such a long absence. They tightened their embrace around him. It was perhaps not a love embrace but an embrace by which one settles accounts, something that makes its way by fractions of an inch into its prey. He wanted to laugh, but his breath shook the discolored flowers in the vases that rose up, chipped and lean, in the darkness of the window. T. went back to playing with her doll. J. sank into an embellishing melancholy, just below the lamp which shed the luxuries of its blazing light on her hair, on her bare shoulders; her nails hung brilliantly from the ends of her hands, like bunches of cherries touched by rain. And it all had a barbaric and expensive little air.

The child went by him spitting genius and gold, drawn off by those vital calls that rise from the thrilled throat of the little strengthless objects that children love to destroy. Why wasn't she in bed yet at that hour? He would have liked to see her sleep, to interrupt that intense quest, which was full of climbing, of fleeting, iridescent exploits. He was . . . in a way . . . jealous, paternally jealous. She ran, she fell, and what happened to her was not yet called, in her mind, falling. The miracle was that little by little she would realize that it was called falling. Perhaps it would have taken little for her to know it already. Perhaps the word "fall" was taking shape in her, without her knowing it. It all bothered him, because it was new, unexpected. T. ran, and space itself seemed to obey the rhythm of a great pulmonary drunkenness. Then she slowed her cadence and came down on her doll, which had fallen from a chair, which in turn fell on her, who also fell. And as she stood up and caught her breath, with the ease of childhood, her gaze gave the impression of rediscovering the toy, it clung to the dress, to the cardboard shoes, to buttons, and to those eyelids whose delicate oscillations produced artificial, leaden sleep, without the lashes. Her little hands sought patiently and gently, in the secrecy of the joints, an ideal attitude, the necessity of which escaped the adult, but which nevertheless was an adult attitude, a woman's attitude. "She's already the child of my child," he said to himself, in a strange way, as he looked at the doll. Both of them, the doll of flesh and that of celluloid, had the same live hands, squeezed together, pulpy, already organized for ruthless enterprises. "She has given birth to it. So she has already given birth." The thought disturbed him deeply.

The icy blade of the knife chilled through his shirt a strip of flesh just above the heart, which beat as if it would burst. AS IF IT WOULD BURST! He saw the redness of things, the redness for which things vie, all things . . .

T. was a budding, still beautiful, and chaste intelligence, for the questionings that succeeded each other there received only the purest answers, an intelligence that set up for itself a slender realm of waves in her gaze, the variations of which extended into initiatives both vain and promising along busy arms and legs, and that finally lit in astonishment on the seed of things, invisible and prominent, ready to fly to the pubescent depths of raw knowledge. And Quinte witnessed that magic impotently. He looked up at J., who was silent, and their tête-à-tête espoused the tart melody born of a fatal combination of boredom and reminiscence to which was now added a surprise, a very vague shame on both sides. She went over to him, he dreaded the moment when she would make a theatrically sharp or evasive gesture which he would be unable to bear, perhaps that of her forefinger pointing to his pocket which was swollen by the addition of a huge, cold knife, standing up. The cartilage of J.'s ears was such that a dense throng crowded at the keyhole to see them turned and twisted between a man's hard, indecisive teeth. Her body seemed too beautiful and too big for him, disproportionate to the force he still possessed to invade it. He dreamed, in an obscure, hesitant way, that he was without work, that they no longer wanted him at the newspaper, that he was really too poor to possess so rich a body. That torrent of life, of beauty, which fled from those creatures in all directions without his being at all involved, what whim of fate could still stop it, could deflect it toward his soul? But because he was there, J. acted as if she were there too, looking very beautiful at the end of the distance. Their drama of contracting partners, "I do" at city hall, "I do" in church, was performed on an irritated stage in a setting of perturbed vespers, and the only dialogue was the whys and wherefores, mentally. He simply felt that he was making a vague gesture with his hand toward that long and patient and remote occasion of possessing a real woman, of living a real love, like the one that is wrecked in the written story of certain extraordinary men, a story almost forgotten in which one learns that what is given and what is received are lost together in an intermediary and personal and ascending construction: love. He played blindman's buff, lugubriously, he sought the shadows of what she could have been for him, in his life, but all he harvested was intellectual little horrors puffed out in his head. Dogs were howling in the immense night of grievances. It was nice to make a raid there, to pillage the few ghosts of a nomadic doubt.

"What's the matter with you?" said J. at last. "Are you in pain? You're livid . . . You're crying."

And T. cried because he cried. T. was not yet asleep. And J. was beautiful, beautiful.

He asked her the following simple question:

"Have I changed?"

"Changed? You're probably sick . . . you shouldn't have . . . The Club . . . it's the Club . . ."

He was now smiling. And he felt like lying to her, since to love is perhaps also to elude others, to be sparing of oneself, since to do that is to lie. It was like a kind of last chance. To love.

"You'll have your vacation," he said to her.

She turned to him, neither weary nor glad. Surprised.

"Really?"

"Yes."

"Will we go away?"

"We'll go away . . . we'll go away . . ." he repeated in a low voice.

She sat down opposite him. His face was no longer the same. It was distorted. Distorted by hope.

"Far?"

"Far!"

She could not see that he was lying. The fabulous defiles took up all the room. The sky's blue management on the roads, the winningness of the plains, the mastabas, the abnormal trees, and in their eyes the sun, that huge fulfillment of all wishes since puberty, the Sun, all that was vacation. She did not want to know more about it. But in the kitchen things made an uncommon sound in her hands. She knew how to make the impact of the utensils merry. And that struck him. It made him feel like going a bit of a way toward her. She was waiting for him in front of the stove.

They looked at each other, he with his lie, she with her hope. They said nothing. The silence whispered to them to say nothing. Their absorbed gestures were those of an indecisive concord, of a joy that fears to burst and rolls around itself, that waits. Silence, thus conceived, was the only true communion possible, love borne to a difficult point of excellence, in the future of love. But would she understand him? She was under the spell of a lightning revelation, the revelation of what ought or ought not to be done with a man like Quinte. By the way in which they agreed to look at each other, he measured the place that remained between them for music, for grace, for the delicate constructions of a dream in common. Suddenly disposed to the incredible, they listened within them to the voices of love, in a suspended time. The most distant of the voices made them think of bards going up the hill of the immediate future; the closest, which were grave and tragic, gave rhythm to the exploration of the past. But they could not meet, for life had corrupted or faked the inner roads. The symphony stopped at the moment and place where gestures and words, extracting themselves from the trap in which chance had put them, got going again, breaking up the design of the absolute songs, sending him back to his eagerness to live and her to the rotting harvest of habits. She suddenly had lots of questions to ask him. But he feared them all, one by one. He suddenly saw her with her arms full of flowers which she began to distribute among at least five crackled vases. The charm was broken.

"Tell me, what was I like . . . yesterday?"

"Yesterday?"

She made no answer. He wanted to know whether he had changed.

"And the day before yesterday?"

"No, you haven't changed," she said at last.

Those words exasperated him. He was right to be afraid of her slightest words. Never did she provide him with the answers required by his insaturable inner life. She did not suspect the existence of even the secret which he carried within him and which had grown so inordinately large that one could have spoken of "danger points," that secret of a breaker of statues. It was not his role to inform her of it. She ought to have foreseen and forestalled because she was his wife. The distance which had grown between them had blurred the targets, it diverted all firing. He felt neither affected nor concerned by what she thought she ought to say to him, in fact it all

seemed perfectly suitable to someone else, to an anonymous monster that flanked him and that was the dump of
all the mistakes, of all her undervaluations and belittlings
of him. The acts and words she aimed at him crashed at
the bottom of a ditch with a frightful noise, but that
ditch had paws, and she always accompanied it like its
shadow. It was himself, as she no doubt saw him, in her
diminutive wifely vision. Someday he would break out
and murder the man he was in the eyes of all those who
loved him or knew him closely. For that man was his
worst enemy.

But perhaps it was she who had changed. She approached him, with a swaying that was unique in the
world. She moved forward, immutable and hard, into his
torment.

He wanted to change, wanted everything to change,
but he was the only one who wanted it, and his own
marriage to variation made their simplest relationships
more and more unintelligible. He wanted a tremendous
quarrel in order to get it over with, but he did not have
the means of setting it off. And besides, it was late, very
late. He imagined a marriage based on actual antago-
nism, on an extremely open struggle for a permanent and
varying conquest relating to the essence of life. He despised happy couples whose lives were uneventful. For
example, he conceived with disgust the union of two brilliant but conflicting minds which, in order to get along,
decided to "understand" each other, that is, to withdraw.
They would proceed by successive resignations of intelligence, they would give each other discounts on ideas
and would thus commit upon themselves, practically
without suspecting it, extortions of vitality, of power, of

nobility. On the way to the end of their convergence, they would unconsciously eliminate their value, their personality. They would finally meet at a frightful point of mediocrity, their love would be perfect, harmonious, two intertwined earthworms, a happiness based on a series of castrations, on the achieved evacuation of the live forces, of the forces that divide. No doubt the fidelity of those poor wretches would be never-failing, for in their case, as in many others, fidelity is only a ghastly *sum of inaction.*

It is true that Quinte and his wife formed a couple which did not resemble that one or any other. They were a couple . . . he himself did not know how to define it, to situate it, either in the present or the future. Both of them simply knew that they were not happy.

"No, you haven't changed."

Yes, he had changed, he was sure of it, but there is a way of changing which there is no mistaking, it is when one changes for the last time, when one changes because one no longer has to change. And that was perhaps what she had in mind.

She saw tears, other tears, which fell from a dish-water of eyes, it was ugly: "I've never seen anyone cry that way," she screamed to herself.

An odd silence set in, they had heard it start, settle down, it was a wrought, fragile thing. He observed a kind of minute of silence for all those who had died of love, he thought, yes, he thought of those extraordinary tombs. He said: "Do I sometimes talk to you about art?" She answered: "No, never." He sighed. He continued: "It seems to me there's an art that's looking for itself in the house. Obviously what I'm saying isn't reasonable." He was jealous of her, of her *success,* he caught a glimpse of a new method in her crannied attitude, a kind of unknown energy which she hid from him, she had a certain way of not being his, of being independent, he no longer even felt himself spattered on her. Their polite, disgusted solitude aired them feebly, driving away, like flies, the last clear ideas they had of each other. She now knew that he was lying about the vacation. "Is it really worth while telling her the bad news?" he wondered. Suddenly his fist clenched around the handle of the broom, his fingers were crushed on it, it was as if his pianist's fingers had been trampled on that huge, cold stick, he saw himself in front of a piano, raising clouds of famous, funereal notes. "No, I don't want to die!" he exclaimed inwardly, in the labyrinth of his fear.

"What about my books?" he asked.

"Burned, you know it very well."

It was true. He had burned everything before leaving, without furnishing a pretext. It was mad.

"Would you open the window?"

She opened it.

"And outside, have things changed?"

No, they had not changed, according to her.

He was no longer listening. His head was caught in the vice of his hands, he did not know what course to choose. Suddenly she declared to him that her stomach was upset, that she was sick, haggard, he watched her move away from him. No, she was still there.

She and the child were there, magnified, terribly spared by the forthcoming event, still untouched by what he was going to commit, untouched by his superhuman strength and inhuman will. Suddenly he felt oppressed, it was like a band of lunatics busily tightening screws in his flesh, he felt oppressed by the question that had not been asked, by the request for explanations that was not forth-coming: "Where do you come from?" Perhaps they would never again empty themselves on him like cartfuls of excess life, perhaps they were dead. Dead in that em-bellishing position, beneath the lamp, near the doll. There was a fine layer of dust on the furniture. Life sud-denly seemed to him flat and dirty like a puddle beneath a zinc sky, there was a swamp of pestilence, broken reeds, slime, marshes, a disturbing, larval silence, the stopped clock. He could no longer bear going back to that im-mense weakness of homes . . . The two of them leaped into his eyes, like cats in a fury. Out of pity they ap-plauded his inadequate act, they enjoyed themselves to the full, he was perhaps grotesque, they laughed, they did not believe in him, he felt the paleness of his harmless image covering all the pages of an outmoded catalogue through which they were both leafing. It was more than he could bear. He will not go home, he went away, leav-ing behind him an empty place in the bed, a place for the one who would replace him, for the First Comer who would bare her breast, who would bite her on the side and on the breasts, and whom she was perhaps already seeing in her dear nightmare, with his panting, salivary, hairy head above her, and around his eyes the marks of glasses which he had thrown aside, and a knife in his right hand.

He did not go home, that was all, he was walking backward, he felt in his back the immensity of the night welcoming him, and the great muttering of the forest, his refusal grew more intense from second to second, he therefore refused to join them for all kinds of said reasons, and in addition to these reasons there were others which he no longer knew, which he had forgotten, no doubt frightful ones. He was no longer walking backward, he went through nameless streets which were knotted in the night, it was the city's most intestinal hour, he plunged into the pure interruption of sounds and lights, he was walking in order to stop thinking, in order to act, in order to be happy to have avoided the worst, which was to return home, in order to recapture the meaning of acts, of the repetition of acts, of the adventure that was roaring diabolical encouragement within him, in order to stop looking reality in the face, in order to conclude. He felt a kind of panic in his organs, a kind of great, sumptuous beating of his blood, he was filled with an ambiguous cruelty, like the prefiguration of an unmixed evil. He jostled a standing sack, a man, who yelled. But that incident could not stop him.

The Definitive Woman

His head almost burst, at 11:15 p.m., beneath a swaying of lanterns, through a few grating streets broken up by vile battles of drunkards and the zooming of hundreds of motorcycles, by indefinable, bluish-green stripes which seemed to fall from the dinosaurian crests of the roofs. Quinte could no longer have doubts about the importance of the appointment. It was his last chance. He ran to it, swept along by his savage desire, which swam, climbed, flew, which formed a slow procession, made circles, millions of circles, in the opposite directions, for those circles did not widen, they shrank visibly beneath his footsteps, it was impressive, thousands, they were now only thousands, hundreds, and my head still isn't swimming, soon only one will be left.

Above web-formed trolley wires, the sparkling of the spiders, only three circles left . . . the penultimate, and, in the middle of the last one, like an axis, a pair of soldered legs around which he turned and turned and turned . . .

The way those legs went up into the dress was of a rare, very rare luminosity, she was tall, darkish, with vast eyes, her gaze lapped up Quinte's yellow-white face like wrinkled milk in a dog's bowl. Her bag was swaying very low and hit her knees, not with a sharp or dull sound but with a wallowing sound; in the dimness of my sight fragrant fish traversed high pitching hairs which were like seaweed; have you ever suffered from the impenetrable movement of a woman's thighs? Out of the corner of his eye he observed the swelling pattern that they elaborated in the skirt; at each step the stockings were ground in that admirable darkness on a level with his desire, my God, the sounds were so finely shrill that they made him think of the mewing of a kitten smothered in wool, and perhaps there was also complicated lace underneath, the roughness of which, as the fingers ran over it, contrasted with the round, vibrant softness of the lighted rump near the otter-like extinguisher. And I had, yes, I had a desire to paste . . . stamps on her huge black eyes, which looked at me as in the past, and my skin in the vicinity of hers seemed to be making signs to her. With his arms dangling, he felt the horrible youthfulness of his body in which the shapeless giants of the stone shuddered among the unfordable rapids of his strength. He already saw the bed and, inside, a strange mass, a kind of heap of pink, inflated inner tubes. "How about it, will you come along?" she said to him. Yes, yes. And he felt that super-abundance of intoxication which transforms everything into gulfs from which voices rise up and dictate to man to fall into them. But she, he did not know why, she was an exception among the gulfs, she was, on the contrary, that terrible swelling of hardness, she grew bigger, she grew bigger before his eyes, she was not an emptiness that broadens out but an embodied *joy* that invades space. He felt the horrible youthfulness of his body. Suddenly there was neither soul nor childhood in that place, everything was heavier, volumes even in the paleness of the hubbub, a thousand tires squeaking together. He would listen to all kinds of surrenders on her vast, sacred breasts, all kinds of artful indifference, and his kisses would be bruised on them like a volley of soft fruit.

The night dried up its lights one by one, it resembled a huge cloud of black dust raised by the frightful galloping of incubi and pierced by a few clusters of circus bulbs, by advertising, by tattoos of sorcerers on negro bellies that had come from far away to stretch out here in the streets where once again the men of sleep merged with those of pleasure. "Moussia, is it you?"

"Yes."

It was indeed she. He was happy, not so much at having found her as at being able to lose her and to lose himself with her. His odd joy turned in his chest like a mad crank-handle. He felt deeply momentary, as if ready for an eternal circumstance. From that moment on, the speed of his visions made him drunk. As they went by they bent rows of antiques set up along the road, they overturned livid things that screamed, but the overturnings themselves were abrupt creations in space, he saw a ghastly portrait on a chest of drawers dance before his eyes, etc. The words "pleasure" and "death," disturbing and hackneyed, dug big holes in his waves of silence where the particulars and clarifications which he no longer asked of life mingled over graveyards of science with figures, with proper names. He thought of the unreality of earlier conversations which had been killed by a winter poetry and of the higher unreality which shadows of events had injected all the way here into a quite illusory story about him. He almost uttered a cry when he saw the hotel.

Finally, they entered a room, in the middle of which stood a stove as black as negroes who give of themselves unstintingly to produce music to the very depths of their loins and who slash sounds to pieces between their teeth, which are born sparks. The one window opened slightly beneath the pressure of a wind that smelled of onion. Moussia gave him the impression of enjoying the encounter in that place which was cluttered with unrecognizable things and which *looked as if it did not want him.*

"Am I disturbing you?" he asked.

"No, not at all. I wanted to see you . . . And now you're here."

He did not know what else to say, how to explain his presence there. He heard innumerable wasps, collisions of thin wings.

"I happened to be in the neighborhood."

With a gesture of her hand she forestalled fuller explanations and said to him:

"It doesn't matter. Sit down . . ."

He sat down on a small sofa.

"Does that light bother you?"

She settled herself next to him and, dipping her hands into fringes, took out a pack of cigarettes from under the seat, she offered him one, which he refused, her own was long and thin in her playful fingers, her crossed legs were a blond provocation against a black background, and wrappings were shiny around biscuits that were falling like jewels from her right hand, her right hand, the more entrancing of the two, because of jewels, real ones.

"Oh!"

"Yes, please do, a glass of nice cold vermouth, it's sweet."

A bottle sprang up from her gestures, which resembled delicate victories of conjuring over fixed matter. They touched glasses, and at the clink of the crystal she emitted a crystalline little laugh. It reminded Quinte of two long, pale lovers; when they rushed naked into each other's arms, the sound was so clear that they seemed to be clinking with their whole bodies. They were like two beautiful champagne glasses, they sparkled, she drank his words and he hers, they emptied themselves into each other in little sips. And when it was over, they were as empty as the drained glasses, but they continued to gleam like the finery of archduchesses beneath the chandelier.

"You're dreaming . . . about a woman . . . ," said Moussia.

"I'm not," he retorted.

"I thought you were," she exclaimed.

She changed the crossing of her knees. Quinte submitted to the eroticism with such brutelike casualness that bits of foul phrases intertwined in his throat, things that pulverized breeding. In a hollow voice she told him fantastic stories which were never quite about love nor quite about death, an astounding mixture of confused, flashing anecdotes from which the only constant that emerged clearly was disgust with living. As she kept talking, her face took on unexpected forms, some of which bordered on ugliness, though its power of enchantment did not suffer thereby in any way. It was then that the words seemed to escape from her in warm trickles, like urine, and that her mouth, with its bright shadows and its red tip inside, was indecent, in the manner of an open fly.

Quinte began to sweat. His role was sinking into uncertainty, he did not manage to break the bonds that had to be broken. He was oppressed by an inability to escape that was more unbridled than freedom. The objects threw themselves violently at his gaze, the growing defects of the furniture, the dense, ensnared pregnancy of the knickknacks.

He learned thus that Ponche had been Moussia's lover, as had Monsieur Cuile, and many others with unpronounceable names. When the list was at its height, he realized that he had been the only one who had not . . . (swabbed that bitch with his eager brush . . .). And a kind of casual modesty no doubt kept Moussia from telling everything, from talking about the blind man and Oswald, about the drunken state in which the painter had found her, about the shop which she crossed virginally, about the corridors in which her footstep was to the tiles what plashing is to water, about Vylinx, about the map on her hip, about the football game, about the bus with the broken brakes, about the barge, etc. On the other hand, she succeeded in making the odor of what she had not told come and go within a certain radius, her suggestions had a terrible odor of act and experience, of unmade bed, of boudoir, they were more than images, they were films of odors forbidden to those under the age of eighteen, full of vicissitudes, for odors too have vicissitudes, and unexpected twists and turns. And it all went by within him, like a procession of beasts stung to the quick, like the hydra of a fabulous sensuality. And to think that he had thought she was pure. And while she narrated, her belly, in which there was no child, was shaken, as it were, by memories of rape.

At a certain moment, Moussia found him odd and told him so. He thought: it's desire. His rapacious senses described in his eyes the ellipse of a black flight. It was a kind of malaise.

"I feel absolutely nothing, don't worry."

Sitting on a couch which was so purple that there seemed to be only purple and no couch, she strove to recapture the threads of her thoughts. Quinte, who had stood up, paced the room, listened distractedly to her flow of talk in which certain words recurred insistently: "felon," "tobacco," "knife," and even "apache." He contented himself with observing, out of the corner of his eye, the successive swellings of her bosom and her dark eyes which thrashed about in a trap of lashes. Jumbled notations fanned his fever: "Moussia has her eye on me," "Moussia's going to run away," or else he regarded the shudders of her dress as exertions of her body. He also had the impression that a key was turning little by little in the keyhole, not to open the door but to lock it. Suddenly he turned around, drawn-looking. Moussia went to the other end of the room. That was what hurt, that printed cloth which squeezed the bifid, pendulous flesh below her waist, that was what hurt. When she came back, he was seated. They ate a few biscuits together. The hard, viril sound he made with his teeth jarred with hers, which was soft and melting, and in that difference, between those two surprising sounds among the myriads of silent flies, another desire awoke, solely the desire for revenge, the brutal surplus-value of some past avidity, he saw fortunes, gold to squander, pangs, furies, torpedoes of rape, mad disembowelers, blood, poultices of moistness between coupled bellies, he saw room for all that in his raw drive.

The seconds went by in double-quick time, ticktock ticktock ticktock.

The anguish was big and full like the sleep of parturient women.

Moussia played with her thin little silver, frostlike cross. She moved about, opened drawers, knocked little bottles of perfume against each other, took out a black stocking which she invaginated, then a girdle, with erratic movements. It was then that he noticed the bed, not far from there.

Thus, even the complicity of things helped him, openly or with the greatest secrecy, unknown to the places where they were, merely by occupying more and more space with fewer and fewer means, merely by taking on new, turbid, poisonous meanings. Like that bed, which was corrupting his soul, the soul of a man of whom his neighbors had said, only the day before: "a decent, likable man . . ." And he burst out laughing.

He felt almost at ease in his body, almost homogeneous, almost adherent to that room, which seemed to him to have been built in another world where freedom is possible only in a cage, a place that was particularly preserved from the hated street, which, during the day, cuts man up into pieces, disintegrates him, that street which he promised himself never to see again except in the form of night. He drained his glass at one gulp, quarts of blood of bulls that had been killed by an ax in broad daylight, yes those ideas in his head, suddenly, and the most questionable colors that were in him, the colors he would be forever incapable of naming, that of his recrements which were moved by love, that of his state of mind, nobody could tell the color of his state of mind, which was unequalably black! Reine had said that, Reine, Reine! a name that he screamed with howling laughter.

She ran her hands over her face as if to settle her features. When she brought them back to her shining knees, she actually seemed more beautiful, a beauty that was endlessly explorable, that kept widening out like the gulfs of an inspired genius. At that moment Quinte had a feeling that it would be long before they could escape from each other or from a common solution.

What he would have liked to arouse was pure desire. Imagine a man and a woman who had been kept in ignorance, ever since birth, from matters of love and who were suddenly parachuted onto a desert island. What would they do? They would sniff at each other, and *that* would be a pure desire. The pure desire of which he dreamed was also a certain inaptitude for thinking and talking, for example, about God, between themselves, for setting God like a trap between two equally voracious sex organs, for having that deviation. But instead of those pure and so new desires there was the red, flabby gullet of a mouth emptying into its poor guts quarts of liquor; instead of those desires there were stammered, incomprehensible, maddening promises of flesh, a kind of lust that was heading toward him like a tribe on the warpath, all of them creeping toward him, with spears, bows, arrows, catastrophes.

It was the owl-shaped clock which was making that sound. It had no hands but was ticking away as regularly as if it were intact. Quinte tried to know what time it was, to perceive the time through that regular, guttural sound, but the thing remained impenetrable, obstinate, barren. He felt like a mountain climber who had no hope of getting to the top. Then, he was savagely interested in not knowing the time, which was always too precise, too aging to please him, and because of the owl's heart that beat in the void, he felt like continuing his efforts farther and farther away, far away in the smallest space and shortest time, in a dot of a dotted line, his place. She began to laugh sadly, she no doubt did not realize what he was thinking, and he, he was beginning to like that strangely strong laugh, he clutched at it as at the tail of a plane taking off fast. Her face shone all the way to him through his big translucent hands which rested on it, with the fingers spread, and her limitless eyes seemed to be reproducing the large lapse of all that they had seen.

Quinte moved his chair closer to Moussia, because memories impelled him, and also because she perhaps thought him ridiculous, so far away from her, examining her like a juror, as when he was a child. She did not measure the exact scope of his desire.

"I had thought you were pure." That was all he wanted to say to her.

"I had thought you . . ."

But he did not finish. As soon as she took her eyes off his, she stood up, rushed to the radio and turned the knob, and even before he opened his mouth to utter the decisive word, the word "pure" or the word "virgin," a big din swept away like straws one or both of those two terms, wailings of wounded negroes. And from their lips, which were shaped like cannons aimed at the blue sun, he saw warlike spells shoot shells of blood and gaudy feathers, and he saw their singing and saltatory power, their paraphernalia of nerves, and life, life, life, all writhing in the light.

Though unsteady on his feet, he had the strength to go over and put his arms around her . . . The jazz, jumping for joy, was digging in his belly to extract the worst instincts, it shook and slapped all his sleeping powers. Never had the trouble he had taken led him so close to the final Dissonance, so close to the Triumph of breakage, all the standing and reclining ugliness proliferated around him, everything that human doubt had patiently won from the temptation of excess submitted to the squirting supremacy of the sounds. His bitterness exploded in salvos, and his pain itself, which was so deep, so inward, went foaming from the chant to the exclamation of the brasses. What long-throttled desire will brew more horrors when it suddenly breaks out? It was as if the impure, fleeting, even carnival-like sensations that the world-as-it-is procures through the soul's willful ecstasies had all at once shot through him, had been totalized in his flesh. This time, in his desire, he contained the whole world, the submersion of subversion, the empires, the development of the species, the death of God, the giddiness of twaddle, high political putrefaction, and other things as well. And while he held Moussia preciously tight, even the themes of forgotten meditations were massively reimbodied in her, there was no universal subject that did not yield to the torments of his body; the rare and the privileged, the unique and the supernatural, suddenly seemed involved in one of her gestures which was in the process of making signs contrary to his, which were eager and neurotic and as if possessed by the need to kill beauty. It was an extraordinary impression, it was as if the purulence of sects and parties were there, within his reach, inciting him to place his lips on enormous wounds with fascinating, enteric textures, it was like an orgiastic emptiness, a gaping carcass, swarming with henchmen marked by wild efforts; thus, he liked even politics as it was, as he found it in the depths of his own infamy, through the blurred prism of his conscience. And thus, faster and faster, he allowed a fit of fury to rise up within him, he did not weary of listening to it rise up within him, it was a nameless and faceless passion, full of mad carriages, of sorts of *rising avalanches,* of luminous imprecations, his whole soul was like a fair ground, and all his flesh too, mythical monsters and rattles, and an emotion in his heart like an armful of reptiles. He was submerged by the tropical genius of the room, by an intense lack of culture which escaped in crooked gleams from his eyes or which ran in his veins or his bones and reached the tips of his senses, which bustled about like millions of small animals on unequalable bellies, he now thought only about love, about its rabic and ingenious nearness, transforming each object into a function of love since there was nothing that did not take part in the passion, his hands and the lines of his hands, his body and the enemies of his body, his watch and the gilded frame on the wall, and the ivory objects, the specters of the past, the coat racks. It all had such a feminine nudity which extended to things and to time that it was not even necessary for him to make a gesture to be on top, in positions prohibited by the Church, and inside, as has never happened to man.

Thus, this vice, which, like certain painters, proceeded by little touches with the aim of achieving a definitive figure, this offensive and difficult vice was passionately identified with the world's vice.

They had stopped dancing. Moussia had slowly disengaged herself with bogged movements of her body. She was lying on the couch, fatigued. He furiously made broad, sharp gestures with his hand. He had the impression of seeing his own fingers detach themselves from his hands and crash against the walls like ill-fitting gloves, they seemed to be hanging only by a thread. But that demonstration had no results. Her hair was disarranged, in front of the huge cheval glass, her dress had never been so close to her skin. In his dazed despair, he imagined that it could all still seesaw. For example, that skin, well, it could still be topmost, could still take first place. "Get undressed," he ordered. It was laughable. She turned around with a look of surprise, framed with a kind of gilded event. It was no doubt the edges of the mirror. And at that very moment he saw to what extent everything remained possible, everything is possible when a woman is taken by surprise in that way, especially violence, cruelty, sadism, particularly as there was not much that held him back, he now hardly felt his past behind him, he was followed by a void, he was afraid, really he was afraid of falling back, while before him, in the dark futurition, everything remained to be done. Suddenly he had a terrible pioneer consciousness, of unlimited wickedness, everything remained to be done in front of him, the frenzied infinite, the big torn worlds, *he no longer knew what a book was*. For many people, what they do is inscribed in the secrecy of the books they have read, only the books know why they have killed, loved, tortured, hated, and the shadow of each of their gestures, even the most spontaneous, hazily prolongs a sentence which they thought had been engulfed, which they thought perhaps they had rejected, and which, having found refuge in the mechanisms of the body, made its way there, clandestinely, and even into the subconscious, which derives its strange power from a big bazaar of abandoned words. But for him, at that moment, there were no more books.

In a state of extreme nervousness, Quinte first laid the blame on the window, which had remained open. In shutting it, he broke a pane and cut his hand slightly. He noticed some tall gentlemen, who were dressed in black, walking up and down in front of the building, they were relatively identical with those who had always shadowed him and whose cheerless undertaking he had thus far been unable to thwart. From time to time they pulled their hats down over their eyes and looked up to the sky. There was quite a number of them and they were taking notes. Quinte snickered and took a firm stand in front of the bed a little more than a yard away from the young woman. The undressing had taken place smoothly, almost unctuously. He had seen and heard everything. He would never forget the scene, thanks to the episode of the brassière, which had been, as it were, burgled from her back by her little hands before dropping unhooked; and when the garter belt snapped open and the stocking shriveled down to the floor, he had the impression of a sudden sublime carnification of space, no never never would that scene fade from his memory, especially the last moments of the dress, which descended by degrees from the most perfect architecture of auric flesh that could be imagined, from a very exquisite and mysterious combination of ovali and volutes superbly sculpted in the iliac mass and both stimulated and corrected by an order of invisible caresses but whose source seemed to be in the gaze which she laid on herself or in the very quivers that ran through her.

"I love you!"

"You're crazy . . ."

She was kneeling on the bed. He also saw her in the cheval glass. He had beauty twice. But he felt rather like throwing himself on the mirror, for it was there that she was more intensely naked. Seen directly, she looked annoyed, and the annoyance clothed her a little. And he repeated to her that he loved her. All the neighbors woke up, first there were dull thuds, then clankings (no doubt metal objects that were moved or knocked over when their owners got up hastily) and finally imprecations, the baseness of which was not distinguishable. It was all reinforced by hammerings of fists against the walls. The protest soon spread to every floor of the hundred-yard-high building, which was perturbed by frightful uproars bordering on delirium. Everyone chimed in, children, old people, the zealots of potent copulation, the sick, parrots, cats, tired civil servants, and barren, yellow-skinned couples with dead trunks who commemorated their antigenetic pact with a sacramental rumpling of sheets, the very ones who went to the park every evening and Sunday mornings, holding on a leash that irreplaceable hairy, faithful, gelded child: the dog. All the dogs barked. But nothing could prevent Quinte from proclaiming aloud his love, the outburst of which exceeded the bellowing of the radio negroes and the impure wrath of the dislocated tenants. That force of love swept the whole interior of his body like a big mobile beacon from the bottom of a gulf of frustrated adolescence. All his botched, grazed, deferred loves, all those monsters of incompetence which had been suckled on shadow piled up in indescribable disorder beneath the cruel light of memory, and they were screaming for revenge.

It did not seem to him that there were other words than those, that he had ever learned others; they summed up the universe, the future, and all kinds of inclusive and individual things. They were also perhaps his first words as a real sonofabitch. They were no longer hackneyed. Perhaps someday he would say "hello" or "all right" in the same way, with the same fervor, and that day he would be saved.

He cried out with his eyes closed, the better to hear what he cried, through the neighboring hatred. But if he did not decide to reopen them, it was also out of fear of encountering his very particular, very autonomous way of being nude, of being silent, motionless, recumbent, astounded. He saw beneath his eyelids, hanging from the blind man's thin molding, Oswald's painting in which Moussia seemed to be the plaything of two conflicting and enraged miracles, in which she had that look of a nun, of a tipsy saint, the contrast of which with what he sensed of her gloomy, tragic inwardness emitted austere magic toward him, the very magic that plunged him into a secret, criminal passion.

"I love you . . ."

But Moussia no longer shared his excitement. She was playing with his hair, without wondering too much about the meaning of the words. Moreover, the rabic ultimatum of the awakened tenants interested her more, even amused her, so it seemed, for she was now laughing, with a laugh that perfected her mouth, that shed a vast levantine light on her teeth, a light that was torturing to him, for he was like a mole in the presence of those big bright things.

It was a dirty love that he felt, a feeling like all the others, which it was impossible to switch toward simple, lovely joy, toward the nobility and grace of innocent abandon.

His senses were bottled up by slugs, which had descended from his soul and were mad with joy in that cellar lined with their shiny streaks. Bending slightly forward, he stroked the arm of a chair, he was performing an experiment, was seeking the degree of sensitivity of his fingers, of his palms. "Are my hands stroking well?" He looked around the room, which seemed to have been the theater of a battle fought with animal lung-power. Thick blood gleamed everywhere on the walls, on the pictures, on the radio. He saw red. The only real light was the purplish drizzle that the hanging bulb, which was like the tongue of an exhausted she-wolf, sucked from his neck with the hatred of a vampire. It was midnight. There were more than one midnight in that midnight, they could be heard roaring like elephants, swelling the handless clock with all the might of their trunks. He wanted to stop up his ears, but his ears would not let themselves be stopped, they resisted the silence, it was as if his organs had suddenly made common cause with his carnal consciousness, as if they were crowding around it to enlarge it. And the whole city seemed dead or in meditation around that perfect din. Even the neighbors, redoubling their rage, seemed expelled from the fête. His cry was heightened only by the murmur of faraway streets, in lands where he had never been because everything had prevented him, including the people who shadowed him. But he was now glad that he had never traveled, he could free himself from that obscure additional failure, there was a screaming within him, he felt like the interrupted feast of those animals, and complete nostalgias made him bring forth tears, nostalgias like great oriental displays, which made him bellow, I love you. All the journeys he had not taken suddenly possessed him, they piled up rotten with sun in his glittering, sunburnt skin, they rose up like sprays of antennae into his imagination. Yonder, the bellies of males were beaten with white-hot cymbals, their rhythms were abraded, yonder there are hypertrophied melons which one has a desire to open with gestures of a mad, swarthy surgeon! To travel! To travel in women, in the south of women, in the south of women's bellies, in those lands where the heavy, putrid darkness of subtropical nights of anguish brews in its terrible pleasure the perspiration of space and of tons of black condiments, the lurching of wild asses and the tetanic olive trees in the sunsets . . . And, in addition, yonder there was perhaps a race of plain people, of true people, of good quality, with the true generosity of the poor and unquestionable rights to a better kind of life, with deep humanity, whereas here, in the city which he had never left, the plain people had disappeared and with them all reasons for being brotherly, the only ones left were unhappy wretches without dignity, wan creatures whose role was to be at the bottom of the scale, beggars, the vanquished who were involved in every corruption, every social betrayal, people who disgusted you forever with fine sentiments and who might have been better, had they wanted to be, if they had dared pick themselves up and fight for the possible good things in life, like those good books they might have been able to obtain, since they are cheaper than bread, but which they did not want, for it was spiritual nourishment, something dubious, useless, a luxury, as they said, and when they said that, there was only one class of people who outdid them in horror, in ignominy, in vileness, the average, mediocre people, a kind of huge family whose members hung like wormy fruit from all the branches of society, "modest," "decent" people incapable of great good as of great evil, who imitated or cringed, depending on the circumstances, and who had a thought-trailer loaded with set ideas and simplistic phobias. No, there were no longer common people or aristocrats in that city, and it was sad. That was why he would have liked to voyage on distant seas. Why, he asked himself in his sadness, why doesn't there exist a sea of concertos, a sea composed of the adagios of all concertos?

When he came back to himself, he tried to return to the paroxysms. He looked at his baleful hands. Moussia's nakedness was infested with purple glints. The odd thing was that she did not ask him for money. In any case, he had none, his empty pockets floated against his sides and he did not feel at all ashamed of it. What would have fretted and frozen any other man in a state of desire would possess, for him, the gift of multiplying his pleasure, for there was room in that singular flesh for a grandiose multiplying of joys by evils, that flesh of his, which had been hollowed by unwonted bad luck but sharpened by the lack of money itself. As for the paroxysms, he still could not find them. They were neither here nor there. He would have liked to be invaded by a wild force comparable to cohorts of picnickers entering a charnel house to have a meat meal there . . .

As casually as can be, he had come near her, after a long journey, and he was almost touching her nipples, as if close to shore. But he did not manage to lay hands on them. He vaguely feared they might fly away, he said to himself ineptly: "What if they were hummingbirds?"

Would acting always mean therefore to hope with violence? He felt a kind of violence blossoming in a kind of hope which was in the process of being fulfilled or disappointed. The gentlemen in black were persistently strolling in the street, but without ever leaving a given perimeter which had been drawn in chalk in front of the building. At times Quinte had the impression that they were taking measurements. For he was near the window. He closed one eye and with the other, which was as inexpressive as a navel, he roamed what remained of pale zones in the darkness. The neighbors persisted in their hostile attitude, they had raised their rumpus to its highest pitch by requisitioning everything they saw and hurling it against the walls. But in some cases, on the lower floors, there appeared to be a great conciliation in the noises and even a tendency to transform what had first been a burst of bad humor into orgies. The fact is that Quinte, who had stopped proclaiming his love to Moussia, could therefore no longer quite understand what all those people had against him. It could be supposed that owing to a fatal sequence of the obstinacy and the noises they would be condemned to put up with them for a long time, since no one wanted to be the first to stop demonstrating his force. In any case, Quinte despised them and Moussia was no longer laughing. The radio had just stopped its broadcast of savage music and a voice uttered non-memorable words which were followed by the first notes of the national anthem. By a miracle Quinte listened to that rather solemn air, not so much because it moved him as because, in a familiar way, it gave body to his torpor. It reminded him of a similar situation of some years before. While he strove to reconstitute the memory, bits of the patriotic song curled in his head, it was like a rosary of licentious ideas told by the devil. It whispered slimy sighs into his ears, the turbid stimulations of a desire for vice. He thought that he had at last found his way back to the paroxysms and that what was going to happen would have consequences, prolongations, the end of which he could not see, situations would be added to situations, he would never again be untroubled, never again the same man twice in succession. He had been dreaming for so long of a far-reaching act, of something which his life would be unable to get out of and which was unwearying.

She lay stretched on the bed. He put out his hand. She watched the fingers, which writhed like asps, move toward her, his dirty nails scratched the light in front of them, she seemed fascinated, but she grabbed his wrists and said softly: "Not so fast." In the way she looked at him her eyes barked gently. When women's eyes bark at you, when they resemble the mouths of puppies that you see yapping behind shop windows, that's the moment to feel desired for any low or noble reason. Presently her whole face started barking in that way, with a delicacy that one can imagine, her mouth, her nose, her chin all opened and shut under the impetus of God knows what agitation of the senses, they were little barks of a damp dog, and Quinte had the sensation of gnawing a bone, he felt like wronging her, like doing her an immense, irreparable wrong, he felt like robbing her, for example, but how could he rob her, how could he inflict such a dispossession on her that it might make her scream, even die ...

She lay stretched on the bed. She was long and loose, free of streaks, her bust was gothically prolonged by the ogive of her slender arms. And her breasts seemed to be to the delicate curve of her whole body what fruits, in Africa, are to the end of a loaded branch. Then she opened, more intensely, sprawled like all the faces of a live folding-board. He remained standing, with his knees digging into the edge of the bed, his arms spread, his tongue hanging out. His fever whorled over his face like a red smoke, his muscles were angular, and his bones jutted from his flesh as from burrowed soil. Never had he felt the edge of his teeth so acutely, their monumental presence in his hostile mouth. He clenched his fists, it was as if his hands closed over his hands, as if he had become twice what he was, as if the second time, which was harder, grimmer, more ancient, covered the other with all its primitive, atavistic vigor.

231

He would not rob her. However, he was further advanced in the disfiguration of morality. His hatred took the same path as his concupiscence, and those two things hugged harder and harder in the strangling of desire. The room was steeped in a pungent odor of broiling, it was in that general scorching that they were going to love each other, in that sulphurous, fleshy odor of medieval wars which was stronger than the old cameral humidity and which won the soul over to absurd murders.

She shook her head, no, not yet. She put out her hand, for money no doubt. He made a gesture of contempt, then emitted an odd, wheezy laugh, like the pain of pigs. Why was she stubborn, there were no more obstacles between them; as a woman, she must have realized it, her determination etched her face with broad demiurgic strokes . . . After all, what dream is not fulfilled if one has really dreamed it? Everything was possible and probable since the only past he had was what he was willing to invent, since he had no past, since there was not even a vestige of his past, since he was frightfully free. He was born of nothing, of nothingness, for baseness and blood, he was planted like a post in the present, in the present of that knife, of that blood, there was heavy traffic in his body, many things moving about furiously, and the discussion of a morbid enthusiasm; he cocked his ear and listened within him, for the last time before belonging to another existence, to beehive tunes which had almost a folk quality, to tossings of dice, and to the gliding sound of rail trucks that moved back and forth in his heaven of flesh, and to the braying of that mournful genius of the heart and mind which is black and hunchbacked and makes its way like a wild ass from birth to death. The act

232

could no longer escape him, the most just act, superb in its justice, which he would not escape this time because it had already begun around him like a spider web in the light and because he was melting at the same time in the core of his body in a major blazing, innocence in its most original aspect, a thing which has not yet been astonished, a privilege owing to which it will not be possible for there to be either shame or misdeed . . .

He recognized him!

At the ends of his hands were no doubt the triumph, the resurrection of Wasmes-Bô, who growled like that, at the ends of his hands spread the deep, *numerical* force of Wasmes-Bô's fingers, of his extraordinary exterminating muscles, in the play of which burst the final stiffness of old paralyses. Wasmes-Bô's silent joy pushed violet torrents against the final dam of doubt, Wasmes-Bô, the Man who said nothing, but whose poison worked its way in the bodies of all who approached him; the shrill, black blossoming of Wasmes-Bô the Beloved finally took place when all seemed lost, it possessed him, it helped him chop that woman's beauty into tiny pieces, and he already felt it becoming increasingly vast and torrid and exasperated within him, full of sarcasms and hatred, full too of the cruel peroration of all his silences which would explode like a long howl in murders, like a cry that contained all the cries of all the nights of infamy. That was what Quinte sensed in his superior anger . . .

But he continued telling Moussia of his love. His big raised arms stayed up, and his killer's grimace froze around his teeth, which were caressed by a kind of strange, sugary breath. A kind of last-minute vanity calmed him in an odd, bitter way and prevented him from perpetrating anything against anyone. There was neither a crime nor rejection of the crime, neither an act nor rejection of the act, but a kind of instant of reprieve that separated dream and fatality, a kind of new distance between what is and what should be. He did not fall on her like a rain of iron, he did not strike her with all his lumbering force, and she did not scream in a fishwife's voice the vile blood-stained words, that vocabulary of rape which used to thrill him in the movies but which had been emitted this time expressly for his own hearing. It was impossible.

The fact is that Quinte no longer quite understood. He questioned himself with a kind of winded candor. Quinte left that strange zone of time where what disappears reigns over what is born. Quinte traversed a vast, devastated region.

Instead of an act which took place under such conditions of potency and intensity that his destiny would thereby have been excited for eternity, what he projected upon the world was at most comparable to some slight symptom of bewilderment. All that remained of the invincible effort which he thought he had put forth in order to live beyond himself and transcend his death was a varying and moderate will that led nowhere. None of the innumerable ways of acting that occurred to him seemed able to introduce an uncommon event. The fête seemed definitely over. He recalled, almost incredulously, the rising of his anger, its excessive, baroque stages. Was it possible that after having desired, willed, and glimpsed so many singular empires, that after having felt other and more luxurious, more finely wrought pains than the existing, inventoried pains of man, was it possible, after all, that failure would prove stronger than life and that it would foist itself upon him with so little grace that it seemed vulgar? The height of irony was that this extraordinary day was ending with an impression of *average man*. His dissolved, battered past was first reconstructed in his consciousness and was already spreading prosaically to the dimensions of his physical and moral being.

He even became aware that he was no longer desirable, for her look was inviting him to take his place on her. It was by that too that he recognized his failure, by that humble expectation of which he was the object, by the little hopes of all kinds that he would bring to life again here and there, depending on his displacements or fixations. The infinite world of hatred and despair was followed by the finite world of love, with its obstacles, conventions, and rites.

He sat down on the edge of the bed and took her hands. "Moussia," he said with exaltation, "we'll go away, won't we, swear to me that we'll go away, far far away . . ." He closed his eyes so as not to see the answer she made with a movement of her head. As if it were yes, he foolishly told her why he had wanted to join the Club, how, before reaching that point, he had had to get rid of innumerable dear things, "values" for the most part. He said that he had "literally destroyed," though without ever specifying what. At times, he stopped in the middle of a sentence, looked at her with desperate tenderness, and murmured, "Moussia, they didn't want me." And she stroked his hair. He retreated to the back of the room so as the better to surround her. How he would have liked to say everything and to love her to the roots of her being! He had hoped to be able to tell her more about it, to explain the situation to her as he saw it in his mind. It was difficult. The time and place were hardly right. And besides, it all contracted in his heart of hearts, like a secret. The massive disapprovals, the inextinguishable outcries which he had had to overcome in men and things only to end in the rather ridiculous position in which he found himself, standing briskly stiff against the mantel, with his feet together, facing a woman who was perhaps repressing a yawn of boredom, the drab, bantering obstacles of all kinds which had combined against him, all of that was now trying to be silent in his renovated memory. He attempted nevertheless to expound to Moussia some views on the person he called the-Man-who-does-not-yet-exist. This man, whom he called *Jean,* was distinguished from all others by his savage, disconcerting exultations. Resisting the huge network of automatic laws which, since his birth, had fixed his place in the world with a discretionary force of tightening and asphyxia, to such a degree that the right to burgeon which had been accorded him was ridiculously pointless, he embodied, all by himself, the faith of those whose spirit demands only the higher marrows, and the obsession of those for whom the flesh is a candidacy every single moment. To look at him, certainly nobody would have been able to suspect the scope of the struggles in which he engaged against the world. He mobilized all the energies of his being for uprootings, soarings, fantastic excisions and grafts whose consequences were unforeseeable, but of which his face and even his daily attitude succeeded in not bearing the mark. Actually, that quiet-looking man, who was not simple and was grave rather than given to laughter, had made the following incredible discovery: *inanition,* a kind of comatose laziness, of essential idleness, which seemed to govern man's relations with his society by a play of reciprocal influences, the mechanism of which was disguised by the unlimited resources of dreaming. The fact is that never had the rate of human bondage been so high as in our time, because it was proportional to the invisibility of the tyrants. Actually, the latter showed their faces less and less, they disappeared behind the countless technical means which they had bought from science to enslave the masses. One could no longer be sure of one's moments of freedom, of invention, one could not even be sure of the expansion of one's chest, for in the air that seemed most breathable there was perhaps a violent poison born of men's will.

By looking about him attentively, by analyzing a few episodes in history, by reading a half-dozen staggering books, this strange character had reached the conviction that despite the speed of life, the flurry of cities and villages, despite and no doubt because of the progress of *mechanical excess* and because of progress itself, man was exploiting his capacities less than ever and was becoming more and more a plaything. Two tremendous powers, one external, the other internal, were vying in the effort to subdue him: the first was called technolatry, the second the spirit of foresight, and because they profited from the victims' complicity in the form of wishes for happiness, everything so concurred that these two monstrosities constantly consolidated their empire. For if men seek happiness in security, it is quite true that what they are capable at most of discovering are the instruments of their weakness and slavery which have been elaborated for them by engineers but forged by their own hands. Thus, in order to overcome human beings the tyrants had also invented a kind of fake tolerance, of fake broadening of outlooks, which were probably born of the myth of equality and which wretchedly permeated the whole century, debasing the higher values to the level of the lower, merging the beautiful and the ugly, causing preferences that raise a vile stew of coarse equivalents. This itching for applause at any cost could not be an emanation of love, the sign of a rapprochement of human differences in the direction of a single light, it was rather the sickening proof of the growing insipidity of life in an age when concessions to baseness, the cult of facility, and profanations of the sacred constituted *Fashion*.

As for the State, it deserved the title of chief robber of men. What interested it primarily, when it broke into them, was their vital faculties. The State's power grows by means of what it steals or cuts away from individuals with creative energy, with primary impulses. This age and this earth offered us the foul spectacle of individuals marching and functioning according to the plans of an authority which, in order to elude the searches of the police of lucidity, had been inexorably decentralizing itself and ramifying for centuries, installing its most harmful agents at the most imperceptible points of contagion, instilling its tenuous but "beneficent" propaganda in one place and its divine lessons of velvety slavery in another. Worst of all, this modern authority involved us in groups in which we were unable to tell whether we remained men or became criminals. Each institution did the thinking for each of its members. One no longer even felt free not to think. We were led to think in such a way that it meant purely and simply the death of thinking. The state of intoxication was over! It was now State intoxication, the crimes which are always perfect, for the culprits can never be found.

Of course, a few rebels blazed out from time to time and bore witness to the rigor of the potential richness of the living, but if one rebelled, it was always with the aim of doing away with the reasons for rebelling. But what would we do without these reasons? Our condition would be even worse!

That is why the man about whom Quinte spoke and whose name, we repeat, was Jean had once dashed about convulsively and why he had opened all his floodgates of pride and will on the world. Certainly that man who was perpetually tormented by fits of voracious anger, but about whom one would have been astounded to learn that they resulted in his spiritual growth, that lone, uncouth man seemed uncharitable and, in short, unamenable to social morality. He had felt it necessary to go through such a stage, for he regarded that commonly accepted morality as a perilous combination of mechanical values essentially unfaithful to human nature, but coordinated and operated at the present stage of civilization by a code of external, weakening, deceitful manifestations, which, in addition, corrupted true virtue, and the only way of overcoming them was by substituting conflicting grandeurs. Had anyone accused him of being inhuman, he would probably have replied that in the inhuman as he conceived it (ambitious, solitary, and insatiably pensive) there was still a man with his promises, possible repentance and living Spirit, whereas in the dehumanized there was nothing left, nothing but matter, the matter of the infinite cruelties of stupidity in the service of dictators, nothing but the works of a huge, impersonal machinery. He was aware that his bad temper was necessary, purifying, that it was the focal point of all the conquering, regenerating dynamisms which would prevail over licit mediocrity, that its quality was other than that of the ordinary bad temper of associations, begetters of wars, other too than that of modern bad temper which is an imbecilic goodness. But, on the other hand, however much he desired to act alone in order to conquer alone, he was thoroughly aware that one is never the possessor of one's acts, and that whatever one may do against others, it is always for them that one does it. He was like an aggressive fortress, for though he defended himself by every means he possessed against the world's soporific assault, though he protected himself with all his might against all enrollments, he also attacked the enrollers, just as he did the occult mass of attackers. And his aim was a great one, for it involved preserving, at all events, what was best and irreplaceable in human sensibility, that sensibility which the present dominating forces wished to destroy and without which, if it is virile and creative, there is no supreme fruition that is valid.

"But that man doesn't exist yet," sighed Quinte.

Moussia had seemed to follow him halfway, then her face had shut, and she was now thinking of something else, of intrigues, of emotional involvements. Perhaps it was only a semblance. She had loved, she was planning to love again, that was all she had to answer. She tapped her right hip with her forefinger. "Moussia, they didn't want me." The people had repudiated him, the singularity of his state had deeply disgusted the upholders of order and even those who were shadowing him. Nobody had been willing to recognize the obscure legitimacy of his hatreds, of his contradictions. She was admiring her own body in front of the big, gilt-edged mirror, admiring her skin which had been curried by male hands. He felt like saying to her: "Come to my arms. We're a youth that exists nowhere else but in us." There would henceforth be a secret, morganatic relationship between them. He shook her arm: "Moussia, we'll go away, won't we, far far away!" She seemed to agree.

Her heavy, moaning body stretched in the blue shadow, he now perceived her tiny smile on the crest of slow, thick, carnal waves. The purity of which she had given the infinite idea and had then belied horribly, that purity was prowling in the warm, fragrant languor amidst the trails of a dubious, wavering luminosity. Quinte coughed. His arms came down with little galvanic quivers, plunged into the sheets to grasp their whiteness, only the whiteness. Not even that. There was thus nothing to seize, not even the death of others. Possession drew back its empire eternally, beyond the reach of his little anxieties, they all flew away, men, corpses, his arms had not dropped with the desired violence, an innocent notion of ineptness had stayed his stony gesture and his sulphured grimace of a desperate man. It was not even worth while starting to do evil, to harm the world. The means, the ends, everything had stolen away. In short, he had not reckoned with . . . his humanity, with that old, tenacious breeding, with the powerful fabric of fears and hypocrisies. He had believed in freedom by liberating himself from the thousands of family and social patterns. But the hardest still remained, his background, his childhood, and all the dramas that had gone through his being like a demand for justice. He had glimpsed a realm where nothing had meaning and where minds tore each other by touching. That was freedom. Then he had turned to the best that man has invented: security in fanaticism. When one reduces the world to oneself, he thought, one finds another dictatorship there.

He stroked her everywhere. He repeated to her: "I don't think I wanted to hurt you . . . I like you."

She had drawn herself up slightly and was watching the delightful work of his hands on her body, its embossing, its inlaying, its boldness which seemed to be *pouring* sensation to her very depths. She felt she was reaching a state of belonging to man such as she had never known. She also had an intuition that between her flesh and her mind the problem was unfurling more insolubly than ever but that this time it was the carrier of a Destiny with its weight of love and death. She felt happy. "Perhaps there are other ways . . . to art?" he suddenly said.

The Return

He got out of bed and
dressed. The room had become saturated with an
extreme sweetness and seemed to contain the growing suspension of all rages, of all desires, and perhaps that enormous silence was Wasmes-Bô returning to his den to die
there of hatred, just as it was perhaps Wasmes-Bô's supreme revenge to create such silence and immobility at
that moment that the most insignificant noises caused
him a great, absurd fright. Moussia seemed to be sleeping
blissfully. He would have liked, however, to say a few
more words to her, words of hope. But he miraculously re-
spected her sleep. Besides, the words remained insane in
the depths of his throat, while the thousand trifles, life's

repeated defections, resumed their weary, paltry bearing. At that hour, the door of the Club was closed, there was no point in going there, in saying to the porter: "I'm Quinte, please inform them that I'm here." He would remain outside the Club forever. He also felt superseded, expelled from the whole room, by the room's slightest details. When he went down the stairs, all the neighbors who had been lying in wait for him swore at him. There was a frightful uproar. "The bastards, they're going to wake her up," he thought. The gentlemen in black had left, their mission had been accomplished. Perhaps they were hiding somewhere and were already tailing him . . . He had gone down the stairs as a wounded gorilla goes down his tree. In the street he now scratched his chest as that animal had probably done, in the same circumstances, casting bleeding looks right and left. Was he putting on an act for himself? It was perhaps his turn to die. That was why they were pursuing him, knife in hand.

"Why are they after me? I'm no longer interested in the acts I perform. Besides, I don't perform them, I let them happen."

He almost threw himself against a parked truck, then began to run, turning around to the emptiness that pursued him, but also pursuing something like the emptiness, he no longer knew whether he was fleeing or chasing. He was living through one of those crucial moments of existence when all the meanings of the world fuse in the symbol of pain. He really found nothing else to live than his own reckless course and the furious dismantling of the laws around him, the trickling of the streets in the night of insults and curses, the night that cannot be retraced, that it is impossible to retrace in order to return to twilight, and rapacious moonlight whirled down from the trees as if they were looking for his corpse. He plunged into things like a rapier, into the space where they had been ignobly laid out, arranged, labeled. He went through the Street of Mad Poetry, his hair was uncombed, his long black arms were dangling, creaking. He ran in his own suffering, in his laughter which was as rigid as bas-reliefs. He swam across stones (he swam so well that he would have had to learn to drown if such had been his desire, a desire not at all improbable), he crossed chromogeneous skies, fields paved with spines, the breath of cowards. He had been running for more than a quarter of an hour, into the legs of skaters, into the gestures of dowsers, at times he had to jump over an obstacle, such as a squatting countess, he dashed forward again, toward horns of animals that were like headlights of cars scouring total darkness, toward something sacred perhaps. Toward well-rigged boats crammed with fruit, toward the neurosis of the seas, toward the sun's sexual obsession, toward its settings which are screwings, toward possessed sharks, toward the Isles of Literature, toward the stampede of possibilities, toward their regrouping, possible death, the possible dramatic turn, possible charity, toward the possible distance which goes from the possible to the concrete and which is impossible to abolish, which is strewn with principles, with fear, with love, with involuntary fraternity, with hypocrisies. Out of breath, collapsing beneath the burden of his very sweat, he nevertheless kept running, clinging to skirts of hell which made him feel life exasperatingly, to limits still unnamed, to unprovable realities, like the sudden birth of his flesh-and-blood person, like the lover he had just been for the first time. He was the only athlete in the city, and he ran away from the finishing-line. His wind croaked, his breath was black, he was riding his last energy. Between shafts of fire he smelled the harness and the droppings, and he had extraordinary nostrils and he had the illusion of living! His steps split the ground into myriads of souls and mysteries, he dashed toward the future tangles of thought in which a frenzied flair leading to unverifiable antipodes of knowledge will circulate, toward the words which he still lacked for expressing his tragedy, which would always be lacking for all the things he still had to say. He stepped over his own gulf of love and hatred, he multiplied the prophetic furies of desire merely by harvesting his slaver in his hand, merely by breaking the pavestones of dismal streets with kicks of his heel. And after each consecration of his strength, he went forward more firmly in order to nip his slackenings in the bud, in order to adore his excess, and the death-pangs of his excess, and his excess of death-pangs.

The street was empty and silent, the wind had stopped blowing, and yet there was an indefinable stirring in the small gardens. He dragged about as if to ask for the right of asylum somewhere, but this crawling itself was also a way of running, an eager quest at the end of which, in order to go beyond life, his face would turn abundantly to death.

The night seemed to be scratching its belly with metallic sounds, glaucous gleams started flowing like pus down phlegmonic façades. Farther off, a kind of whitish border seemed to set bounds to the muffled multiplication of the darkness. A pale, anxious-looking man emerged slowly from a bush behind which he had been watching for the childish beginnings of day and the first pouts of the wakers as they opened their doors to see what the weather was like. He seemed attracted by the railroad which ran nearby and he stared for a long time at the rails, between the ties were some skinny weeds. He followed the track for a hundred yards in the course of which he bent down three times to pick up big gray stones which he tossed into the stream. Finally, as if moved by a resolution that rejected a savage, voluptuous temptation, he took the road to town.

When he got home, the door was open. He crossed the foyer and entered the living room in which a night-light was burning. The house seemed uninhabited. Yet a fresh sensation of care and order grazed his closed eyelids. Without opening them, he recalled, like a distant cousin, like a former friend, each object, and the place of each object, its shape, its color. The little gadget at the bottom of the vase, the faded designs of the wallpaper, and the oldish things that were dying uncertainly in corners, he recognized them all, they were the spitting image of his memory. He sat down and the very sound of the broken springs offered him such a portrait of the sound that he almost said: "So it's you . . ." He stayed there for an hour, perhaps longer, overcome by a kind of uneasiness, no doubt because of that lost job, a nasty emotion. From time to time, he cast painful glances at the foul night-light, from which they rebounded into the large mirror with broken corners at whose intercession he tried to distort whatever fatal and motionless presences were behind him. Then he stood up painfully. He seemed taller, thinned by the silence, by the foul stretching of the tick-tock of the clocks which were three to one against him, and the shadows maneuvered by the harsh light dabbed the sadness of his face as if he had a wound. He thrust his hand into the inner pocket of his jacket, opened the pink drawer of the commode with feigned piety, and placed a kind of oblong paperweight, which resembled a knife, on the scattered stamps of an inherited collection. The night-light slightly diabolized the scene. Then he went to the bedroom. He opened the door with a mixture of decent bewilderment and boldness that the neighbors knew so well. He cast an exhausted, gray, muddy look inside. They were sleeping. "It's they," he grunted. They were sleeping. The hair of the younger tallied, at the other end of decades, with that of the elder: same pompous idleness on the pillowcase, same assiduous wave. It's they, he grunted. And for the first time he felt curiously jobless, superseded. He was afraid to touch himself, to graze himself, lest he fall to dust. He was not crying. They were sleeping like the dead, not like the dead, he corrected, "but each like someone who forcefully foretokens his awakening." He closed the door and went back to the commode, which he opened tremblingly. *The knife resembled a paperweight.* He closed the drawer again, almost majestically. He sat down and waited. Everything waited. He waited, the other two waited, his anguish waited, his hatred waited, the tightening of his heart waited, only Death did not wait.